# REUNITED

## Ruby's Journey

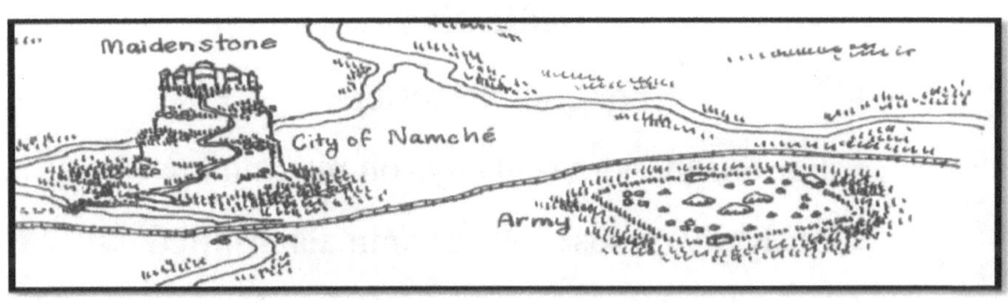

# Acknowledgements

I wish to thank Maeve Pascoe for her splendidly evocative artwork on the cover, interiors and map of the Skygrass Country.

Ruth Sonnenberg, the author's mother, did the drawing of Angelion.

# Dedication

For both my sisters

For Susan, who is always on my mind &

For Kelly, whose love of animals inspired

the character of Ruby O'Doyle

# Settings

| Talin | Sab-ra's home, village along Green River |
|---|---|
| Namché | City where Maidenstone is located |
| Maidenstone | Ancient Lamasery |
| Natil | The King's Valley |
| Skygrass | Location of the blue diamond mine |
| Halfhigh | Way station on journey to Skygrass |
| Lost Lake | Valley in Blue Mountains |

# Major Characters

| Sab-ra | Child Spy, Maidenstone Novice, Empath, Healer |
|---|---|
| Ellani | Sab-ra's grandmother, Midwife |
| Silo'am | Sab-ra's Grandfather, Head Silversmith Guild |
| Ruby | Sab-ra's twin, they were separated at birth |
| Hent | Sab-ra and Ruby's uncle |
| Dani | Sab-ra and Ruby's father, died in ice crevasse |
| Ashlin | Sab-ra and Ruby's mother |
| Hodi | Sab-ra's spy partner, killed by Kosi Shunned |
| Conquin | Sab-ra's best friend |

# Characters at Maidenstone

| | |
|---|---|
| Mistress Falcon | Head of Maidenstone, Priestess, Empath |
| Honus | Cook at Maidenstone |
| Brother Jun | Empath Teacher |
| Brother Marzun | Head Empath |
| An Mali | Physician at Maidenstone |
| Te Ran | Priestess, Far Seer |
| Gordo | Skygrass gemstone merchant |
| Ten-Singh | Bearer who takes Ruby to Talin |

# Characters from Army & Twelfth Valley

| | |
|---|---|
| Grieg | Captain of Army, Obsessed with Sab-ra |
| Justyn | Grieg's Translator, in love with Sab-ra |
| Ruisenor | King of the People in the Twelve Valleys |
| Verde | First Queen of the Twelve Valleys |
| Ion'li | First Consort, Second Queen |

# Kosi Warriors

| | |
|---|---|
| Say'f | King of the Kosi Warrior Tribe |
| Lord Rohr | First Blood Arrow and Sab-ra's Guardian |
| Lord Sta'g | Second Blood Arrow |
| Hozro | Chief of Kosi Shunned, White Eyed |
| Ghang | Kosi guard at Maidenstone |
| Lord Norgay | Horse Captain to King Ruisenor |
| Wirri-won | Kosi Healer |
| Kim-li & Kensing | Sayf's daughters from first wife |

# Months in Skygrass Kingdom

| | |
|---|---|
| January | Moon of Snows |
| February | Hunger Moon |
| March | Vernal Moon |
| April | Waking Moon |
| May | Planting Moon |
| June | Flowering Moon |
| July | Ripening Moon |
| August | Thunder Moon |
| September | Harvest Moon |
| October | Red Leaf Moon |
| November | Black Twig Moon |
| December | Long Night Moon |

# Prologue
## Part I, Ruby's Story

When seventeen year-old Ruby of Viridian discovers that she was born a twin, she is furious with her mother, Ashlin, who kept the secret for so long. Ruby's mother confessed that she left Ruby's twin sister, Sab-ra, behind when she was forced to leave the city of Namché in the Blue Mountains because the infant was too weak to travel. Ashlin had always believed the baby died, but recently she received a letter from the Mistress of Maidenstone saying that Sab-ra lived. Hoping to find Sab-ra, Ashlin sends Ruby to Namché to find her sister.

Meanwhile, Sab-ra, who barely escaped an Avalanche that buried the mystic valley of Skygrass, is travelling across the Blue Mountains with Lord Rohr, one of her husband Say'f's guards. They are travelling to Natil, the Valley of her People's King. The Warrior King, Sab-ra's husband, refused to leave the Skygrass Valley when Sab-ra did, vowing he would find and kill Captain Grieg who had abducted her. When the Gate stones to Skygrass slid closed—Say'f stayed behind. Sitting astride his huge black warhorse as the snow and ash swirled around him, he vowed, "I will meet you in the Valley of the King."

# Skygrass Kingdom Map – West

# Skygrass Kingdom Map – East

# Chapter 1

## On the Isle of Verdantia - January

Seventeen year-old Ruby O'Doyle lay cuddled in a mass of hand-pieced quilts with her young setter puppy, Maeve, sound asleep beside her. Ruby's red hair cascaded over the embroidered linen pillowcase, her eyelashes dark against her fair cheeks. A freezing rain fell outside the window taking her deeper into slumber, but a brisk knock on the door and her mother's voice brought her from her dreams.

"Get out of bed now, Miss, it's time you had breakfast with your family."

"Ma," Ruby groaned. "What time is it that you are waking me on my school break?"

"Don't be bold, and it's Mummy, not Ma. The breakfast is ready. Get yourself down here. Your Da and I have some things to talk to you about."

Ruby looked at her clock gloomily. Nine o'clock on a bloody Tuesday morning. During holiday vacation no less. What in the world had induced Ma to make a full breakfast in the middle of the week? She put her feet on the wood floor, winced at the cold and reached for the skirt and sweater on the floor she had discarded the night before. She stepped into her clothes, yanked a comb through her curly red hair and stomped down to breakfast. She looked at the table in dismay. There were rashers of bacon, sausages, eggs, black pudding and toast—burnt to a crisp. Baked beans, fried tomatoes and brown soda bread were already on her plate.

"Do I have to eat all this? What's the occasion, Ma?" she asked, looking at all the food.

"Don't be giving me grief my girl, and it is Mummy, as I told ye before. Sit down while I get your Da his tea."

Ruby's father, a tall skinny man with freckles and an easy smile came and joined them at the table. It was an eat-in kitchen with a pine table and four old gray chairs. The table had been scrubbed so often, it was nearly white. Glancing out the window, Ruby noticed that last night's rain was turning to snow. The snowflakes seen through antique leaded glass windows made the world look soft and out of focus.

"Morning, Ruby."

"How ya, Da."

"Say grace, you," her mother said.

Ruby recited the usual prayer, crossed herself and dug in. "So what's the big deal to get me up out of bed at bleeding dawn?"

Ruby's mother didn't answer. She was unusually quiet, looking out toward the back garden. She was in her late-thirties and still youthful. Her red curly hair had only a few silver threads. Her eyes were far away. Then she straightened her shoulders and exhaled as if she had been holding her breath a long time.

"Okay, here goes, my girl. I have a tale to tell you and I don't think it's going to be easy," she hesitated. "When I was about your age, my older brother Linc talked my Da into sending him on a trip to see the Far East. He had dreamed of seeing the Blue Mountains since he was a tot. Da was sick with the cancer and wanted Linc to have his dream. Half the place was on the dole, but Da had some money stashed away so he buys Linc a ticket. Linc was beside himself with joy. He was headed to this place called Namché."

"Can ye not come to the bleeding point here?" Ruby said, rolling her eyes and thinking about meeting her boyfriend Shane later at the shops.

"Language," Ma snapped. "I was planning all the time on following him, but I didn't tell Da. I figured I had to wait until he was welcomed into heaven before I left. Linc and I were going to live together when I got there, the pair of us. Linc was all for studying the animals of the place, Goddess love him. Nobody thought those animals were real, but the day I found my dear brother, I held a baby white cave lion in my hands. You can't image how beautiful he was."

Her voice was soft and dreamy. For just a moment, she looked seventeen again, holding a cup of tea, the warmth making red tendrils around her face. Tears came to her eyes and she blinked them back.

"Ma, I swear, I'm going back to bed if you can't come to the point," Ruby half rose to leave.

"Did I say you could leave the table?" her mother asked.

"Sit girl," Da said calmly. "Your Mum is trying to tell you something important here. Go ahead, Ashlin."

"So, we hadn't heard from my brother for almost half a year. Sure, we'd no phone when he left, so how would he ring us? And he always did things in his own time. At first, we thought he was just not for writing, but when Da died and Mum turned fifty and we still didn't hear a word, I left our beautiful Isle of Viridian to find him. Makin' a long story short, for Miss Impatience here, I found him up in the Blue Mountains. He had died of starvation, giving all his food to the cave lions."

"Jaysus. Oh Ma, I'm so sorry. I knew he died, but this is awful, truly awful."

"I'll go on then, shall I? Unless this little wagon needs her bed more 'un the story."

"Okay, okay, I'm staying," Ruby said, settling in for the duration.

"There was this big Monastery, part school and part hospital in that town. They called it Maidenstone. When I got to the city of Namché, a monk took me to the Wool Market and we found this man, named Silo'am. He had brought his wool down from the high range to sell. He had a grown son named Dani, young and dark-haired. Oh he was lovely, he was."

"Ma, you didn't, did ye? Did ye fall for this dark mountain lad?"

"Maybe I best tell the next part," Da said gently, patting Ma's hand and she nodded.

"Dani guided your mother up into the Blue Mountains. It took weeks, even in summer, but eventually they found her brother. It was like she said. He was lying dead of starvation in a mountain cave. They had no choice but to bury him with rocks, trying to save his body from the mountain lions eating him. They call them Angel-lions in that country."

Ruby looked at her mother who gazed down at the table, blew her nose and wiped the tears from her face.

"Your Ma and Dani found this baby Angel-lion near Linc's body. The lion's Mum and her baby ran into the deeper tunnels and disappeared. They coaxed the baby out, stayed and took care of the wee one. When he was big enough they left him to fend for himself."

"We named him Sumulus," Ruby's mother said softly. "He had the most beautiful eyes and the tips of his ears had white fur tassels on them. When he played in the mountain meadows, I would sit down on the grass and after a while, he would come and put his head in my lap. His eyes were near to silver. My Dani loved him too." Ashlin's voice was low and sweet. Ruby could feel the room grow tight with her mother's profound love for the little lion.

"Ah, you were a bold little rebel then, were ye Ma?" Ruby said.

"Now, Ruby, none of that. Your Ma and that boy Dani fell for each other hard," Da looked away for a minute. His face wore a wretched expression, almost a wince. Saying this seemed to hurt him even after all those years.

"You'll be having another cup of tea, Frank," Ma said. Da nodded. Ashlin stood up and re-filled his cup, handing him a ferocious dark brew.

"Go on then," Ruby said.

"So, they got married, your mother and Dani and your Mum got herself pregnant."

"Hold on a minute here, Mum. You were married to somebody else before Da?" Ruby asked. She felt the palms of her hands start to sweat.

"Ah now, Ruby girl, you have to try to understand, it was an eon ago and a long ways away from our beautiful island. I was terrible lonely, I was."

"So how did this fall out? What happened to this Dani, to the dark-haired lad?" Ruby asked. It troubled her deeply that Ma had married someone else besides her beloved Da.

"Dani died in a mountain climbing accident," Ma said, her voice low and sorrowful. "He screamed my name as he fell," her tears came down hard. After a bit, she cleared her throat and said, "I tried to climb down after him, but the rocks were slick with ice. I called until my voice went. I waited above that crevice for a week, until all my food was gone. He never moved."

"And you are the kid, Ruby," Da said, his voice so gentle, so very kind.

"Am I not your child then, Da?" Ruby could hear the anguish in her voice as she turned to her father, tears filling her eyes.

"No, Darlin' you're my child all right. I adopted you right off the bat. Your Ma used to say I fell in love with you before I even knew for sure I loved her."

"So what happened when you left," Ruby said, with a worried frown on her face. She dreaded what other deeply buried secrets she would hear.

"I had you. When you were old enough to travel I came back to Viridian, to tell my own Ma what happened to Linc and to show her my baby. Ah, but you were a sweet little dote, a giggly small one. I met your Da and we got married right away."

"I can't take this all in, Ma." Ruby stood up. Her stomach clenched and her hands left sweat marks on the back of the chair. She felt desperate to leave the kitchen. "I want to go talk with Gran about this."

"You're going nowhere, you. There's more to tell. You were born a twin, and I am going to Namché in a few weeks to get your sister. There," she said. "Now I've told you."

"What?" Ruby looked at her parents in stunned silence, sitting down suddenly.

"You have a twin, a sister. They named her Sab-ra. It's been seventeen years. I thought she had died, but I learned last week that she lived."

Ruby sat at the table, shaking her head, unable to say a word. Nothing in all the years she had been the child of these two had even even hinted that she wasn't an only child. She shook her head, trying to register a sister, a twin. Everyone was silent and Ruby nibbled on her toast as if in a worrisome dream.

"If I have a twin, why isn't she here?" Ruby demanded, lifting her face to her mother angrily.

"When she was born, she was very poorly, a weak little thing. Couldn't even raise her head. I left her with the Mistress of Maidenstone in the city of Namché, because they didn't think she would live. I thought her dead all these years."

Ashlin continued saying, "It was a horrible time and there was a war in that country. The Army ordered all the white people to leave the city. I brought you back here to our Island and married your Da. It broke my heart to leave your sister behind." Her voice trailed off into silence.

"I don't understand. It's been seventeen years and suddenly you remember this child that you left. Could you not just give this up? After all, you gave her up," Ruby's mouth tightened in disapproval. She glared at her mother.

"You have no idea how hard this has been for me, Ruby. A few months ago, I wrote to the Mistress of Maidenstone and she sent me back a letter. That's when I learned your twin lived. Her name is Sab-ra, and she's been raised by her father Dani's parents. They have been training her to be a Healer. I got the letter and ever since then, I've been dreaming about her. In the dreams, she is calling me, needing her Mum. I'm going to the Blue Mountain country and I'm bringing her back to Viridian."

"So, Ruby girl," Da said, "You are going to take language lessons so you can speak to your twin when she gets here."

"Oh Da, no," Ruby wailed. "If Ma can even find this girl, can't she leave her there?"

"I'll get the letter," Ma said, "You'll see why I have to go. There is war in Namché again and your sister left the city almost a year ago. She was travelling up the mountains to warn her People about the Army that plans to invade the high country."

# Chapter 2
## Sharing the Story

Ruby stalked down the cobbled streets with their brick houses and narrow-minded windows that watched her splashing past in the freezing rain. She was enraged and stomped in all the puddles. Water soaked into the sides of her boots making her toes ice cold. She reached her Gran's yard just in time to see her leaving by the front door. Ruby called out to get Gran's attention and her grandmother turned around.

"Ruby, darling I'm about to go to the market. Did ye need something?"

"I need to talk to you," Ruby said and at her despairing tone, Gran knew her granddaughter had at last learned the family secret.

"Come in, I'll get your tea," she said putting her arm around Ruby's shoulders and leading her into the kitchen. "Take off those boots and your coat before you catch your death."

The teapot whistled as Ruby removed her wet things and sat on the red painted stool at the old yellow linoleum countertop. Pouring the tea, Gran sat down across from her granddaughter. "So your Mum told you the whole story, did she?"

"You knew all this time?" Ruby said, frustration apparent in her rising tone. She felt her heart beat faster.

"Yes, dearie, I knew. I have told your Mum a hundred times you needed to know."

"She says I'm not Da's kid."

"That's not true. He's your Da. He adopted you right away. I am glad you know. I've been waiting years for your Ma to tell you."

"Ma got married to some dark-haired boy from the mountains when she was my age," Ruby's voice was outraged. She dried her hands on Gran's soft old dishtowel and ran the towel across her forehead, wiping away the raindrops.

"Yes, she did and had the two of ye—you and your sister. Her husband's name was Dani and he died in a mountain fall," Gran's voice was calm. "It happened a long time ago, Ruby, and your Mum was all alone in that God forsaken country."

"So was she married in the Church at least?" Ruby asked.

"No, darling they don't have out Church in that country."

"She probably wasn't married at all, Gran. They were just sleeping together. I know it. Oh, God, it means I'm illegitimate!"

Gran rose and walked over to Ruby's side of the counter saying, "Nonsense, Ruby girl. You're grand, yes you are. You know your Ma believes in other things—something she calls the Sacred Feminine. She doesn't even go to church with you and your Da. And you've been baptized, you will go to heaven, I have no doubt."

"How do we know this Dani lad is even dead? She could be married to the both of them." Ruby felt her body grow hot and queasy at the horrible thought of bigamy.

"He's gone from this earthly life. Your Mum saw him fall into a dark crack in the mountain. She told me she tried to climb down to him, but she fell and could hardly escape. She waited at the top of the crack for weeks and nearly starved herself to death before she gave up."

"Sister Margaret says if a girl lets a boy have her before their marriage, she cannot be cleansed of that sin. Sister says a girl's greatest treasure is her virginity and that boys are just nasty little burglars! Oh Gran, my Mum is going to hell," Ruby cried.

"Ruby, your Mother is much like me own dear grandmother who was of the old Celtic people. My grandmother believed she saw the face of the Goddess in the spirits of animals. She lit a candle every night to a white statue of a lioness she called the Goddess of Fertility. It worked, you know. The woman had twelve little children. And, my grandmother had the Sight."

"The Sight, it's all pagan nonsense, that's what the Sisters tell us."

"God's Church was built on the foundation of those old beliefs, Dearie. You know the Church honors the spirits of animals. Last year they had a Blessing Mass and your brought your Irish setter, Maeve, for the Priest's blessing, didn't ye?"

Ruby nodded reluctantly. Bitterness made the corners of her mouth turn down.

"What matters now is that your Mum has told you about your sister. You have no idea how much your Ma has suffered worrying that the little dote died. She had the light of the risen Lord on her face when she showed me the letter from the Mistress of Maidenstone."

"I'm still mad. She kept this dark secret from me my whole life, and then she expects me to forgive her!"

"Give yourself time, Dearie. She's your Mum and a fine one. It will be good to have another young one around here. The only thing I can't understand is why she isn't sending you."

"You think I should go?" Ruby's eyes widened. "I wouldn't set foot in that God-forsaken country."

"I think it would be the greatest adventure you could ever have," Gran's eyes crinkled as she smiled.

*I would chain myself to the altar of the church before that happened*, Ruby thought.

Two weeks later Ruby pulled her Diary from her nightstand drawer to write down her jumbled thoughts. She had managed to avoid anything but the most trivial conversations with her parents.

*Dear Diary,*

*It has been weeks since I heard the devastating news that Da is not my father and Ma married a mountain lad (or maybe didn't even. I am still disgusted with her) and got herself pregnant. I talked with my Gran, my best friend Jackie and me boyfriend, Shane. I told them all about it. Shane just kept kissing me. He was trying to distract me and make me stop crying. He tried to unbutton my shirt and I said, 'Would you ever just hump off.' He left me, all mad.*

*Jackie said I should have known my mother had been with another man before me Da. She reminded me Ma taught all that old Celtic stuff at the University and those people thought a woman got a child from a god, a tree, or some such heathen nonsense.*

*My mother bought her tickets to go to Namché after confessing her sins to me. At least her conscience was clear. I was still furious. Da defended her to the hilt, like all'us.*

*I went to see Fr. Patrick and told him all about it. He said I was right. Ma was a truly sinful woman, not even believing in the one true God, but he said I was guilty of keeping the sin of anger. He told me to pray for the wisdom to forgive my mother. He said he would talk with her again about her pagan beliefs. He thought she might give them up and join the church. I have my doubts.*

*Signed "Hard Done By" Ruby*

Several weeks went by as Ruby sulked in her room, refusing to speak to her parents before she wrote in her Dairy again.

*Dear Diary,*

*It's been over a month now since I heard my mother's big news. Despite myself, I have reluctantly agreed to go to the Blue Mountains in the Far East. After Ma got her tickets, she got the bursitis in her shoulder and the doc said she couldn't go. Ma begged me to go with tears in her eyes from a hospital bed. Gran turned in Ma's tickets and bought me a boat ticket and the train tickets. Da said I was too young to go on such a long trip; something bad would happen to me. Gran said he was living in the past. Girls took protection with them these days, like knives and that. In the end, Da said it was my choice, but he didn't want me to go. It wasn't really a free choice for me though, Ma forced me. She said she could never forgive herself if she didn't try to find my sister. A mother's tears, how could a daughter refuse?*

*I had to meet with all my teachers. They gave me stuff to read and I'm going to have to take a passel of tests when I get back, but they didn't think I would lose the whole year. My Science teacher said I should have known. When we did Genetics last year, she told me I couldn't have these dark eyes with two blue-eyed parents. When I find this Sab-ra person, I am going to tell this mooching sister that she can just stay in her country. I'll be giving out when I see her, you can just bet.*

*Signed "Still Outraged" Ruby*


*Dear Diary,*

*I leave for the Far East in the morning. Mum is still in hospital from the bursitis. Now she's got pneumonia too. I wanted to stay and see her home from hospital, but she said she didn't want me to wait any longer. She gave me her small green book; the one she reads at night. I couldn't read the language it was written in, but Ma had drawn pictures in the flyleaf. They showed grass as high as her shoulders and grasshoppers flying in formation. In the margins, she drew a picture of the Lion Baba, with his mane and tufts of hair on his ears. She wrote his name, Sumulus. She wrote other shocking stuff too, I closed the book it was so bad. Something about how she felt when Dani made love to her outside in the grass, no less. Good thing Fr. Patrick doesn't know that stuff.*

*Signed, "Shocked and Dismayed" Ruby*

## Chapter 3
## The City of Namché
## February

It was a gray misty day when Ruby and her father left the house for the docks the morning of her departure. The previous day she had visited the hospital and seeing her mother's white face on the pillow, kissed her good-bye. Da was so sad looking Ruby almost decided not to go. He told her it would take two weeks to get to the Blue Mountain country. He brought her young red setter dog, Maeve, with them to the docks and Ruby could hardly stand to say good-bye to the two of them. She felt the tears well up whenever she looked into her dog's dark loving eyes.

"When the Ferry reaches the mainland tomorrow, you're going to have to get from the wharf to the Train Depot. You should hail a cab. Just show the driver this, it's the schedule for the train. I still think you're a right eejit for going." He shook his head.

"Da, you are looking absolutely shook. I'll be fine. Now, you have to promise me not to get langered every night while I'm gone. Only have a pint or two with the lads of an evening, will you? Please keep track of me dog until Ma comes back from Hospital. And I need you to write and let me know she's getting better."

Da begged her to promise she would return as soon as she found her twin. She nodded, eyes brimming.

Long after the boat pulled away from the dock, Ruby stood at the railing and waved at him. He was a dark speck, still waving, when the storm clouds hid him from sight. The winds were horrendous, the boat wallowed and Ruby threw up over the deck railings repeatedly. Her red

23

hair was soaked from the rain. By the time the boat landed on the mainland, she was exhausted, already regretting having left Da, her Mum and her dog Maeve.

She hailed a cab and showed the cabbie the picture. The little puck took her from the waterfront to the train station. He held out his hand after, wanting money. She pulled some silver groats from her bag and he took two, smiling and bowing. The train station was so big and dark it looked like the mouth of the Fiend himself. There were like a hundred trains. She found the ticket office by reading the signs and handed the small gnome-like man her ticket.

"You already have your ticket, girlie, just get on the train," he said looking at her like she was mental.

"Which one?" she asked.

"It's that one there," he said pointing.


Once on the train, Ruby talked with a man in a uniform who took her to a little private cubicle. It had a tiny couch made of green metal with bright cushions. There was a big window to the outside. Above the seat, Ruby noticed cupboard doors. She pulled them open, inside there was a fold-down bed. The tiny room had a sink and a pitcher full of water, but no latrine, not even a hole in the floor of the train. *Barbarous form of transport*, Ruby thought.

Gran had sent apples, hard bread and cheese. She figured she would run out of food in about an hour. She wished she had done as she had thought initially and chained herself to the altar in Viridian's High Church. In the night the train stopped. Ruby dashed from the rails into the brush and did her business. She was climbing back on board when the uniform stopped her.

"Ticket," he demanded.

"It's in my room," she said outraged, whispering 'eejit' under her breath.

"All right then," he said. "I'll come by later to punch it."

Ruby was walking along the swaying aisle when a woman with a backside the size of a sheep, opened the door into the hall. Ruby looked in and saw a whole row of toilets. It was the jacks for everyone. Heaven forbid the boys used it too!

When the uniform came, he took her ticket and cut a little circle out of it. "You don't have to stay in here the whole time," he said. "You can sit in the regular seats if you want."

The next day, when she was bored of looking out the window in her alcove, Ruby discovered the part of the train where rows of benches faced each other. She was surprised to see two of the Garda lads sitting in the seats. The boys were police officers, the law-keepers on Viridian. They smiled and tipped their hats to her. They wore black uniforms with golden triangles on their caps. The color of the uniforms surprised her, usually the Garda wore blue uniforms.

"Where are you off to then, Girlie?" one asked after her.

"What's it to you then? Bold 'un."

"We wuz just wondering if you were going as far as the east. We're going all the way to the folded land."

"Fair play to you," she said walking down the aisle and taking a seat. Shane had warned her off the police fellas. He said the Garda were a bunch of bollix who were getting above themselves because of the uniforms. She had to admit the uniforms were sweet.

The Garda moved seats until they were sitting across from her. They opened their lunches and offered her poms and nuts. Ruby accepted the good eagerly. Her food was already gone.

"Give us a kiss then for the pom," a red haired freckled one said. "Or at least tell us your name."

"Ah, he just never shuts his gob," the dark-haired one said. He hit his friend in the head with the flat of his hand saying, "I'm Jaime and this numbskull is Carmac. He thinks he's God's gift. I'm the one who knows how to properly kiss a girl."

"I'm Ruby," she said and laughed at them. What harm could it do to speak to the lads? This stupid trip was already starting to feel like it would never end.

"We're going to a Garrison where all the soldiers went on some bloody quest up into the Blue Mountains. They all died, so the call came out for soldiers wanting a bit of action to come and help man the Garrison. That's why we are wearing the black uniforms."

"It's in this god-forsaken culchie town called Nam something or other," Carmac said.

"It is Namché?" Ruby asked.

"Tis," Jaime agreed.

"I'll be going along then with you then," she said. "I'm headed there myself."

The young men looked at each other and at her, grinning.

"You can sleep in our bunks if you're tired like," Carmac said, with a sly smile.

"I have my own bunk and I expect you to watch out for me like I was your little sister and not be a bunch of jackeens. I'm below the age of consent and Fr. Patrick will be waiting to be sure I've done no sin when I get back."

"Yah, sure, we will. We were just teasing you," Jaime said. "You'll be safe with us."

Later, when Ruby returned to her small cubicle, she pulled out a pen to write in her Diary.


*Dear Diary,*

*I've met some Island lads on the train today. They are Garda and going to Namché too. They like to act like bold maggots, but I think they will watch out for me. It's making the trip go easier. Yesterday we passed the first set of mountains. The train went up and down like a little toy engine crossing miniature hills. The Garda told me I could eat one meal a day in the dining room. The cost was included with the ticket, they said. Gran might have mentioned. I was darn near to having a weakness before those boys gave me some of their food.*

*Da had this language teacher come to the house before I left. She taught me how to say, "My name is Ruby," and "I'm want to go to Maidenstone," and a bunch of other phrases like, "Where is the toilet?" I actually got quite good, at least I could understand it, but when I spoke the language my accent was funny, apparently. Still, the Garda lads were most impressed.*

*As soon as I get to Namché and see this twin sister, I'm going to make her promise to stay where she is. I'll turn right around and go back to Viridian that very day..*


*Signed, Ruby the bold girl*

# Chapter 4
## Arriving in Namché

Ruby opened her eyes to a cloudy sky when the train came to a stop in the city of Namché. The train station was very small compared to those she had seen on the trip. The town had been built in layers, like a wedding cake. A wavy wall made a circle of protection around the city. Terraces that looked like massive green lily pads stuck out from the sides of the mount. At the very top of the layer-cake mountain, Ruby saw what looked like a bracelet of towers linked by bridges. The bridges must have been made of prisms because when the sun hit them, rainbows covered the structure and it looked purely magical.

The Garda lads walked with her to the Army barracks. The Garrison was comprised of four buildings placed around a graveled square. On the right side was a two-story block building. To the left there was another building which must have contained the dining area. Ruby could smell food cooking. She thought the third was probably the soldiers' sleeping quarters. At the back of the square, a fourth building served as the stable. Ruby saw a Garda leading a horse inside. A fenced enclosure stood in the center of the open square.

"So, Ruby girl, will ya' kiss us good-bye then," Carmac asked, grinning at her.

"Don't you be kissing him, I'm the best kisser," Jaime gestured to his lips.

"Are you boys leaving before taking me to this Maidenstone place?" Ruby's excitement at arriving in the city had suddenly evaporated and she felt apprehensive as the cool wind hit her face.

Jaime put his arm around her, wanting a kiss good-bye. Surprising herself, Ruby kissed him back. Carmac hit his friend's arm and pointed across the graveled square. A short soldier with medals all over his chest walked toward them and barked out some orders. He must have asked for their papers. After looking over their papers, the decorated soldier nodded at Ruby and gestured for the lads to follow him. The fellas looked back at her, a bit ashamed to be leaving her alone, but marched after the Lieutenant or Captain or whatever he was.

"Sorry, Ruby, we have to go," Carmac called. Following the soldier, they looked back and waved at her. "Come back and see us sometime."


Ruby walked the ancient cobblestone streets toward the market. She could smell the scent of bread baking. Street musicians played a cheerful tune and children ran toward her carrying small open vessels. She dropped a coin into each leather bowl. The dark-eyed little ones were just plain enchanting. There were many shops selling beautiful silks, spices and vegetables. The proprietors bowed to her as she passed. She got up her courage at one shop that sold wool. She entered and touched the yard goods, finding them softer than any she'd felt on the Isle of Viridian A young woman came out of the back and chattered to her. Ruby was delighted she could understand some of her words. Those language lessons Da made her take had paid off.

"I need to go to Maidenstone," Ruby told the clerk. She thought she had said it correctly, but the woman looked confused.

"Maid – en – stone," she said. The girl nodded and pointed to the massive circle of colored towers at the top of the mount. She took hold of Ruby's arm and led her through the confusing array of streets and alleys, until they reached the bottom of an enormous stairway. Ruby had to tip her head back to see the whole of it. Rainbows from the glass bridges came half way down the mountain—truly lovely it was.

"Thank you," Ruby said and reached for her. She took the girl's face in her hands and kissed both the girl's cheeks. It was a customary manner of giving thanks in Viridian. The clerk seemed startled but then smiled. Gesturing to the staircase, which was at least a hundred steps tall, the clerk dashed back into the maze of alleys.

Ruby took the steps slowly, feeling the importance of this day. She was returning to the place where her mother had left her sister seventeen years ago. She thought of her mother, just her age, walking these steps to the top. Had she been pregnant the day she arrived at Maidenstone? *It must have been hard to walk up so many steps carrying twins in her belly.* She looked up at the first landing and then up again. Suddenly, Maidenstone seemed to call her as a mother called her child.

Above the market, beautiful houses covered with flowered vines stood on each terrace. Another fifty steps higher, Ruby looked down seeing a kind of mist that hung around the base of the mountain. It looked solid as a snowdrift. When she finally reached the top, Ruby saw six colored spires standing in a circle. A taller white tower stood in the center. A web of shining bridges connected them. The rainbows glinting off the structure were blindingly beautiful. Ruby was walking toward the yellow tower when she heard a woman's voice call out.

"Sab-ra, my goodness, how is it that you have returned?"

Ruby continued walking.

"Wait," the woman called and Ruby turned toward a dumpy woman in a pale blue dress. She had a white cap on her gray hair and looked like a grandmother. She walked quickly toward her with outstretched arms.

"Oh," the woman stopped suddenly. "You aren't Sab-ra, are you?" She touched Ruby's hair. Then she said, "I know who you are." She took Ruby's hand and giving her no chance to refuse, led her to a door with a curved top that opened into the yellow tower.

Once inside, they walked down beautiful stone-flagged halls until they reached a heavily carved door with a silver doorknob. When the pudgy woman knocked briskly and opened it, Ruby saw a beautiful raven-haired woman in a dark blue gown. She wore a complex white and ivory braided belt at her waist. The woman stood up from behind her desk and breathed out audibly, her mouth making an "Oh" of astonishment. Together the two women looked at Ruby in amazed silence. Ruby just stood there, wondering if they were mental. The women talked together but she caught only a word or two. Then the dark-haired one spoke to her in her own tongue.

"Ruby?"

"Yes, I am called Ruby." She was feeling irked at this continuing inspection. She wondered if these two snotty cows were going to offer her something to eat or drink. It was time for tea, after all.

"I am Falcon, Mistress of Maidenstone. This is An Mali, our Healer. Is your mother called Ashlin?"

"Yes, that's me Mum." Ruby felt a stab of homesickness. Why had she ever agreed to leave with her mother in hospital?

"Did you know you have a sister?"

"I came to see her. As soon as I see this twin, I plan to leave. I'm in bits already from the long journey."

Although they both seemed a bit off, they gestured for her to follow them, leading her to the kitchen where thank heavens, she saw a kettle boiling and smelled clover honey. Ruby sat down at the table, nearly stepping on a small white dog lying on the floor. She reached down and picked him up. "I'm sorry," she told him and he licked her chin. He settled in her lap, unwilling to be put down again.

"His name is Cloudheart," Mistress told her. "He is Sab-ra's dog. He seems to recognize you. He doesn't love everyone," She smiled gently.

After eating their simple meal, Mistress took her up a curving flight of steps to a small room. Inside were two beds with white sheets and blue wool coverlets.

"This was your sister's room when she was a Novice here," Mistress said. She seemed sad.

From the window, Ruby could see the Garrison and the train station. Beyond the city, she could see wave after wave of the Blue Mountains. After the woman left, she laid down on one of the beds. She was exhausted and a wave of emotion swamped her. Cloudheart had followed her up the stairs and settled between the beds with a contented sigh. Ruby trailed her hand down to pet him. She felt happier touching the little dog's soft fur.

Just before she fell into a warm river of sleep, she prayed to meet her sister soon, so this wretched trip would be over and she could return to her own country.

# Chapter 5

## At Maidenstone

When Ruby opened her eyes the following morning, for a moment she didn't remember where she was. Then the memory came flooding back. She was at Maidenstone, the ancient school and hospital where she was born and where her mother had left her twin sister. She got dressed, went downstairs and arrived in the kitchen, having gotten lost twice. The maze of corridors at Maidenstone was terribly confusing.

She walked into the room seeing two women wearing white aprons bustling around in the minimal kitchen. They told her their names were Honus and Kieta. Honus was a chubby smiling woman with dark hair cut shot. Kieta was taller; the planes of her cheeks were flat and her eyes were slanted. They showed her where to sit and brought her a little toasted sweet cake and a cup of black coffee. There was a red fruit too. She asked the name of it.

"Sapritet," the cook said. "Delicious." She smiled and rubbed her round belly.

Ruby ate the sweet cake and fruit slowly wondering what the day would hold. The Mistress of Maidenstone entered the room and the cooks fell silent. They seemed intimidated by the tall dark woman with her air of mystery. Turning to Ruby, Mistress said she had several things to tell her. They walked down the hall to her office. She gestured for Ruby to sit on the other side of her desk.

"Ruby, it's unfortunate that you came to meet Sab-ra at this time of year. Sab-ra is not in Namché now. She left here at the end of the Waking Moon, over a year ago. A Kosi Warrior took her north. She was going to warn her People about the Army attack that was coming to the high country."

"I know about this war. I came to Maidenstone with some soldiers coming to re-supply the Garrison."

"Yes, many soldiers and civilians died in the quest for the blue diamonds led by the evil Captain Grieg," Mistress grimaced. "I have not heard anything from Sab-ra since she left, but I would know if she died. She lives."

"You considered she might be dead?" Ruby asked. This place was scary and dangerous. She wouldn't stay a minute longer than necessary. A wave of homesickness hit her hard.

"Many people die during wars," Mistress told her calmly. "Even you should know that."

"I am not a thicko," Ruby said. She felt irritated at the tone of the woman's voice. When there was no response, Ruby continued, saying, "I have to see Sab-ra. My Mum, I guess I should say *our* Mum, is very sick and she made me promise."

"Well, it is too cold now to travel to the high range. You will have to stay here until spring is further along. Then you can go north. In order to stay, however, you must contribute. Can you cook? Can you teach? Are you trained as a Healer?"

Ruby tried to control her temper. This poxy female acted as if she was in charge of her life. "If you didn't want me, you only had to say. It's not a bother on me to leave now," Ruby said angrily. She felt her cheeks redden.

"You don't understand me, Ruby. You have to have a guide and none of the Bearers would take you at this time of year. You will stay here for at least two months before you can go north."

Ruby thought for a few minutes and sighed. She knew she needed this arrogant woman's help. She took a deep breath and lowered her shoulders. "If it's money you are asking me for, I have some."

"I would not take money from Ashlin's child," Mistress said coldly. "You insult me."

A short silence ensued while Mistress and Ruby regarded each other, until Ruby's eyes fell.

"I can cook some things," she said "But what I do on the Isle of Viridian is go to school or help Mum with housework or go to church. Do you have a church here?"

"We worship the Goddess here, in all her myriad forms. There are many Goddesses in our metaphysics. Some are spirits of water, rocks and plants. Some are the essence of wind or snow. There is only one Great Goddess though, and she is the spirit of the Dhali Ra, the tallest peak in the Blue Mountain range. Do you understand?" Mistress looked at her intently.

Ruby was frowning. "Yes, but in my country the Priests, our spiritual leaders, tell us there is only one God and he is definitely not a woman. If a person believes anything else, they go to the Demon Fires when they die." She felt her face flush as she defended the true religion.

"We believe there are many roads to the afterlife," Mistress' voice was calm and she seemed amused by Ruby's passionate defense of her faith. "Our Priestess, Te Ran, taught Sab-ra the art of the Far-Seer. Your sister can see the future."

Ruby felt her lip curl in disgust. "That is black magic and no good person uses it."

"You may keep your own beliefs, Ruby, but it is discourteous to disparage the beliefs of those living here, especially when we are providing you with a room and food," Mistress said coolly. "Today, you will help

Honus and Kieta in the kitchen, but soon I want you to meet Te Ran. Perhaps with her help you could see where your sister is living now."


The next morning Ruby woke early, dressed and headed directly for the kitchen. Maidenstone House was enormous with its twists and rising staircases that ended in closed doors. Arriving after three false turns, guided only by the scent of cooking food, Ruby finally reached the kitchen and said good morning to the two cooks, Honus and Kieta. They handed her plates and silverware and told her to set the table in the dining room for the students. When the table was set, Ruby sat down to await her breakfast.

Honus came into the dining room and shook her head, gesturing for Ruby to come with her. Apparently, she wasn't allowed to eat with the other 'la-di-dah' students. She had to eat in the kitchen with the cooks. At least it was warmer there and Cloudheart came out from under the stove. Ruby was happy to see him.

Peeking into the dining room as it filled with students, she discovered there were only five students studying at Maidenstone. Asking Honus about them, she learned that four came from the city of Namché. The fifth student arrived before the Occupation. Her name was Deti. She was thirteen, tall and slim as a reed. When Ruby served her, she noticed Deti wore an expression of stillness, as if she were listening to someone calling her from far away. Honus had called the girls Novices. Ruby was scandalized. A Novice was a girl called to serve God by becoming a Sister, a female officiate. These girls were being taught sorcery. They did at least give a prayer of thanks for the food, she noticed, but they prayed to some Goddess or other. It was all heathen nonsense.

After helping serve the food and clean up the kitchen, Honus told her to go to Mistress Falcon's Office. She walked part way with her talking about Sab-ra, although Ruby didn't catch all of it.

Ruby managed to stumble upon the right corridor, practically by accident and knocked on the door.

"Enter," a cool voice ordered.

Ruby walked into the room, seeing Mistress Falcon seated at her desk. A tall coffee-skinned woman stood beside her, clothed in ivory linen. She was very thin, had fine features and skin was the color of redwood. She looked like the gypsies that moved from town to town with their little camper trailers on Viridian.

"Ruby, it is customary in Namché to bow your head to a Priestess."

Ruby clenched her teeth, not wanting to demonstrate respect to this eastern witch, but at Mistress' unflinching gaze, she finally ducked her head.

"This is our Priestess, Te Ran, a talented Supplicant and Far Seer. Te Ran, this is Ruby, Sab-ra's twin sister."

"I greet you sister of Sab-ra," the red woman said, looking at her for a long time.

Ruby nodded, unsmiling.

"Starting tomorrow, you will work with Te Ran each day after washing the breakfast dishes. She will test your abilities. This is a gift, Ruby. If the Far Seer permits, you might see Sab-ra in a vision or trance. It is proper and appropriate to thank me, and you will kneel to Te Ran." Her voice was deadly serious.

Ruby felt anger rise inside her. She hadn't wanted to come to this God-forsaken country in the first place and now she was supposed to kneel before a coffee-skinned pagan who told the future like a carnival gypsy.

"Ruby," Mistress Falcon's voice commanded, "On your knees."

Ruby shook her head. Te Ran took Ruby's arm and with astonishing strength forced her to the floor. Her knees banged on the cold stone. Ruby got a shock from Te Ran's touch.

"Ouch, you are hurting me," she cried, angrily.

"If you don't demonstrate more respect, next time, I hurt you more," the Priestess said and Ruby felt her breath quicken. The hair lifted on the nape of her neck.

"You are dismissed, Ruby," Mistress said and she fled.

# Chapter 6
## The Temple

After breakfast and helping wash the dishes the next morning, Honus told Ruby to go to the Temple. They walked out of the yellow tower together and the cook pointed to a soaring white building nearby. Ruby walked to it, feeling apprehensive. Te Ran was waiting for her just outside the big door.

"I greet you, Ruby," Te Ran said. "Come with me into the sanctuary." The Priestess walked purposefully to the front of the nave.

Ruby followed her into the large open room with many seats in rows for the worshippers. That was the only proper church-like about the place. It had no true altar. The windows were old and wavy and not one window had been made of stained glass. The place felt alien. The corners of her mouth tightened in distaste, but she tried to suppress her response to this tosspot's wrong-headed religion.

Suddenly, the sun came out from behind a cloud and all the wavy glass in the windows scattered a thousand crescent moons on the stone floor. It was glorious. Ruby found herself unexpectedly moved by their beauty. She felt a lump in her throat, wondering how long it would be before she would kneel before the altar in Viridian again.

"Come," Te Ran called over her shoulder walking to the front of the sanctuary.

On the altar, Ruby saw a silver bowl placed on a translucent rock shelf. Ruby felt her stomach clench but walked forward. She felt as if she were pulled ahead by an invisible cord. Te Ran drizzled oil around on the top edging of the bowl.

"Watch while I light the rim," she said and struck a flint against a rock. The rim caught fire and flames danced along the edge of the vessel. In the center of the bowl, floating in the clear liquid, Ruby saw a wick.

"Now, you will light the center flame. To do this, you will need to stop the fire from burning your skin."

Ruby had no idea what the irritating gypsy woman meant. She took a lighted candle and inserted her hand and arm directly through the rim flames. Once the wick ignited, she stepped back. A blue blaze rose high into the air, nearly to the ceiling.

Te Ran looked at her meaningfully and Ruby knelt. She wouldn't wait for Te Ran to drag her down to the stone floor this time, although she felt a qualm. By kneeling in this place, was she being a traitor to her faith? What would Fr. Patrick think?

Then Te Ran picked up a small saucer filled with burning leaves. The scent was delicious, like dried hay on the fields in Viridian. The Priestess bent her face down to the rising white smoke and inhaled sharply. She shivered as she intoned some syllables. Her eyes rolled back in her head.

Suddenly Ruby felt a brush of warm air and the Priestess' body rose in the air. It was terrifying and Ruby trembled all over. She desperately wanted to escape, but her body refused to move. The poxy gypsy woman had placed her in some type of paralysis. Despite herself, Ruby's eyes rose to Te Ran's face. It was transcendent with joy. She swallowed convulsively in fear. Shuddering, Ruby felt a great power inflame her spirit. Seconds later, Te Ran's body returned to its usual size. She touched Ruby's forehead in blessing.

Feeling the Priestess' touch like an electric spark, Ruby stood up and raced out of the Temple. She was desperate to escape the frightening place. Te Ran darted after her and grabbed her shoulder, pushing Ruby down to a sitting position.

"Talk to me," she demanded. "Tell me what you saw?"

Ruby was trembling and could not speak for a moment. She shook her head.

"Tell me," Te Ran ordered. Her voice was loud and Ruby turned her head away, afraid to look at the Priestess.

"I saw you get larger. I felt something," Ruby voice was grudging with resentment as she said, "I felt a power. It was like what I imagine the Rapture will be."

Te Ran looked at her appraisingly and reached into the pocket of her robe. "This is a Far Seer orb," she said. "Look into it. Tell me what you see."

Ruby looked at her sadly. "Te Ran, I cannot do this. When I knelt in the Temple, I felt I had defiled the true religion." She looked away from the Priestess and up at the sky. To her horror, she saw that it was already dark. She had spent a whole day in the Temple, thinking it had been an hour.

Te Ran gripped her shoulder saying, "I ask you, sister of Sab-ra, please to look into the glass. Once you do, you may leave the Temple. Hold the glass in your hand. The moon is already rising. Twist it back and forth. When the light of the moon falls on the glass, look deeply inside."

"No, this is wrong. It is against God. I should not do this." Ruby felt her back muscles tense and her shoulders hunch up.

"It is only the power of the Goddess," Te Ran told her gently and gazed into her eyes until Ruby's eyes fluttered in trance. Te Ran eased her gently down to sit against the exterior walls of the Temple.

"What do you see?" Te Ran whispered quietly.

Ruby's voice sounded dazed as she whispered, "Red-haired girl. Big with child. She rides beside a large copper-skinned bloke."

Te Ran snapped her fingers and Ruby returned to the present.

"Did anyone in your family have what the People call the Sight?" Te Ran asked, a curious expression on her face.

"Supposedly, my Great Grandmother had it, but the only thing she could tell was whether a pregnant woman would have a boy or a girl. It was nothing, a cheap con, a carnival trick." Ruby struggled to display her formerly suspicious attitude, but something powerful had happened to her. She couldn't quite shake it off.

"Be that as it may, Ruby, I think you have the true gift," Te Ran said seriously. "You may go now."

Ruby struggled to her feet and walked back to the yellow tower, trying desperately to hold in her mind a memory of her father saying grace before the evening meal.

After helping Honus and Kieta serve breakfast for the students the next morning, Ruby walked out of Maidenstone's yellow tower. She was still badly shaken from her encounter in the Temple the day before and had hardly slept. She needed to talk with someone from her own country. Standing on the forecourt, she looked down at the hundred steps and saw the Garrison off to the west, near the railroad tracks. It looked as if it would be easy to find, but she knew there was a rat's nest of alleys between the bottom step and the Garrison.

When Ruby reached the bottom, she dodged her way through numerous alleys in the market and after many wrong turns, she chanced upon the Garrison. Walking up to the two-story building, she told the soldier on guard she had come to see the two Garda lads from Viridian.

"Their names are Carmac Gifford and Jaime Fitzjohn."

The guard nodded and left. Ruby stood on the stoop, trying to regain her equilibrium, enjoying the sounds of street musicians tuning their instruments and the smell of bread baking.

"Hey, Ruby Girl," Carmac called out, running across the open graveled yard from the dining hall. He looked happy and windblown. "Jaime is working in the kitchen, but they told me I had a visitor. Hoped it would be you, I did."

"Can we walk somewhere?"

"Sure we can, Ruby darling. What's wrong? You look a bit shook."

"I just need to talk a little."

"There's a park near here where the almond trees are blooming."

They walked together down the tree-lined streets. Carmac reached for Ruby's hand and she squeezed his fingers. Her hands were cold and his felt warm. The scent of the flowering almond trees rode the wind. Their pale pink blossoms looked incongruous on dark leafless trees that stood in melting snow.

"How is it going, Ruby?"

"I got to the Maidenstone School and they gave me a nice room, but the Mistress made me go to this Temple. I didn't want to go. It isn't a proper church and I was afraid Fr. Patrick would be mad, but she said I had to."

Carmac's blue eyes were intent on her face as he listened.

"This woman, Te Ran, they call her a Priestess, but I think she's a gypsy witch, I do. Anyway, she made me light this wick in a bowl filled with oil. When I lit the flame, it rose nearly to the ceiling. Then I saw the Priestess rise in the air, like a balloon."

"What?" Carmac asked. "You saw her floating up in the air?" He frowned.

"That's the only way I can describe it. She made me tell her what I felt."

"What did you feel?" he asked.

"Bloody terrified is what. She touched my head and I must have blacked out for a moment, because I saw this twin of mine. I told you that I came here in search of my twin sister, didn't I? Anyway, my sister was riding in the mountains with a giant copper skinned bloke and she was pregnant. Then this Priestess asks me if I have the Sight."

"Do you have it? One of my old relatives had it, Mum said."

"I'm not sure. Gran told me her Gran had it, could see the future like. Carmac, I'm scared of that Temple place."

Ruby was visibly trembling and Carmac put her arm around her shoulders.

"Then you shouldn't go back to that culchie place."

"You think?"

"Sure, just tell the magic floating woman to fly away somewhere. Tell her you want nothing more to do with her."

Ruby wondered if it could be that easy, as easy as simply refusing. She gave a big sigh and felt the tension in her neck and shoulders ease.

"Thank you, Carmac, I will give it a try," Ruby said, but she had a funny feeling she might not be given a choice in the matter.

"Come give me a kiss then for the good advice," Carmac grinned at her.

Ruby melted into the soldier's embrace. When she pulled back, she had tears in her eyes. Carmac's body felt so much like her boyfriend Shane's. She brushed her tears away and smiled.

"Don't tell Jaime," she giggled, "He's the one who boasts he's such a good kisser."

As Ruby walked back up the hundred steps she thought about Shane, back on Viridian. Carmac was a better kisser than Shane was, for sure. Cuter, too, with his red curls and dark blue eyes. Very handsome in his uniform, too. She managed a grin, feeling better.

# Chapter 7
# Labor Pains

In the middle of the night. Ruby sat up in bed groaning in pain. She looked out the window from her room at Maidenstone. The moon was very bright and the stars were thick. Their light came through the dark sky as if they shone through tiny pinholes. The pain hit again and Ruby clutched her stomach. An Mali, the elderly Healer who met her the day she arrived, had showed her the clinic at the top of the ancient building. The Healer said that if a Novice was ill, she came to the Infirmary. Ruby lay back on her bed watching the moon, forcing back screams as the pain got worse and worse. Realizing it was impossible for her to lie still, she got up and paced the room.

Giving up at last, Ruby decided she would find the blasted Infirmary. She felt faint from the pain and terrible nausea. She walked slowly down the hall, clutching her stomach, searching desperately for the circular staircase. By the time she reached it, she was bent double in pain. Walking up the three flights of steps was excruciating. She opened the door to the Clinic, holding her hand over her mouth. She barely made it to a sink in time to throw up.

"Who is it," An Mali's sleepy voice asked.

"Help," Ruby cried. She could not stop throwing up and the pain was worse than any she had ever felt before.

An Mali came out of her small room, looking concerned. "Ruby, what is wrong? Are you sick from food, do you think?"

"This terrible belly pain is beating the living shite out of me," Ruby managed. An Mali put an arm around her and led her to one of the beds. Ruby threw up all over the floor and began to cry.

"I am so sorry, An Mali."

"Show me where it hurts?"

Ruby pointed to her belly. When An Mali touched her stomach, she screamed.

An Mali went to the Medicine table and brought her some little white pearl-like pills. "These are made from the poppy flower. It will stop the pain," the Healer said. Ruby swallowed them eagerly.

"The pains. It comes in waves," she managed. An Mali sat beside her, stroking her forehead. Slowly, as the poppy took her pain away she slept.

At dawn, the pains were gone. Ruby felt refreshed and calm, happier than she had been since leaving home. She got up, dressed and headed for Mistress Falcon's office. She only took one wrong turn before entering the proper hall and felt proud of herself. She was beginning to learn the crazy layout of Maidenstone. Mistress' door was ajar and Ruby could hear two voices. Mistress was talking with the Priestess, Ten Ran. Ruby slowed down and stopped, knowing she should not listen to their conversation, but was unable to stop herself.

"I believe Ruby has the ability to see using Vision, Mistress," Te Ran said. "I didn't even give her monkscaul to breathe, and still she saw. What is more, she did not see something momentous to come, as I do. The heathen girl saw her sister immediately. She rode with a Kosi warrior and Ruby could tell Sab-ra was pregnant."

"Sab-ra is pregnant. Interesting. I wonder if she married. She had a strong connection with the Goddess, perhaps she did not feel the need of a husband," Mistress Falcon said.

*Her sister was having a kid and she wasn't even married?* Ruby was mortified. *Didn't any of these people have morals?*

"Did Ruby say anything about our religion?"

"She seemed to consider me little more than a carnival fortune-teller. However, when I asked her to light the inner flame of the Supplication bowl, she didn't hesitate. She put her hand directly through the fire and lit the wick. She didn't seem feel the heat. It took Sab-ra months to learn how to do it, and she burned herself repeatedly. When Ruby lit the wick, it rose higher than I have ever seen it. The blue flame nearly reached the ceiling of the Temple. It was staggering."

"I find myself completely perplexed," Mistress said. "Here we have a young woman carrying a commission from her mother, a girl who rejects everything we believe, and yet has enormous talent. It is a puzzling problem."

"It is." Both women were quiet for a few moments and Ruby was about to run down the hall and leave until she heard Mistress speak again.

"I am happy to know that Sab-ra lives and is with a Kosi. I wonder if it is Ghang's child she carries. He took her up into the high range, you will recall."

"I could put Ruby in a trance to find this information, if you wish."

"No, Te Ran, we cannot do this simply to satisfy our curiosity. I was going to wait until summer before sending Ruby into the high range, but now I think she must go soon."

"I agree. Will you send Ten-Singh with her? I could go along if you wish."

"No, the high range is alive with wounded and dangerous men. You must remain here, although I would be grateful for anything you see in the Scry."

"As you know well, Mistress, the Scry is not for finding an individual's path, it is only to discern the fate of nations," Te Ran's voice was calm. "I find it astonishing that Ruby could have such a talent, hidden under the layers of her monotheistic religion."

"As do I," Mistress said, deep in thought. "However, when she speaks of her God, I feel her certainty. Although it is very different from our beliefs, there is power in her faith."

Ruby turned and ran down the hall. She didn't want this so-called Vision talent. It shook her down to her boots. Mistress said the mountain was alive with dangerous men and yet she planned to send Ruby there? She quivered and clenched her sweaty hands.


A few days later, Ruby and Cloudheart were sitting in the grass near the fishpond in the back garden of Maidenstone, when the young Novice Deti opened the door and came outside. According to Mistress, Deti came from an unknown valley in the Blue Mountains. While she was away at school one day, Harn soldiers had attacked and burned her village to the ground. The shock of finding her family all dead and her home smoldering in ashes had rendered her mute.

When she arrived at Maidenstone, the Monks worked with her for some time, eventually learning that she had been in training as an artist. They had encouraged Mistress to foster Deti's artistic talent. Ruby had watched her draw one day, impressed by her ability to capture the essence of a person in a few strokes of a paintbrush.

"Mistress said to give you this," Deti handed Ruby a letter. The stamps were from Viridian and Ruby knew it was a letter from her Da. Ruby walked up to her room and sat on the bed. What would she do if her Mum was worse? God forbid she died. Ruby's breath came quickly and her heart beat faster.

Ruby felt a sick desperation and her heart twisted inside her. She felt a wave of homesickness for her Mum, her Da, her dog, her friends and the lovely isle of Viridian. She trembled, thinking her mother might already be dead. She paced the room, trying frantically to think of what she should do. She took her small purse and checked the money inside. It was enough to send a telegram.

Running down the hundred steps, Sab-ra went directly to the Garrison. She was panting hard when she arrived. Her red hair blew across her face and she brushed it away impatiently.

"I need Carmac," she told the guard and he nodded.

A few minute later, both Carmac and Jaime came walking across the gravel.

"So how are you today, Ruby?" Jaime asked. Carmac reached out and gave her a hug.

"Boys, I have had a terrible letter from me Da. Mum has been in hospital and a surgeon was called to do an operation. Ma doesn't want me to come home yet, but I am frantic to know if she made it through the surgery. I want to send a telegram to me Da and ask him to send one right back here. Can you help me?"

"Sure we can, come with us."

The three of them set off walking through a haze of scents from the spice merchants, to a tiny stall in the Market district. A thin man bowed repeatedly to all three of them. It took some time, but at last he sent Ruby's telegram.

*"Is Mum better? Twin not here. Want to come home."*

They waited for several hours. At one point Jaime went to a food stall and brought them all something to eat. Ruby was ravenous. She paced around the telegram station, unable to sit still. The sun was setting when the bowing man gave her the return telegram.

*"Mum better. Stay there. Find sister."*

# Chapter 8
## Meeting Brother Marzun

"Where have you been?" Mistress asked her angrily when Ruby returned and reached the top of the hundred stairs leading to Maidenstone. She looked tall and imposing with her black robe swirling in the wind.

"I went to send a telegram to me Da. My Ma is sick in the hospital. I needed to know if she survived the surgery." Ruby knew her voice sounded sulky. She resented having to tell Mistress why she left or what she did. It was no business of hers, snotty cow.

"Te Ran told me that you saw Sab-ra pregnant in the Temple and An Mali said you had severe abdominal pains last night. Do you think your pains might be connected with Sab-ra?"

"I did wonder if it was because my sister was having her baby. Me Gran would call it sympathetic suffering," Ruby admitted reluctantly.

Mistress looked thoughtful. "I planned to try to get you to Talin before Sab-ra delivered, but if you think it's too late, perhaps you should stay here longer. The white tresses of snow still lie upon the foothills of the Dhali Ra. Before I make a final decision, I would like you to talk with Brother Jun."

Another one of the fey people, Ruby thought resentfully. Her mouth twisted but she followed Mistress back to the Yellow Tower.

"Go now and help Honus and Kieta finish cooking dinner," Mistress said.

She's using me like a galley slave, Ruby thought sourly, although she admitted to herself she was in no hurry to leave. If she stayed at Maidenstone, she could see the Garda from time to time, especially Carmac, and if Da sent a telegram about her Mum, they would bring it to her. Once she left the city to go higher in the mountains, she might never get word of Ma's condition.

A young monk in a red robe was waiting for Ruby outside the kitchen after she finished washing the breakfast dishes the following morning.

"I am Brother Jun," he told her calmly. "Will you walk with me?"

As if I have a choice in the matter, Ruby thought sullenly. She followed the monk with little Cloudheart pattering behind them. Jun heard the click of Cloudheart's toenails and looked over his shoulder. Ruby thought the Monk might send the little dog packing, but what he did instead was startling.

"Cloudheart, I greet you," he said quietly and actually bowed to the white dog.

This place completely baffled Ruby. *Who bowed to a dog?*

They exited the Yellow Tower and walked across the lawn to a Green Tower. Jun opened the door and ushered her inside. They proceeded across an open stone-flagged space and climbed a circular staircase. It went up many stories until they reached an eight-sided room at the top of the spire with windows on all sides. The view of the Blue Mountain range in bright sunlight was stunning.

Jun looked at her with a gentle smile. "Te Ran tells me you have the Sight," he said.

"No. I don't. It's just that culchie Te Ran who says so," Ruby heard the crankiness in her own voice.

"Do you fear the Sight?" Jun asked.

"Would be a silly thing to be afraid of something I don't have," Ruby said defiantly.

"I want you to talk with Brother Marzun," Brother Jun said. "Would you let him see into your mind?"

Ruby felt an immense frustration. She hated all this nonsense, seeing into People's minds. It was ridiculous. She took a deep breath and said, "I am only here because I have a twin sister. Sab-ra is her name."

"I know her well," Jun said, his eyes sparkling.

"My Mum is in hospital but she said I have to stay here until I see my sister. I would go back now, but she made me promise to find Sab-ra before I returned. I hoped she would be here in Namché, but apparently my twin left a year ago. Mistress is keeping me here until it is warmer and then I will go up into the mountains to find her." Ruby felt peevish and reached down to pet Cloudheart. Petting him always made her feel better and eased her longing for her own red dog.

"Would a weapon help you on this journey?"

"Yes, it would. Could you give me a gun or at least a knife?"

"No. I meant a mind weapon. Brother Marzun could give you a weapon of the mind."

*Better than nothing, I suppose*, Ruby thought, exasperated.

The following morning Jun was waiting in the hall when Ruby left the kitchen. Again he took her to the Green Tower. After walking the circular staircase inside the tower, Jun opened a door to the outdoor bridge. They were going across the bridge to the White Tower, he said. Brother Jun stepped forward and floating tendrils of mist rose to his waist.

"Follow me," he said.

Ruby took a step into the fog and felt it pull her forward gently. When they reached the white tower, Jun looked at Ruby.

"Don't the glass steps with no hand rails frighten you?" he asked, with a perplexed expression on his face.

"What I see is a broad white bridge made of glistening stone. It is wide enough that a team of horses could have ridden across it."

Brother Jun looked at her in amazement and murmured, *This girl sees beyond the spells we put upon the bridges.*

Inside the White Tower, they walked up more flights of stairs. These steps were made of yellow glass. Like Jun said, there were no handrails, but Ruby felt peaceful as she climbed. The sun hit the steps and yellow prisms were everywhere. Ruby's resentment of being at Maidenstone left her then, like a gull in flight. She was entranced by the beauty of tiny circular rainbows floating up the walls. The reached an eight-sided room with windows all around it.

"I will leave you here, Ruby. Brother Marzun will come for you."

Soon a door opened and a fat little monk entered the room. His small eyes were dark. They twinkled. "I am Brother Marzun," he told her. "When you look at the beautiful Blue Mountains, what do you see?"

"A bunch of little valleys, running along a green river." Ruby's voice sounded bored.

"You can see that far?" Brother Marzun seemed amazed. "The Twelve Valleys country is ten days ride above Namché."

"Is Sab-ra there?"

"If you count the valleys from west to east, Talin is the third valley. That's where Sab-ra came from."

"The little valleys are so beautiful, like a necklace of jewels strung along a green river," Ruby said.

"Like a necklace, indeed," Brother Marzun said. "And like a necklace made of blue diamonds, it is desirable country. Up in the highest range there is a blue diamond mine which belongs to the Twelve Valleys people, although no one knows its exact location. They mine stones there called Skygrass stones. The war with the Harn Army was fought because they sought possession of the blue diamond mine."

"Will I go up into the Blue Mountains in the spring?" Ruby asked, quivering a little at the thought of the trip.

"Mistress will send you there when the weather improves," Brother Marzun said.

"Will I take a train? I took many trains to get to Namché."

"No, Ruby, there are no trains above Namché."

"Then how will I ever get there?" Ruby felt dismayed.

"On horseback. It's about a ten day trip."

A ten-day trip in the mountains on a horse would be a nightmare. She hated this whole thing. Why couldn't her mother have gone to find this sister by herself? Ruby gritted her teeth. Then she felt guilty when she realized she resented her mother's dire illness. She felt a headache coming on.

"I dread this trip," she admitted, looking down, "But I promised me Ma I would find my sister, Sab-ra, so find her I shall. If I were on Viridian, I would ask Fr. Patrick to bless my journey." She felt a sadness that made her chest feel heavy.

"Then I shall do so in his name," Brother Marzun told her gently. He drew a circle in the air above Ruby's bright curls.

"I have a question for you," Brother Marzun said. "It may seem odd, but I want to know if you know me?"

*What kind of a question was that*, Ruby wondered, irritated.

"No, of course I don't know you. How could I? I only just met you," Ruby found herself increasingly irked by Brother Marzun's gentle questions.

"Look into my eyes," the monk's voice was soothing.

Ruby gazed into his dark eyes. They were like small pools and after a moment or two, she gasped.

"What do you see?"

Ruby's voice was low and sounded tranced, "Why, I do know you. You are my Grandfather." Soft amazement filled her voice.

"Yes," he smiled at her. "I was once married to a beautiful wife. She died giving birth to our second son. The midwife who attended her felt terrible remorse over her death. I could not work and take care of two young children, so I asked the midwife and her husband to adopt the infant. I named my son Dani. I am Dani's father and your Grandfather."

Ruby's face filled with amazement. She couldn't speak for a moment.

"A year after the midwife and her husband adopted my infant son, I felt the Universe nudge me and heard the call to enter the Monastery. I took my older son to the Valley of Talin. Sab-ra's grandparents adopted him also. The two boys grew up together. My eldest son was named Hent. He is your uncle and their parents are your adoptive grandparents." As Brother Marzun spoke these words, Ruby felt her eyes grow heavy. "Tell me what you see," he said.

Her voice had a singsong quality as she spoke. "Mum sits in fields of flowers with a dark- haired boy. They play with a wee white lion."

"Would you like to stay and work with me?" Brother Marzun asked her kindly. "There are many things I could show you." He snapped his fingers.

"Yes," she breathed out a long sigh of relief, coming back to the present.

"Our time together will be a journey of great import. For both of us I think."

# Chapter 9
## Going into the High Range
## April

It seemed to Ruby only a few days had passed since she began working with Brother Marzun when one day she noticed that all the snow was gone. Small yellow sativa flowers were blooming in the kitchen garden. There were red flowers on the sapritet bushes and the other trees were topped by a cumulous of green leaves.

"What month is it now?" she asked Honus. She felt confused and troubled about the dramatic change in the weather.

"The Planting Moon has already begun," she answered.

"What month did I come here?" Ruby asked.

"You have been here two moons already," Honus said.

Ruby frowned. She had started working Brother Marzun only a week after arriving in Namché. Horrorstruck, she realized she remembered nothing since she began spending her days with the old monk. She walked across spring green grass to the White tower and ascended the circular staircase. When she reached the top room, Brother Marzun was sitting in his chair looking out as the verdant plants of spring climbed the Blue Mountains. Except for the highest peaks the mountains were now completely bare of snow.

"Brother Marzun, according to Honus, I have been coming here every day for over two months, although it only feels like we began days ago," Ruby's voice shook. "I remember nothing of that time. What is happening to me?" Tears sprang to her eyes. She blinked them away.

Brother Marzun's serene countenance wore a sudden frown.

"Did you hear me? I don't have any memories since we met! Two months according to Honus," Ruby wailed.

"I will get Brother Jun," he said. When he came back, he asked her to tell Brother Jun what she had told him.

"I remember meeting Brother Marzun and finding out he was my Grandfather. Other than that I remember only a few times helping in the kitchen and one day with Cloudheart in the garden."

Brother Marzun sighed quietly and said, "Ruby, I fear you have the Far Seer disease." His face creased in sympathy.

Ruby was disgusted. *Working with the old monk had given her a disease? What had happened to her Ma in the last two months? Was she even alive? Had she received any letters or telegrams?* She was about to ask, but Brother Jun spoke, breaking her chain of thought.

"The Far Seer disease is not a true disease, Ruby. It is what happens to extremely talented Far Seers who cannot control the Sight."

"Exactly," Brother Marzun said calmly. "You have a rare form of the Sight called the Vision. Most of the acolytes that study with Te Ran learn to Scry, to see momentous events in the future. You have the ability to see what is happening to others in the present. When Te Ran took you to the Temple, I understand she asked you to look into her crystal orb and tell her what you saw. She said you saw a pregnant red haired girl who rode with a dark Kosi warrior. We believe it was your sister, Sab-ra."

"I remember that," Ruby said tentatively, seeking desperately to understand what had happened to her.

"The Far Seer disease comes because the Seer actually enters the consciousness of the person she sees. For the last two months, we think you have been inside Sab-ra's mind, living her life."

Ruby felt her cheeks redden and tears of rage begin to form. "This Vision thing took my life," she wailed. "When I agreed to work with you, nobody told me that a huge block of time would vanish. I never would have agreed to you probing around in my mind if I knew this would happen."

"None of us knew it would happen," Brother Jun told her gently. "We have not had this happen before to any of our acolytes. But don't be afraid. It can be managed."

"What matters is what you do from this time forward," Brother Marzun said crisply. "Listen carefully, Ruby, this is important. You need to control this. You must never seek the Vision again, unless your own life is in danger. Are we agreed?"

"Yes," Ruby told him firmly. She feared this awful Vision business. *Avoiding it would not be a loss. Crazy fey stuff,* she thought.


Mistress Falcon was waiting when Ruby reached the door to the Yellow Tower. "There is no need to delay your trip up into the Mountains any longer," she said.

"Who is going to take me up into the Mountains," Ruby asked, suspiciously.

"One of the Bearer people who works for me. Ten Singh is his name."

"I cannot leave Maidenstone on a trip alone with a man," Ruby wailed in horror. "My Da would be scandalized."

"Deti will be going with you also. I would like you to take Cloudheart along and bring him to see Sab-ra, but I am not sure he will leave Maidenstone. Call him and I will ask him to choose."

What nonsense, Ruby thought, giving the dog a choice. "Come to me, Cloudheart," she said. He ran to her. She lifted him up in her arms. She smiled down at his bright eyes.

"Set him down now," Mistress said. "Cloudheart, come here," she called, but he would not leave Ruby. He sat at her feet, fixing his eyes on hers lovingly.

"My true companion," Ruby murmured. Cloudheart's loyalty had helped her feel less homesick.

"Then you may go with Ruby, Cloudheart," Mistress said, speaking directly to the dog.

"Mistress Falcon, have I heard from my father in the last two months? I'm terribly afraid of what happened to my mother."

"Yes, child. Your mother has recovered enough to leave the hospital. She and your father are together at home. You may write them, if you wish. I will send the letter."

That evening Ruby wrote a long letter to her parents, telling them she was leaving Maidenstone to travel into the high range. She described Brother Marzun and told her mother that he was Dani's father. She said she missed them terribly, told them to kiss her Gran, hug her dog and say hello to Shane for her.


It was late afternoon when the small cavalcade going to the Blue Mountains got underway. Ten Singh, Deti and Ruby walked down Maidenstone's hundred step staircase with little Cloudheart trotting beside them. It was a warm breezy day and the sky was blue and cloudless.

Ten Singh was a slim man with intelligent brownish green eyes. Mistress told Ruby he was one of the high range Bearer people who took messages from one settlement to another. Ruby wondered if he could defend her from the dangerous men Mistress said were in the hills. Then she noticed how his muscles bulged and how easily he lifted her from the last step on the staircase to the ground.

Three ponies stood tied to a post nearby. One had a dark woolen roll on the back of his saddle. All three animals looked around wildly, jerking on their laces. Their eyes showed white whenever a blowing sound came from inside the tunnel.

"This is your pony, Ruby. She is a gentle sort, named Star."

"She doesn't look very gentle now," Ruby said, fear filling her stomach. "Do we have to go into that dark tunnel?" She gestured to a circular opening, filled with a boiling mist.

"Yes, but Star will be fine once we get inside. Have you ridden much in your country?"

"Once or twice," Ruby said. "They have small ponies at the parks and kids can ride them. Mum took me sometimes when I was a wee little thing."

Ten Singh's mouth twisted and he frowned. "I will keep our pace as slow as I can, but Mistress said there was some urgency about getting you to Talin. This first day we will ride only for about four hours. I am going to lead all three of the ponies into the tunnel now. I will hold your hand until we get through. If you are frightened, close your eyes. Deti, will you be all right walking beside me?"

"I'm excited to go on this trip. I haven't been out of Namché since I came here before the War." Holding Cloudheart's leash, Deti skipped ahead in clear delight.

White fog boiled out of the tunnel entrance, and Ruby shivered. Once they were inside, it was completely dark. Ruby felt cool air wetting her eyelashes and found the thick white vapor hard to breathe.

"Keep your eyes shut," Ten Singh reminded her.

When they were out in the bright day again, Ruby sighed in relief.

"Don't turn around," Ten Singh commanded her brusquely.

"Why?" She had almost turned back.

"The Leopard Gate frightens most people."

"Not me," Deti said, bravely, but Ruby noticed she didn't look back either.

In front of them, a guard was checking people leaving the city. Past the checkpoint there was a multi-arched stone bridge spanning a water barrier. Beyond the bridge, Ruby saw a huge wall. It wavered in the sunlight and seemed made of fabric.

"What is the wall made of, Ten Singh?" she asked. "It looks like some kind of metallic cloth."

"It is a magic mesh and no arrow or even bullet can penetrate it. When the Harn Army came, we could have defended the city, if enough citizens had joined the Resistance. Instead, they opened the gates." His voice sounded bitter.

Beyond the wall, Ruby was relieved to see a road. The ponies clopped along slowly, leaving dusty hoof prints behind them. Soon, she would see Sab-ra. What would she feel when she saw her sister, she wondered. She was anxious to get this trip over with so she could return to her parents and her friends, but knew she would be sad to leave Cloudheart when the time came to return to Viridian.

# Chapter 10
## The Trip to Talin

The rain started slowly but then pelted down. Ruby's travelling cloak was quickly soaked. Her shoes squished against the flanks of her pony. Her red curls were plastered to her forehead.

"Ten Singh, can we stop soon. I am perishing for my tea." She kept hollering until at last Ten Singh told her they would stop soon.

They arrived at a poor farmstead about an hour later. A peasant dressed in rags came outside and told them to dismount. Deti jumped down and dashed around exploring the farm with Cloudheart. He found a hen and barked at her. The chicken was sitting on some eggs on the muddy ground. Ruby looked around in dismay. *Was this dirty farmhouse where they were going to sleep?* Even though they had ridden only about four hours, her bottom was terribly sore. Dismounting from Star, Ruby was unsteady on her feet. The farmer gestured and they followed him into the dank wooden structure. There were only three rooms, and none of them had doors. Ruby shivered, thinking about sleeping in this dark place with two grown men.

"Where do we wash, Ten Singh?" she whispered.

"There is a spring behind the house, use that."

"Won't the water be cold?"

"Of course," Ten Singh said looking at her with a wry expression, partly amused, partly irritated.

"I am sore," she whispered and patted herself on the bottom.

"I will ask the farmer for some milk-bag unguent."

*Something from a cow's dirty udder?* Ruby thought, feeling uncomfortable about what the farmer would bring her to use on her sores. When Ten Singh returned, he had a piece of what looked like cowhide folded into a packet. Opening it, he showed her a dollop of black tar. Although Ruby dreaded applying the sticky substance, and the cowhide smelled disgusting, she forced herself to rub the gel into her skin. Revolting it was, but she had to admit it helped.

Ten Singh took the dark wool roll from the back of his pony.

It was a type of tent, Ruby realized, watching him erect the shelter. Inside it was very dark, but clean and warm. Ten Singh spread some furs on the floor saying it was where she and Deti would sleep. Cloudheart settled himself between them with a sigh. Ten Singh said he would sleep in the farmer's house with the farmer. Deti would be sleeping with her.

When the farmer pressed Ruby to take the rest of the unguent the next morning, she thanked him and took it. Despite it coming from a common dirty cow, she knew she would use it. They faced many more days on the road.


The following afternoon, the sun came out as they entered an area of harsh black sand and enormous boulders. Ten Singh called it the Garden of the Gods. Ruby looked around for any type of house or inn. There was nothing but wind and raw nature. The tied the ponies to small trees. Ten Singh started a campfire and told Deti to get some water from a nearby stream. Ten Singh handed each of them some bread. He had spread cheese on it and warmed it over the fire. It was a long way from a proper tea, but Ruby was grateful. The bread was delicious.

"I was near to having a weakness," she told Ten Singh. He shook his head, unused to girls who complained as much as Ruby.

After dinner, Ten Singh led her away from the campfire to a small spring bubbling out of the ground. The water was icy cold.

"I will leave you. Remove your pants and sit down in the water. It will help."

Ruby practically screamed when she lowered herself into the water. She jumped out several times, but made herself get back in. The water did help and after applying the black unguent again, she found herself more comfortable. She walked back to the campfire and asked Ten Singh where he was going to set up the black tent.

"It's called a dweli, Ruby, but tonight we will be sleeping beneath the stars," he grinned at her startled expression. He led both girls deeper into the grass that encircled the gray guardian stones. They followed a slim little trail, hardly visible in the fading light. At first the grass only reached up to her waist, but deeper into the green scrim, it towered above her head. The grasses parted and Ruby saw a large circle of flattened green rushes. It looked as if something had stomped them down. Ten Singh spread their sleeping robes on the flat grasses and went back for the ponies.

"This is a Ghat bed," Deti whispered.

"What are Ghat?" Ruby asked, feeling alarmed. She wasn't about to sit down until she knew what the heck a Ghat was.

"Wild oxen."

"Will they be coming back?" Ruby heard terror in her voice. She envisioned cattle running in the night, stepping on them with their cloven hooves. How she wished she had never left home. She wondered if her parents were sitting down to tea and ached to be with them.

"Ten Singh wouldn't have us camp here if the Ghat were coming back. You are a silly scardy cat, Ruby," Deti said.

Cloudheart kept leaving them to run into the tall blades and Ruby called him back several times before trapping him and setting a big stone on his leash. He tugged against the rope and looked at them, pleadingly. Both girls shook their heads. Cloudheart sat with his head hanging down. It was unusual behavior for the little dog, Ruby thought. He was normally so well-behaved.

Lying on furs, looking up at the stars through the moving circle of the grasses, Ruby saw a dark vee formation in the colored sky of sunset.

"Are those birds, Deti?"

"No. They are grasshoppers. They are as long as your arm. They are all black, except for one. The lead hopper is yellow. They are carnivorous, but they only attack bee hives and wasp nests."

"Look at the stars," Ruby marveled. "They look so close."

"Those aren't stars, they are called Firebrand," Deti told her. "They are as big as birds, but are bees. They bumble through the air like small fuzzy puppies."

Ruby thought about her mother's notations in the green book. Ma had written about grasses taller than her head and grasshoppers longer than her forearm. *My Mum was here before me*, Ruby told herself. *She wouldn't have sent me if she didn't know I'd be safe.* Lying back on the furs, she saw herself walking in the steps of her small red-haired mother from decades ago. "Perhaps it won't be so bad to have a sister after all," she murmured.

The next day, Ruby noticed the great grass plains were changing. The earth had begun to roll up and gently down. The hills grew larger, becoming a wave of rising curves before they cascaded against the great Blue Mountains. By late afternoon, the land changed again. They rode through enormous ferns and white-barked trees. At sunset, they reached a cluster of gigantic boulders with water cascading down their stone faces. Green mosses covered the gray granite. At the base of the stones, a pool had formed from the spring water. The water was turquoise blue and so clear they could see all the way to the white sandy bottom.

"We have reached the Springs of Natrun," Ten Singh announced. "We will camp here tonight."

Ruby took off her boots and put a toe in the water, expecting it to be frigid. To her delight, the water was warm, almost hot. It smelled like Sulphur. She wrinkled her nose. Ten Singh said he would leave so they could bathe and the girls happily dove into the water. When they emerged, their bodies were red as strawberries. Ruby applied the last of the black oozy ointment to her bum, but she hardly needed it any more. Later, they ate some sort of chicken bird that Ten Singh cooked over the fire. He said it was called chanry.

*I'm changing,* Ruby thought. *I am actually appreciating this wild country of my sister's.*

"We are more than half-way to Talin now," Ten Singh told them. "Soon you will see your sister and your family from the Twelve Valleys."

Ruby had not thought about having family in Talin. It was a pleasant notion. But every day carried her further from Viridian. She thought the nearly uninhabited country in her sister's land lovely, but she wondered if she would ever see her own land again.

# Chapter 11

## The Great Kosi Grasslands

Horrible life-ending screams rode the air the next morning as Ruby, Ten Singh and Deti were gathering their supplies and preparing to leave their campsite near the Springs of Natrun.

"What is that ghastly sound, Ten Singh?" Ruby felt an awful trepidation. Her heart beat faster and her breath caught.

"I don't know, but I've been told the Kosi have a stronghold near the Springs of Natrun. We must avoid them at all costs. They often take young women." His voice was low and ominous.

The cries continued the entire time Ruby and Deti gathered up their things and packed them on their ponies. Cloudheart stayed so close to Ruby she tripped over him several times. Her fingers kept fumbling with the horse's saddle girth. Drops of sweat formed on her forehead.

"Hurry," Ten Singh commanded.

The horrible shrieks ceased for a moment and they all stopped working, wondering why the heart-rending sounds had stopped. Then they heard a whip crack and a long howling ululation, followed by the sounds of men yelling and children screaming.

"I'm going to see what is making those cries," Ten Singh said. "Stay here." He rode off. Half an hour later, he returned.

"It's the Kosi Shunned. They are driving a group of women and children in front of them. You two must ride south or risk capture from their scouts. I will find you later today or tomorrow," his voice was dark with dread.

The girls mounted up. Ruby had trouble getting back on Star with Cloudheart in her arms. He was struggling and fell to the earth, flipped over and ran after Deti. Ruby followed, feeling her throat close in suppressed panic. When she and Deti had ridden for several hours and Ruby could see Cloudheart was completely tuckered out, they stopped.

"We can stay here until Ten Singh comes," Deti said. They hobbled the horses. The weather worsened, storm clouds rode the skies.

"We better set up the dweli," Deti told Ruby. "We will be here all night."

The girls struggled to set up the round structure. The wind became their enemy, blowing the dweli down every time they almost had it secured. Finally, they succeeded, crawled inside and yelled for Cloudheart to come in. He did not appear.

"I'm afraid Cloudheart has run away. He probably believes he can find Sab-ra somewhere." Ruby's voice was flat and discouraged. She had a feeling her sister was nearby too.

"I am going to ride north a little ways, maybe I can find Cloudheart," Deti said. Her words were confident, but Ruby knew she was frightened too.

"Deti, please don't leave me," Ruby pleaded. Her heart thudded against her ribs.

"I told Sab-ra when she left Maidenstone that I would keep Cloudheart safe," Deti's mouth was set in a stubborn line. "Just stay in the dweli."

"No, please don't go," Ruby said. "I can't stay here alone." She started to cry.

Deti opened the slit door and peered out. Rain was beginning to fall. "I'll be back soon, Ruby," Deti said. Her slim body was a shadow as she disappeared into the grayness of the rainstorm. Ruby wailed, but Deti did not return.

That evening Ruby opened the flap a hundred times until the moon rose. There was no sign of Deti or Cloudheart. Finally, exhausted from fear, she fell to the furs on the floor of the dweli, sobbing. All night she waited, sleeping on and off until dawn came in—pink and golden.

She walked outside, saw Star hobbled nearby and picked some long grasses for the horse. She took some food from her pack for herself. Star was struggling against her restraints and Ruby wondered if she was thirsty. She untied the hobbles and fumbled with Star's packs, trying to reach her water skin. As she did so, the neck rein slipped from her hand. When she turned back to offer water to the pony, Star whirled and disappeared into the grasses. In seconds, they swallowed her whole.

"No," she screamed, but it was useless. It was as if the pony had never existed. The grass muffled even her clopping feet. The only sound Ruby could hear was a low keening wind. Now she was completely alone. Deti, Cloudheart, Ten-Singh—all of them gone, like the world she had come from.


Deti came upon Cloudheart in late afternoon, still running north toward Talin. Jumping from her pony, she grabbed him and hugged him hard. The rain had stopped and a watery sun came out.

"You are staying with me, you little monster," she told him. He struggled and growled quietly in her arms. She was unmoved. She put a long thin rope around Cloudheart's neck and told him to find Ten Singh. Following Cloudheart's lead, she came upon the Bearer guide late in the day.

"Deti," Ten Singh said when he saw her. "I'm glad to see you. The mob of Kosi rode off," he said. "The party was going northeast. Only the Kosi warriors were mounted, only the women and children were walking. Where is Ruby?"

"I left her at the dweli, straight south of here."

They rode knee to knee until it was too dark to see the trail. Although Deti protested saying that Ruby would be terrified if they didn't get back to her that day, Ten Singh found a small grove of stunted trees and they tethered the horses. They didn't make a fire, worried the Kosi would spot the smoke. In the misty half-light, they ate their cold food, rolled themselves in furs and slept.

That afternoon, Ruby thought she heard the faint sounds of horses. She jumped to her feet and walked outside screaming, "Ten Singh, Deti, I am here."

But when the blades of grass parted, it was not Ten Singh. It was not Deti. It was an enormous dark-skinned savage riding a black horse. He was bare-chested and his face was narrow and linear. His nose curved like a hawk's beak. He had a longbow on his back and a quiver of arrows hung from his saddle. A serrated silver knife was stuffed in his belt. His eyes snapped when he saw her. He uttered a few guttural words.

"Mother of God help me," Ruby entreated and fell to her knees. She kept her eyes on the ground, praying he would ride off, but he didn't. She saw his leather boots come closer.

He grabbed her by the hair and lifted her up.

"Let me go, you are hurting me," she screamed, twisting away from him.

He put his arm around her waist, pulled a piece of leather from his belt and gagged her. He tied her hands together and lifted her on to his horse. He spotted her backpack and tied it to his saddlebag. He gave a piercing whistle and a tall rangy dog came out of the reeds. He mounted behind her and they rode northeast.

The next morning Deti and Ten Singh continued south. The weather had improved and both were in better spirits.

"We should reach the dweli in another hour," Deti told Ten Singh cheerfully. "I told Ruby to stay there. She's such an easily frightened little thing. Not brave like Sab-ra at all."

But the dweli had a funny abandoned look when they spotted it. They tied their ponies to bundles of tall grass. Abruptly, the reeds parted and Star trotted into the clearing. Ten Singh grabbed her, holding the reins until she stood quietly. He petted her gently, calming her fears. Deti pulled open the dweli door calling Ruby's name, but the dweli was empty.

"Ten Singh, she's gone," Deti said, despair rang in her voice. Together they read the signs of broken grasses and trampled foliage.

"Did she leave any message?" Ten Singh asked. "Where is her little diary book?"

"Her pack is missing. The book was in her pack. I feel terrible, I should never have left her."

"One of the Shunned Kosi scouts took her," Ten Singh told Deti. He looked away in shame.

"Oh Goddess, no," Deti wailed.

"From the pattern in the grasses, I see that he rode northeast when he left. He travelled in the same direction as the captives we heard." His voice was old as death.

"What should we do?" Deti's face was white.

"We need to go on to Talin. I can get help there to go after the Kosi scout. It must have been a scout who kidnapped Ruby."

## Chapter 12

## The Green River Camp

The copper-skinned barbarian removed the leather strap that tied Ruby's hands and the gag from her mouth on the second day. He gave her some inedible food that she threw fiercely into the fire, looking at him in contempt. Later he gave her water, which she gulped down, although bitterness still waved across her features and caused her teeth to clench. The man spoke seldom and when he did talk, Ruby didn't understand a word. She was outraged at her abduction. She wanted to stab the savage with a knife, but the idiots at Maidenstone had sent her on this journey unarmed.

Late on the third day, they approached a river. Ruby saw the flashing light of the rippling water running through the forest. Across the waterway, she spotted twenty or more hide tents and many dark-skinned people. The savage aimed his horse straight down the vertical slope from a high ridge and splashed through the lime green water to the edge of the encampment.

Women ran toward them with loud cries of excitement. The men surrounded the warrior's horse. One savage pulled Ruby off the horse and she stumbled, her feet unsteady on the white sand. Many of the women were bare-breasted and Ruby was horrified. *All of these women were filthy pagans*, she supposed.

A Kosi woman led her into the largest tent. There were no men inside, for which Ruby was grateful. Then she noticed an ivory-skinned woman sitting quietly in one corner. The woman had black eyes and hair. Her whole being seemed flat, like a black and white picture in a school book. Ruby fastened her eyes on the woman's face and caught a tiny blink of recognition.

"Sab-ra?" the woman asked. Her voice was so quiet, it was almost a whisper. She displayed no feeling, not even curiosity. Ruby found it unbelievable that in this camp of savages she had actually found a person who knew her sister.

For a moment or two, Ruby was unable to respond. The kidnapping, terror and hatred had reduced her to almost an animal state. She sank to the floor, shaking. Finally she said, "I am not Sab-ra, I'm Ruby."

The woman rose slowly and walked over to stand beside her. "I thought you were Sab-ra, but now I see I was wrong," she said.

"How do you know Sab-ra?"

"Yes. I am from Talin and I have known her since she was a child. My name is Nyria," the woman said. Her voice was flat. "I have been with the Kosi tribe for many years now. Where were you captured?"

"I was travelling through the grasslands on my way to Talin to find Sab-ra when the beast took me." Ruby felt disgust curl her lips.

"The great grass plains belong to the Kosi. They take anyone who travels it without their permission." Nyria's voice was dull and matter-of-fact. She showed no emotion. Living with the savages had sapped her vitality, leaving a ghost of a woman, half-alive, half-dead.

"Have you ever attempted to escape?"

Nyria flicked her eyes toward a cluster of Kosi women and shook her head. She put a finger to her lips and whispered, "Quiet. Some understand."

Later a muscular Kosi woman approached and motioned for Ruby to follow her. Ruby didn't want to go with the woman, but two of them grabbed her by the upper arms and practically carried her. They left the tent and walked down toward the river. Then the women tugged on Ruby's shirt, trying to pull it up over her head.

"Stop," Ruby cried, frowning at the woman and pulling her shirt back down.

The woman stepped back and in a single graceful movement, drew her long dark dress over her head. She wore nothing at all beneath it. Ruby was scandalized. A group of Kosi Warriors stood by a smoldering bonfire, laughing. Ruby was horrified at the woman's calm nudity, outside no less, and in full view of the men. *Did the woman have no pride at all?*

"No," she said again, when the woman tugged at her shirt, her voice rising in panic.

The Kosi woman called others and together the women ripped all Ruby's clothes off. They pushed her down into the river. It was stingingly cold, almost brutal on her skin. They scrubbed her all over using sand to scour her clean to the delighted amusement of the men who came closer to watch. Ruby was furious. Once released, she stomped up the bank and stood with her hands on her wet hips glaring at the men.

Nyria came up with a dark red gown and helped her dress. She and Ruby returned to the large tent and sat together in the back corner, watching through an open tent flap as the Kosi women prepared the evening meal by the campfire.

"Why did they drag me to the river, Nyria?"

"You have to be clean for the wedding."

"What are you saying? I'm not staying for a wedding. Somehow we have got to escape," Ruby's voice was low and frightened.

"He has decided to marry you," Nyria said. "They washed you so that you would be clean for the breeding," she said.

"What?"

"The Chief of the Shunned Kosi is going to marry you. I pretend I can't understand the language, but I can."

"I would never marry a dirty savage. I shall unequivocally refuse. I came here from an island far away and have a Ma and Da there. They would have to give permission and I am going to get married in a church in a long white dress..." Her voice trailed off, knowing to her sorrow that she was a long way from becoming a bride in a pure white dress.

"The Kosi don't ask a woman's permission," Nyria said flatly. '"He thinks you are Sab-ra and that you married his rival, the Kosi King, a man named Say'f. They say Say'f is dead and has no claim on you now. He would be the new King of the Kosi Warriors and has decided on you as his Queen."

"Would he force me, then?" Ruby asked. She felt the blood drain from her face.

Nyria looked at Ruby and nodded sadly. "Most of the Kosi women can't have children. Kosi Warriors steal women from the Twelve Valleys to be the mothers of their children. That's why they took me, but I never became pregnant after leaving Talin. They finally stopped trying."

"We have to get out of here," Ruby said. She felt faint and put her head down between her knees.

"Did anyone travel with you to the land of grass as tall as men?"

"A man named Ten Singh from the Bearer People and a little girl named Deti."

"Would they come after you?"

Ruby exhaled in relief. "You are right, Nyria. They will come after me. All we need to do is wait until they arrive. I'm sure they will come." Her heart was beating fast, but she made herself calm down. Allowing terror to completely overwhelm here would be of no help.

Later a Kosi woman entered the tent and motioned for them to come out to the campfire. They walked outside just as a group of large muscular men rode into camp on enormous horses. They rode as if merged with their mounts. Dead chanry birds hung from their saddle horns. The men removed the birds' feathers and the women tied them to a pole across the campfire. The smell of the roasting fowl and chanry meat turning on a spit and sizzling made Ruby's mouth water.

"Which one is the Chief of the Shunned?" Ruby asked Nyria in a whisper. Nyria pointed to a large muscular man. As he turned toward them, Ruby saw he had a white eye. The eye didn't move as he looked at her. She found his deformity disgusting.

"His name is Hozro," Nyria said. "He is the beast who killed my son. My boy's name was Hodi." Her face seemed carved in stone and even her chilling words produced no change in the expression on her face.

Late that night as Ruby lay in the Kosi women's tent Nyria whispered, "I don't think a lone Bearer person could take us out of here."

"Then we should try to escape before they get here. If we travelled south, we might find Ten Singh," but even to herself Ruby's voice sounded small and unconvincing. This country was so vast. Finding Ten Singh would be like spotting a tiny light in an endless forest of darkness.

"I think we would be re-captured before we got very far. When Hozro heard the rumors that King Say'f was dead, he went to the Citadel and forced the Kosi who were waiting for Say'f to swear allegiance to him. Those who wouldn't, he killed. Many women died there too. He took the rest to this camp. He is a vicious brute."

"Did he truly murder your son?" Ruby's whisper was shocked.

"Yes. Hozro killed my little boy and put his body in the garbage," her gentle voice was so soft Ruby could hardly hear her words.

"Dear God, Nyria, I am so sorry."

"The Bearer People brought his remains back to Talin. I have a husband there."

"So, you were kidnapped from Sab-ra's village in Talin?"

"Yes, it was many years ago, but unlike many of the captive women of the Twelve Valley's country, I never stopped hating this ugly, brutal culture. Now I am ill and fear I will die here, never seeing my husband of the village of Talin again."

"We won't let that happen," Ruby's voice was fierce. "We will escape." Her rage at the death of Nyria's son took away her despair. *I have the Vision*, she told herself. Brother *Marzun said so. I see can what is happening in the lives of others.* It was time to chance the Far-Seers disease. For that to work, she needed a bowl of liquid to reflect the light.

At midnight, Nyria crept from the tent, disturbing a sleeping Kosi guard. He asked her what she wanted.

"Brin," she said and the Warrior laughed. Nyria told Ruby that she would try to get some of the intoxicating liquid the Warriors drank to blur the harsh outlines of their lives. Women were not usually allowed to drink Brin, but the Kosi laughed at her request. Ruby heard the sounds of him pulling his water skin from his belt and Nyria sipping the liquid and coughing. They sat together drinking and talking. When she returned, Nyria had a small bowl filled with amber liquid.

They waited for another hour to be sure all the rest of the women were sleeping. Then they lit a tiny candle. The light from its flame spread across the golden brew. "What can you see, Ruby?"

Ruby didn't respond. She had entered a dream state in which she voyaged across the great grass plains. Later Ruby's voice, sounding drugged and slow, woke Nyria. "Four people come to the Green River camp. Two dark warriors, one Bearer and one old woman with long white hair. Singing she comes."

"Ruby," Nyria nudged her awake. "Wake up. You said that four people are coming here."

"Yes. I saw them," Ruby said, emerging from her trance. "All we can do now is wait and pray. Pray as hard as you can to your Goddess and I will pray to the one Lord who rules us all."

Hearing Nyria whisper her prayers, Ruby asked God for deliverance from the Green River Camp but feared her rescuers were a long ways away and that her prayers would go unheard, unanswered.

# Chapter 13
## Alive in the Green River Camp

The following day, Ruby crept away from the camp, took the little green book from her pack and pulled out a pencil. She swallowed hard, knowing she would probably not survive and that nobody would read her words.

*Dear Diary,*

*I don't know if anyone will ever read this. I've been captured and sit on the sand near a green river while bunches of filthy half-naked copper skinned Kosi savages work around me. Some of the women wear long gowns, but nothing beneath. No knickers at all! Apparently, those are the married women. The unmarried women wear trousers like the men, but walk around bare-breasted. They have no shame. I am blushing myself scarlet being so scandalized.*

*A man named Ten Singh brought me into this god-forsaken wilderness, but he and Deti left me alone in the tall grass plains and a dark-skinned warrior kidnapped me. Gran, I know you would be pleased to hear that I have reluctantly admitted to myself that I have the Sight. Last night, in a Sight vision, I saw Ten Singh returning. He was the person who took me from Maidenstone, trying to get me to Sab-ra's village..*

*If anyone finds this little book after my death, I beg you to send it to Viridian. I want Ma to know that I forgave her for keeping the secret of my sister from me. My Da needs no assurances; he knows I love him dearly. Gran, I say farewell to you with the greatest sorrow. I am crying now, thinking of my family and my beautiful red setter dog, Maeve.*

*I met a woman here whose name is Nyria. She actually knows my sister, Sab-ra. She told me that the Chief of the Shunned plans to marry me—without my consent, I must add. The brute's name is Hozro. He thinks I am Sab-ra who married another Kosi Chief. He thinks the other Chief is dead now. At least my sister got married before having her babies. I was glad to hear she had some morals. What could have made her marry a filthy savage I have no idea. Maybe she had no choice.*

*Hozro is a big ugly buck with a white eye. Nyria told me he killed her son, a boy named Hodi. My heart goes out to her. This place has taken all the juice, all the sap from her personality. It's like talking to the walking dead. She is like a black and white photograph. Every time I look at Hozro, he is looking back at me. I'm like a juicy goose he is waiting to cook and eat.*

*Nobody can read here, so I can put me plans down on paper. After talking myself blue, I have finally convinced Nyria to try to escape. We are going to make a break for it after dark. She has been making friends with a horse, bringing him little crab apples and such. She thinks we can both ride him. Without a saddle, I have my doubts, but we have to try.*

*We are going to wait until the camp sleeps. Then I will swim through the river to the other side. Nyria will bring the horse later, leading him through the water. She thinks the sounds of saddling could wake some of the men, but since the horse is the fastest mount they have, she says if we don't fall off, we will be able to get away. It sounds all well and good, but I just found out she has never ridden a horse, and he is a big stallion. I pray hourly for deliverance.*

*I won't be able to write again and I will have to leave this book here. I've made my last amends and prayed for my soul to join the heavens.*

*Signed, Ruby's Final Entry*

At moonrise, the women went down to the river to bathe. Ruby and Nyria went with them, talking quietly as they walked a sand path through whispering shrubbery.

"Should I try to swim across the river now?" Ruby asked.

"Yes. The mist is rising already. When the Kosi women swim out deeper into the water, get across the river and wait. I will come later with the horse."

"If I remove my clothing to swim, I won't have anything to wear except my knickers once I get to the other side."

"It isn't that deep, you can walk. Make your gown into a bundle and hold it rolled up above your waist. Don't go until the moon slides behind the clouds."

As the Kosi women stripped and walked laughing into the moonlit water, Ruby looked carefully around. She and Nyria were alone. The mist was already up to their knees. Ruby pulled her gown up and rolled it around her waist. She whispered good-bye and walked down to the river. She sat on the bank and slid down with a splash. The water was icy cold and the bottom of the river slippery with clay. She forced herself to walk deeper into the current, keeping one hand on her rolled dress. She turned back once, but it was too dark to see Nyria. She kept on, fighting against the muscular cold water that wanted to pull her under. As Ruby approached the other side, the water grew warmer. She seemed to sense her sister beside her, pulling her across the water to safety.

She emerged dripping and ice cold on the other side. Reeds and marshy ground rose slowly all the way to the bottom of a tall ridge. Ruby stood and pulled the dark red gown down, covering herself. Shivering convulsively, she made her way to the base of the escarpment. Once she almost slipped into a tiny spring. It was colder than the river. She put one foot into the water, testing to see if it had a solid bottom. Icy swirling sand pulled at her foot. It was quicksand. She pulled her foot up out of the water frantically. Fear gave her legs strength and she pelted through the reeds and emerged onto solid ground.

Panting, she sat down near the base of a silvery shrub. She was too cold to sleep, but sat shivering, resting off and on until nearly dawn when she fell into a light doze. When she opened her eyes, it was morning. She saw the back of a Kosi Warrior. He was squatting on the ground in front of her, starting a fire. When he turned around, his white eye burned her. It was Hozro. He pulled her up beside him and looked deeply into her eyes.

"Saah-brah," he said and satisfaction showed in the brutal lines in his face

Ruby screamed.

Hozro tied Ruby's hands behind her back and marched her across the river into the Shunned camp. She looked for Nyria but didn't see her. The horse she and Nyria planned to use stood calmly in the circle of thorn bushes the Kosi used to contain their mounts. Nyria had never even gotten him out of the corral. Ruby closed her eyes in despair as tears dripped down her dusty cheeks.

One of Hozro's women came up to him and said something in the Kosi language. He handed Ruby to the woman. She took Ruby by the upper arm, leading her to the women's tent. In a back corner of the shelter, Ruby met Nyria's eyes. Her face was covered in bruises. Nyria pointed at her foot and Ruby was horrified to see that a broken bone stuck out through the skin. The Kosi had maimed her only friend. Ruby shoved the hand of the Kosi woman off and ran to Nyria. Her eyes were so dull, she looked half-dead.

"Did they break your foot?" Ruby asked in shock.

"Yes."

"Can you feel your toes?"

Nyria shook her head.

"Was it because we tried to escape?" Ruby asked, repulsed by the Kosi violence.

Nyria nodded, "But Wirri-won is coming."

"Who is Wirri-won?"

"Kosi Healer."

The few words seemed to have tired Nyria even further.


Later that day, the tent flat opened and a woman who looked a hundred years old strode in. She was tall and commanding in appearance. Her face was white as soap. The top of her head was bald as an egg, but long white plaits grew from the back of her head, nearly reaching her waist. Each plait had a silver ring at the end. They clinked together as she walked. She wore a long gown made of a yellow fabric. Many silver rings shone on her fingers. Tattoos decorated her upper arms. Ruby recognized her; it was the singing woman she had seen in the Vision.

"Sab-ra?" the old woman called out and strode to their corner.

"No, my name is Ruby," she replied, stunned to find this ancient woman knew her sister.

"Bow you head, Ruby. She is Wirri-won, great Kosi Healer," Nyria managed to say. Ruby bowed.

Wirri-won knelt and examined Nyria's leg carefully. She removed the binding with a single cut of her knife and shouted at the Kosi women in a rage. She knelt by Nyria and aligned the bones in her foot, holding them tight until there was a snapping sound. Nyria screamed and then was silent. Then the Healer rubbed some type of green plant mixture into the place where the bone had protruded.

"If foot bone snaps again, you will die," Wirri-won said to Nyria. "Don't stand on it." Then she turned to Ruby and said, "Hozro wants to marry you."

"No, Wirri-won," Ruby pleaded. "I can't marry." She thought desperately for a reason the woman might understand. A sudden insight made her say, "I am pledged to the Church."

Wirri-won turned to Nyria and they talked in low tones.

"Hozro says he will fight other husband. This man named Church," Wirri-won told her.

"No, pledged to Temple. To Te Ran, to Goddess," Ruby said prevaricating wildly, desperate for anything to keep from falling into the hands of this brutal criminal.

"Then no marriage," Wirri-won said and Ruby nearly fainted in relief.

"Beg her to take you to Talin," Nyria whispered. "Do you have any silver parthats?"

Ruby walked over to her bag and pulled out all the money she had left. She held it out in her cupped hand. "Wirri-won, please take us to Talin."

The Healer looked at her scornfully. She grabbed Ruby's bag and upended it on the floor. After scrabbling around on the ground for a bit, Wirri-won rose triumphantly with Ruby's mother's little green book. Ruby shook her head.

"Let her have it," Nyria hissed.

"No," Ruby said and held out her right hand on which she wore a small silver ring with a rounded garnet stone. It was Da's gift to her when she left for Namché. Reluctantly, she drew the ring from her finger and held it out to Wirri-won. Her stomach clenched as she offered this ancient woman the last vestige of a world that seemed to spin further and further away.

Wirri-won took the ring and nodded but continued to go through the items from Ruby's pack, at last finding a small bottle of pain reliever Ruby brought with her from Viridian. The Healer took two pills and gave them to Nyria, pocketing the rest. Then she strode from the tent, her robe swirling around her bare feet.

# Chapter 14
## The Last Dance

That evening the Kosi put on a kind of savage celebratory dance. Everyone sat around the fire and an old man wearing only a dirty orange loincloth beat a large metal pot in a complicated rhythm. Two young boys had finger drums that echoed to the rhythm of the larger drum. Three naked Kosi warriors with white painted patterns on their skin, walked into the circle of light. They began to dance, slowly and then faster. The Kosi women began to sing a hauntingly sweet melody.

Another warrior marched three women, bound together with leather thongs, into the firelight. The men circled around the captive women in their dance. A more highly decorated warrior entered the dancer's circle. He slashed downward with his knife, cutting the leather thongs that bound the women to each other. He cut one woman's dress from the neckline to the base and tore away her gown until she stood naked in the moonlight. The Kosi roared and their women shrieked in glee. The Warrior seized the woman and ran from the firelight with the woman lying across his shoulders, screaming.

The dance resumed. Over the course of the night, warriors stripped the other two women and carried them away, leaving only Hozro dancing to the drums. The tempo beat faster and Hozro spun in circles, his white eye left a circle of light in the air, following the speed of his spin. Suddenly, the music stopped and Hozro strode over to Ruby and pulled her to her feet.

"Wirri-won," Ruby screamed and the ancient healer came forward. Wirri-won raised her hand in the air, palm forward and put it on Hozro's chest. He and Wirri-won argued loudly. Ruby stepped back to stand beside

Nyria. She said something under her breath and Ruby bent down to hear Nyria's translation.

"Wirri-won is telling him you are Sab-ra's sister. She says you cannot marry. You are pledged to a Temple in Namché."

Hozro took out his knife, gesturing with it, touching the blade to Wirri-won's breast. Then he drew it along her jawbone leaving a long thin cut that seeped red. She remained as still as if she had been carved from ice.

Nyria whispered, "Wirri-won is explaining that you have given your virginity to the Temple where you will become a Priestess. He does not believe her."


A sudden hush stilled the camp the next afternoon as everyone heard the thudding sounds of horses running fast down the ridge. Two men rode into the clearing—both were Kosi. The women screamed and ran into the tents, except for Ruby and Nyria, who stayed where they were. Nyria could not walk now without help. Ruby felt a sense of relief. The Vision had proved true, she had seen these two warriors coming to the Green River camp in her trance. They were coming to rescue her.

"The name of the smaller of the Kosi warriors is Argo," Nyria said. "He's the Kosi assassin. The other Kosi is a man named Ghang."

Ruby remembered that name. Mistress Falcon told her that a Kosi called Ghang has taken Sab-ra up into the high range at the beginning of the war.

The smaller of the Kosi warriors dismounted and pulled out his knife. His eyes were proud and he had a haughty look. He appraised Ruby and Nyria disdainfully, narrowing his light gray eyes. Suddenly, he charged toward Hozro, his knife raised. Men ran from the circle to grab bows and knives, but Hozro held up one hand and all the men stopped moving. He and the small Kosi warrior began circling each other. Both had knives and jabbed them forward into the air.

Hozro sliced into the side of the Kosi assassin. Argo grunted in surprise. Blood ran down his dark skin in a red curtain. The knives flashed so quickly it was hard to see what was happening. Then Hozro gave a cry and went down on one knee. Argo stood back, giving him time to rise. Hozro's warriors began to surge forward, but Hozro held up his hand again and slowly got to his feet. He lunged forward with his knife outstretched but stumbled and fell. With a single stroke, the smaller Kosi stabbed his knife into the back of Hozro's neck. Hozro fell to the ground without another sound. The warriors moved forward warily toward the killer. He raised his arms in the air, screaming triumphantly.

Argo knelt down and hacked viciously at Hozro's neck until he severed his head from his body. He grabbed the head by its long greasy hair; showing Hozro's face to each warrior. Several blanched. The women of the Kosi screamed. Hozro's white-eye was open, horrifying even in death. Argo walked to his horse, grabbed a leather bag and put Hozro's head inside it.

Wirri-won stepped between the small warrior and the others. She uttered some fierce words.

"What is she saying?" Ruby asked Nyria.

"Wirri-won says now that Hozro is dead, the group must follow to the old Kosi ways. If King Say'f lives, he has one moon to come forward. If he is dead, his Queen must name and then mate with the next King."

"Who is this Queen," Ruby asked, faltering. Something told her she didn't really want to know the answer.

"It's Sab-ra," Nyria said. "Your sister is Queen of the Kosi."

*Good Lord,* Ruby thought. *How on earth had her sister become Queen of this dirty tribe? Was she the only civilized person in this God forsaken country?*

Ghang walked to the center of the circle and began to speak. Nyria translated his words.

"I am Ghang. I serve the Queen Sab-ra of the Kosi. I call upon you, Green River Kosi, to return to the service of King Say'f. Come forward and kneel before me. I will take you to Halfhigh. The true King will be waiting."

At last one old battered warrior walked slowly forward to Ghang. His chest showed evidence of many scars. He knelt before him saying he would pledge to serve the King. One by one, the rest came forward and knelt. Each warrior threw his knife into the fire to show their loyalty. In the end, there were only three women who refused. One was Horzro's chief wife. Her flashing topaz eyes looked contemptuously at Ruby and Nyria. The women who would not swear loyalty to Say'f followed Wirri-won to the horse enclosure. Wirri-won mounted her elegant silver mare and led the small band away.


By late afternoon the camp was packed and the Kosi who swore loyalty to King Say'f were mounted. Ruby and Nyria, her foot still unable to bear her weight, were bundled into a wagon with raw red meat and the bodies of dead chanry birds. Ghang and Argo led the cavalcade splashing across the bright river and up a trail to the top of a high ridge. Ruby's heart pounded as the Kosi mares pulled the wagon up the near-vertical incline. When it hunched over the edge between the trees, she sighed in relief. She was leaving the Green River Camp. And Hozro, the man who planned to take her against her will, lay dead, his head in Argo's saddlebags.

When the caravan stopped at evening, Ruby climbed out of the wagon and stretched her arms above her head. Then she helped Nyria down. Supporting her weight by an arm around her waist, Ruby took her to a nearby tree. They sat underneath its welcome shade. Ruby noticed a bad odor coming from Nyria's foot. She feared it was infected. Watching the Kosi women assemble a meal for everyone, Ruby asked Nyria to translate their conversation.

"The women say the Kosi King was lost in an Avalanche last year. He and Sab-ra were in the Skygrass valley, the location of Talin's blue diamond mine, when the Avalanche struck. Many People and Kosi lost their lives that day."

"What will happen if the King doesn't appear?" Ruby asked.

"When a new King is crowned, he chooses twelve Blood Arrows as guards. They must offer to give their lives to protect him. Most of the Blood Arrows for King Say'f met the soil during the war with the Army or later in the Avalanche. According to Kosi law, Sab-ra must marry one of the surviving Blood Arrows."

"Perhaps Ghang thinks by bringing all the warriors to Halfhigh, Sab-ra will name him King and marry him."

"When Hozro's killing spree at the Kosi Citadel ended only Ghang, another Blood Arrow named Rohr and Argo still lived. I learned that your sister ordered Argo to bring Hozro to Talin. She and Rohr have gone there."

"Then we owe her our lives," Ruby murmured softly.

The caravan trekked on. Nyria began to recognize the countryside and told Ruby they were on a trail above the Twelve Valleys. Once a young boy rode up to see who was passing through. When he saw the Kosi, he darted away. Later Ghang sent a Kosi Warrior ahead of the caravan to scout the trail. When he returned he spoke to Ghang.

"Stop the caravan," Ghang shouted and the Warriors stopped. Several Warriors dismounted, walked up a small hill and lay down, looking northeast, bows at their sides. Argo ran forward, joining the men on the hill, preparing to ambush the person coming, but Ghang put out his arm to hold the assassin back.

Ruby caught the word, "Bearer." Nyria told her the Bearer people were neutral in the tribe conflicts that plagued the country. They were allowed safe passage everywhere. She felt her body ease. She remembered her trance dream in which a Bearer came to the Green River to save her. An hour later, Ten Singh reached the caravan. After greeting Ghang, he walked over to Ruby.

"I am so happy to see you alive," he whispered. "I feared you dead."

"Please take us to Talin, Ten-Singh. Nyria has a husband there. She is afraid she is dying and wants to see him once more. Her only hope would be to amputate her foot and apparently only Wirri-won could do that."

Ten Singh and Ruby walked over to the wagon where Nyria lay. In the last half day she had lapsed in a coma. He knelt beside her and looked carefully at her foot. "She wouldn't live through the rest of the long trip to Talin, Ruby," Ten Singh whispered sadly. "I am sorry, Ruby but she is already dying." He looked down at the ground and then off toward the sun falling behind the mountain. Ruby felt warm tears run down her face.

"Could you go after Wirri-won? Bring her back her to help Nyria?"

"No, Ruby. I cannot find this Wirri-won person. She left here days ago travelling east. Mistress hired me to bring you and Deti to Talin. Deti is already there. We will go tomorrow."

Ruby saw his fixed expression and knew he would not budge. "When do we ride?"

"In the morning."

"Can't we take Nyria with us? Maybe in the wagon?"

"No, Ruby," he shook his head, his eyes full of pity. "She floats the Black River already. She is too close to the entrance of the world beyond. We cannot save her. All you can do is tell her husband in Talin that she never stopped loving him or trying to escape."

"Then may God have mercy on her soul," Ruby whispered, wondering if she herself would survive to make her way back home.

# Chapter 15

## Leaving the Kosi for Talin

The next morning, Ten Singh told Ghang that he and Ruby were leaving the caravan. He had been commissioned by the Mistress of Maidenstone to take Ruby to Talin. Ruby walked into the women's tent slowly. Nyria had slipped ever more deeply into a coma. Her breathing was slow and ragged. Ruby sensed Nyria would probably be dead by the end of the day. Ruby knelt down and kissed the woman's forehead. She promised to tell Nyria's husband of her unending love when they reached Talin.

When Ruby mounted Star and she and Ten Singh rode from the camp, she heard a high ululation ring horridly from behind her. It sounded like Nyria's voice, Ruby looked beseechingly at Ten Singh, but he shook his head. Her face was a mask of regret and the tracks of tears.

By evening, Ten Singh pointed out Talin's high plateau lit by moonlight. Ruby had dreamed the previous night of Nyria, smiling in the arms of her husband, but even dreaming she knew it was not the Vision. Ten Singh cantered up the slope into the village with Ruby close behind him. The moon was rising. The whole village lay asleep. No one came from their houses to greet them.

"Come," Ten Singh whispered. He dismounted and led his pony toward a small wooden stable behind the crescent of white stone houses that encircled the plateau. Ruby followed him. The warm scent of hay and horses drifted toward them as Ten Singh slid the stable door open. He lit a candle lamp and they walked inside, the sound of their ponies' hooves deadened by the straw on the floor.

"Look," he whispered pointing into a stall.

A bright red mare tossed her head when she saw them. A small male colt nursed at her side.

"How beautiful he is," Ruby whispered and a tiny smile came to her face. "A right perfect little dote."

They climbed the ladder into the hayloft and bedded down there. For the first time since the night with Deti and Ten Singh on the great grass plains Ruby felt calm.

"Why didn't anyone come out to greet us?" she asked Ten Singh.

"It's probably too late and they are sleeping, but usually someone is on guard," his voice was thoughtful.

Deep in the night, Ten Singh woke her, shaking her by the shoulder. "Ruby, wake up. You are having a bad dream." He could not rouse her and she continued talking in a tranced voice.

"Nyria rides the black sailed boat, her eyelids are closed."

"Ruby," Ten Singh said, but she had slipped back into sleep.

When Ten Singh woke in the morning, Ruby was standing in the doorway to the stable. The rising sun outlined her body. She turned back to him, centuries of sadness coating her young face in shadow.

"Nyria's gone," she said sadly and Ten Singh nodded.


Later they heard a voice calling from outside the stable. Ruby climbed down the ladder from the haymow and opened the door.

"Ruby, is that really you?" Deti's eyes widened. Cloudheart stood at her feet.

"Deti, I am so happy to see you and little Cloudheart. I'm so happy you both made it." A warm rush of pleasure ran through Ruby's veins. "Is Sab-ra here? Is everything all right?"

"Sab-ra left Talin a week ago for a place called Halfhigh. Since she left, a terrible disease has struck Talin. The People get large rounded purple growths on their skin and die. It's awful. Nobody knows how to cure it. Your grandmother went up the mountains searching for plants that might help."

Ruby climbed down the ladder and took Deti in her arms, kissing both her cheeks.

"No, don't touch me," Deti said, twisting awkwardly away.

"Why?" Ruby's voice sounded hurt.

"We don't know how a person gets the Mottled Sickness, but we are afraid it comes from getting to close, or kissing someone. Hello, Ten Singh," she greeted him.

"Are you well, Deti?" Ten Singh asked.

"I am. According to Ruby and Sab-ra's Grandmother, I have already had this disease. They found a small purple welt from years ago on my body. Apparently, you can't get it more than once, but I could still carry the infection. That is why I fear touching you. I can't let you come inside the house, but I'll make you some tea and bring it to the stables."

"Can't I meet Sab-ra's grandparents?" Ruby asked, sounding troubled. She thought Talin would be a safe harbor, but once again tragedy had demolished her hopes.

"They will come to see you when they can. I will bring blankets and food. I'm sorry, but until Grandmother returns, I am afraid to let you leave the stable." Deti turned and ran back to the semi-circle of houses.

She returned shortly with tea, blankets and hot bread. She climbed the ladder up to the haymow and the two girls sat together in the opening, dangling their legs in the sunlight, careful not to touch each other.

"Why does Sab-ra want to reach this Lost Lake valley?" Ruby asked.

"She thinks the King of the Kosi, the father of her children, is sealed inside the valley, unable to escape."

"I saw her pregnant in the Sight, but you said children. Did she have more than one baby?"

"She had twins and they are so beautiful. Grandmother says Quinn, that's her little boy's name, is the future King of the Kosi. And little Crimson is a Kosi princess. Your sister left her children here in Talin when she left for Halfhigh."

"I would love to see them," Ruby's voice was warm.

"You won't be able to hold them or touch them, but I will bring them to the stable so you can see them."

"Have any People of Talin died from the Mottled Sickness?"

"Almost a third of the village is already gone," Deti's voice was low. "Luckily, Ambe, the woman who is nursing the twins, is unaffected. She and her husband will leave Talin soon, taking the babies. They won't return until the illness runs its course."

The following day Ruby stood watching from the second floor haymow window as a tall elderly man helped bring supplies out to a wagon. A young couple with a toddler were getting ready to depart. After the woman finished saddling her pony and filling his packs with supplies, she walked off toward one of the houses. When she returned, she had two papooses wrapped up in her arms. She walked to the stable so Ruby could see the babies. Both of them had sparkles in their eyes.

"Hello, Ruby. My name is Ambe. The babies are Sab-ra's, Quinn and Crimson. I wish I could bring them up to you, but my husband and I need to leave for Halfhigh."

The elderly man walked down toward the stable. "I am Silo'am, Guild Master of Skygrass and your ...Grandfather," his voice hesitated before saying the word. "We are afraid for Sab-ra's babies. My son Hent and his wife Ambe are taking them and their own son, Manny, away from Talin. We think they would be safer in the upper range."

"Could I go with them?" Ruby asked, hopefully

"No, I don't think so. Ellani, your Grandmother, will be back today. She will want to meet you and will be awfully disappointed if I sent you north."

Ten Singh came up behind Ruby. "Silo'am, I am Ten Singh. I am leaving Talin soon to return to Maidenstone. Are you sure Ruby is safe here? I could take both girls back to Namché with me."

Deti was walking toward the stable, leading a pony. "Deti, do you wish to return to Maidenstone?" Ten Singh asked.

"No, I like it here. Flashes of my former life come to me and I have been drawing every day," Deti said.

Ten Singh looked disturbed at the thought of leaving both girls in the center of a deadly disease. "I urge you both to reconsider," he said. "I think both of you should come back with me to Namché. I can bring you back to Talin after this sickness has passed."

"No," Ruby said slowly, after considering his offer. "I must stay. I want to meet my Grandmother who raised Sab-ra. If I leave with you, by the time we get back here both my Grandparents could be dead. And I have yet to meet my sister."

"Then I will wait another day, in hopes that your Grandmother returns. I don't wish to leave you here. You are in grave danger from the disease."

"I will not change my mind." Ruby's voice was firm.

Silo'am returned to assisting Hent and Ambe with their packing. When the pair rode off the rim of Talin's plateau, Ambe held two little papooses in her arms. Her husband carried their toddler who rode in front of him on his pony.

Deti ran to the rim, watching them leave and drawing little circle blessings in the air.

Ruby felt a profound sadness. Everything in this pagan land seemed to conspire against her finding Sab-ra. And until she saw her sister, she would never feel right about returning to Viridian.

# Chapter 16

## Deti

The following day Ten Singh left for Namché. Late in the afternoon a Bearer rode into Talin. Ruby watched from the haymow door as her Grandfather Silo'am walked out to meet the man. She heard the messenger say he had encountered Ten Singh who had directed him to the Valley. He said he had a letter for Ruby from the Mistress of Maidenstone.

"The People have the Mottled Sickness," Grandfather told the man. All the color drained from his face. Trembling, he handed Grandfather the letter. Forgoing tea or a meal, he left immediately. Grandfather brought the letter to the stable shortly thereafter.

Grandfather was starting to look better, Ruby noticed. His raised sores were fading and his cough was less persistent. Deti lowered a rope and Grandfather attached the letter to it. As Ruby opened the letter, sealed with the silver crest of Maidenstone, reading it carefully before Deti, who was tapping her foot said, "Ruby, I can't stand the suspense. What did Mistress say?"

"A telegram came from me Da. It said Mum was completely well. He reminded me that I am to find Sab-ra and if she is willing to come, to bring her back with me to Viridian. Do you think that is possible, Deti?"

Deti frowned. "I have known Sab-ra for many moons now, and I don't think she will leave the high country whether she finds King Say'f, her husband, or not. Even if he is dead, she will stay and rule the Kosi."

"I thought the King of the Kosi was dead. Would she try to rule that filthy savage tribe alone?"

"I believe so," Deti said, solemnly.

Ruby gave Deti an 'are you mental' stare and shook her head. "My sister and I are so different, Deti. I only want to do what God says is right and to find peace for myself. Sab-ra must be a cheeky little wagon to think she could do such a thing without a husband."

"It's not so much that she is arrogant," Deti said, quietly. "She only wants her life to mean something. She wants to be remembered after she is dead."

"Seems to me she is getting above herself with such notions. She should be preparing her soul for the day she stands before God," Ruby said piously.

"In her own way that's exactly what she is doing," Deti's voice was so soft it was nearly inaudible.


Two days later, Grandmother returned to Talin from her trek up into the mountains to find plants to help heal the villagers of the Mottled Sickness. The girls saw her unsaddling her horse. A young boy took the animal to the stable.  An hour later, the woman stood in the grass below the haymow and called their names. Ruby came to the doorway and looked down. "I am pleased to see you at last, Ruby. My name is Ellani," she said, profound pleasure in her face.

"I am happy to meet you," Ruby replied. "I have come a long way."

"The Mottled sickness is going away. Both you girls can leave the barn and come up to the house now." Ruby and Deti hugged each other in happiness.

When they entered the kitchen, they saw a large tub of steaming water. "You may bathe," Ellani told them. Both girls were grateful for the hot water and soft linen rags Ellani brought them. Once they were out of the water, Grandmother took all their clothes and washed them in the tub.

She gave the girls long nightshirts, soft things of Sab-ra's, and sent them to hang their clothes out to dry.

Hanging up their clothes outside in the clean wind, Ruby said, "Deti, I can't stay in Talin much longer. This trip has already taken months. I am becoming desperate I am, to see my Mum and Da. I need to go to Halfhigh. Since the Babas are there, Sab-ra will come to them in time. I can see her and my promise to me Ma will be kept."

"It's a five day trip to Halfhigh. You don't know the way."

"Will you go with me, Deti?" Ruby felt her breathing quicken.

Deti stood hanging the last piece of their clothing with the wind and bright sunshine all around them. "I will, but I want to show you something before we go."

The girls returned to the stable and Deti scooted up the ladder into the haymow. She returned with a rolled sheaf of drawings. They walked back up to the house together. Once inside, Deti unrolled the hide parchments on the table. The drawings were of Ruby, Sabra with her babies, Mistress Falcon, Talin and the mountains. They were so beautiful, they took Ruby's breath away.

"You are only talented, you are," Ruby said and felt a smile warm her face. Grandmother came over to see Deti's drawings.

"Deti, did you draw these?" she asked. Deti nodded, smiling shyly.

"I believe you may have come originally from the Valley of Quatar. It's the fifth valley and the training school for artists is there."

Deti tipped her head to one side, struck by Grandmother's words.

"I saw your face change when I said the word Qatar. Do you remember that word, Deti?" Grandmother asked.

"Something about it is familiar. Ruby wants to go to Halfhigh," Deti said. "I would like to see this valley of Qatar you mentioned, but could someone take us to Halfhigh first? I want to see Sab-ra and give her these drawings of her babies. Then I'd like to see Qatar."

After dinner that evening, Ruby sat at her Grandparent's table to write in her Diary.

*Dear Diary:*

*My last entry was not the last after all. I am here in Talin, the place where Sab-ra was raised. I had to spend nearly a week in the haymow of a barn, before they would bring me up to the house. It was to protect Deti and me from the Mottled Sickness. While we were living in the barn, a couple named Ambe and Hent took both of Sab-ra's Babas to Halfhigh. Sab-ra went to Halfhigh before we arrived and I plan to follow.*

*Deti showed me her drawings of the village of Talin, the Elders and Sab-ra's twins. Deti is bleedin' talented, she is. If I can't get my sister to return to Viridian with me, I'll bring me Ma the drawings so she can see her grandbabies.*

*I keep thinking about my home, me Da, me Ma and of course my beautiful dog. That life seems a million miles away. I have a terrible fear that I am forgetting it. Some days I have a hard time remembering my Gran's face.*

*Signed, Ruby the rescued.*

<h1 style="text-align:center">Chapter 17</h1>
<h2 style="text-align:center">Leaving for Halfhigh</h2>

Deti and Ruby rode out of Talin the following morning. They were going to Halfhigh where Hent and Ambe were staying with their son, Manny, and Sab-ra's twins. Ruby's grandmother had asked virtually every person in the village if they would guide the girls. All were either too ill, or working to provide food and care for those still recovering. Ruby insisted she would go alone if need be, but she was going. Sab-ra was at Halfhigh and she had given her mother a pledge that she would see her. Deti thought they could make it—just the two of them.

They left little Cloudheart behind in Talin, afraid of losing him on the trail, but at the last moment decided to take Dusk, a beautiful Kosi gazehound Sab-ra had found at the Kosi stronghold called the Citadel.

Ruby and Sab-ra's grandparents made a detailed drawing of the country to help the girls find Halfhigh. The map was beautifully drawn, but Ruby wondered if the landmarks that were so clear to the People of Talin, would be obvious to her. Such notations as Elder Oak and Gray Sands were not very encouraging.

The first day they rode north toward the final bend in the Wool Road. Riding on the broad well-travelled trail, Ruby felt her cares evaporate. It was the last stage of her journey; soon she and Sab-ra would be together. Her Grandparents, Ellani and Silo'am, sent food with them and a black dweli tent rolled up behind Ruby's saddle.

Deti rode a small red pony called Naj and Ruby rode Star, the pony she had ridden out of Namché. It seemed eons ago when she left Maidenstone, a little mouse frightened of everything.

The day was clear and both girls were in good spirits. They had no trouble finding the first campsite, or the spring for drinking water. They set up the black dweli, made a campfire and sitting by the firelight they taught each other songs. Deti found a tree with a white trunk and peeled some sheets of bark. She sketched Ruby's face in the firelight using black char from old campfires.

The next day they travelled through a northern remnant of the great Kosi grasslands. The whispering grasses moved in the wind, cresting like waves on the sea. In the afternoon, the girls heard the thudding of horse hooves.

"Who do you think it could be?" Ruby asked.

"I've heard that sound before, I think it is a wild horse herd."

Ruby trembled, fearing it might be the remaining Kosi outlaws from the Green River camp, but when the grasses parted, a glistening wave of horses rode through an opening in the high prairie. There were about twenty foals and colts, most were less than a year old. The majority were white, but a few were black or silver gray. A large mare, smoke colored with a black mane and tail drove them. She raised her head and screamed when she saw the girls' mounts.

Despite Deti's efforts to hold him back, Naj trotted forward, his eyes locked in euphoric transcendence on the lead mare. The mare cantered after the colts, nipping the stragglers, urging them forward. Naj bucked and reared throwing Deti to the ground and disappeared, running after the herd. The stirrups from his saddle flapped in the air; his reins fluttered behind him.

"Deti, are you all right?" Ruby ran to Deti who was lying on the ground. She sat up, rubbing dirt out of her eyes. They looked around at the endless plains and Star, whose reins were still in Ruby's hand. "Star almost got away too," Ruby said, gripping her reins tightly.

The careful map had blown away in the wind. They looked everywhere on the ground but found only one little scrap of ant'l hide. The rest had been trampled to shreds by the wild horses. The remaining piece showed the way out of Talin and the first day of the trip.

"What are we going to do," Ruby wailed.

"We are only a day or so away from Halfhigh," Deti said. At Ruby's dismayed expression she added, "I remember most of the map." The girls gathered their supplies, Deti mounted Star with Ruby sitting behind her and calling to Dusk, they continued north.

By evening, they reached the edge of a large sand-filled basin. It stretched away to the horizon. The Wind Goddess had scalloped the sand into tiny ridges and miniature gullies. Lines of white crystals tipped the ridges. The sunshine made them sparkle.

"It's salt," Deti cried out happily. The girls ran and picked up the small transparent particles, tasting them on their tongues and laughing. "I think this depression must have been a salt lake many eons ago. Perhaps this is where the gray mare was taking the foals. Horses like salt."

"I think this is Gray Sands that they put on the map," Ruby said. "It was about two thirds of the way to Halfhigh."

Early the next morning, they saw the herd again. Naj stood out. He was the only one with a red coat. He trailed the gray mare, still lost in adoration. The girls walked forward silently, with Star trailing behind them, her reins held tightly. When they got within ten paces of the herd, the wild horses moved away, surging like a wave. After an hour of silent approaches, followed by the herd sliding away, Deti tried calling Naj. He didn't even look in her direction. The gray mare pricked up her ears at the sound of Deti's voice and began to direct the herd toward them.

"Naj," Deti called as the enormous wave of horses came running right toward them.

"Run," Ruby cried. She darted out of the path of the herd, but Deti stood motionless with her hands outstretched. As the herd parted around her, Naj ran by. She grabbed his saddle horn and threw herself in the air, landing on his back. She strained against the reins, pulling backward and although he bucked, she hung on like a limpet. As the rest of the herd dashed away, she rode him back to Ruby. Once he had settled, she dismounted and started to undo his saddle cinch.

"What are you doing?" Ruby shrieked at her. "Don't do that, he will get away for sure."

"I know," Deti said, calmly. "I just need to remove his saddle and bridle. He is mine no longer. He has joined the wild ones."

"Deti, you are crazy as a cow. We are a thousand miles away from Namché, alone in this vast country and you are going to let your pony join a wild herd?" Ruby was incredulous.

"I can't trust him anymore," Deti said. "He will run away again if he ever has a chance."

*Deti is one crazy thicko*, Ruby thought. *Why, oh why did I ever leave Viridian?*

They spent the night in the Gray Sands, rising early the next morning. Dark edged clouds filled the northern sky. They could smell rain on the wind.

*Adventures,* thought Ruby sulkily. *Gran said it would be the greatest adventure I could ever have. She failed to mention that adventures are often cold and wet and make you miss your tea.*

By afternoon, a heavy rain began. The girls were soaked in minutes. Ruby wanted to stop set up camp, but Deti persisted saying they were almost there. Several hours later, the rain stopped and as the sun went down, huge and blood red. The girls stopped at the base of a flat-topped mountain.

"This must be Halfhigh," Deti was smiling. They could see white stone houses and a black dweli atop the mesa. They rode Star up the inclined trail.

"Ambe, Hent," Deti called out repeatedly. No one responded. The evening sky was darkly ablaze, hungry as a forest fire. Deti put Star in the horse corral with Hent and Ambe's ponies. There was no sign of the adults, the toddler or the twins. The wind rose and a very large black dweli, apparently a permanent fixture at Halfhigh, groaned in the wind. They opened the flap door, saw the bedstraw and decided to sleep there.


The sound of Ruby's singsong voice woke Deti as the gray light of dawn hit the mountains. She was talking in her sleep. "Black spots run red. The leopard roars."

"Ruby, what is it. What do you see," Deti shook her arm. Ruby blinked and returned to the present.

"A leopard is here, Deti. I saw his footprints earlier. I think he attacked Hent and Ambe."

"Goddess, don't let it be the babies," Deti cried softly.

"What are leopards afraid of, Deti?"

"Fire. They fear fire," Deti said. She opened the flap to the dweli, went outside and ran part way across the mesa to a cluster of small trees and silver leafed shrubs. She tore off some branches with dead leaves and brought them back to Ruby.

"I'm going to make torches," Deti said, striking a fire stick against a flint stone. The sparks tumbled against the dead leaves on the branches and the blaze caught. Both girls walked hesitantly around the perimeter of the camp holding the blazing branches. A thin scream scorched the air.

"Ambe," Deti yelled. "Hent. Where are you?"

They heard a second high-pitched cry. It sounded like one of the babies. The girls ran to the stable. The door was ajar, creaking in the wind, metal hinges moaning. Through the half-open door, they saw a large shadow on the floor. It was a man's body. Ruby thrust the torch into the building. The coppery scent of blood filled the room. A massive black leopard stood over Hent's body. It threw back its head and roared.

Like lightning, the leopard came running at the doorway. Both girls screamed and Ruby dropped her torch. The straw on the floor ignited and made a terrifying sound. The flame lit the air making a whooshing sound. The animal darted past the girls. Ruby saw the tip of his curled black tail vanish over the rim of the mesa. Thin screams rode the wind, the door banged repeatedly against the doorjamb.

Deti pulled the door fully open and fell to her knees by Hent's body on the stable floor. "He's alive, Ruby. His pulse is like a thread, but he is alive. Climb up the ladder into the loft. I think Ambe and the babies are up there."

Ruby stood frozen as the flames licked the straw in places throughout the stable. Her eyes were huge.

"Now," Deti screamed.

And Ruby ran, jumping over patches of fire. She scrambled up the ladder. Her heart beat so fast she heard it thudding in her ears.

Ambe lay curled in one corner, seemingly unconscious. Sab-ra's baby Crimson was sitting beside Ambe. Her brother, Quinn, stood in front of her, a long wisp of straw in his hand like a tiny sword. Ruby got her arm around Ambe's shoulders, lifting her up to a sitting position. She coughed, retched and started to cry.

"Ambe, we have to get the Babas out of here. The leopard is gone." Ambe struggled, lurched and got shakily to her feet. Ruby picked up Quinn, tucked him under her arm like a sack of grain, carried him across the floor and started to climb down. He struggled to escape.

"Hold still, Quinn," she screamed. She looked down to see Deti dragging Hent's body outside through the doorway. Ruby's breath came fast and her palms sweated, making it hard to keep hold of the ladder and the baby. The fire had heated up the room and smoke rose. Ghostly tendrils of death were already halfway up the ladder to the loft. She forced herself to keep climbing down, reached the bottom rung on the ladder. The fire was all around her.

"Deti," she shrieked. "Come get Quinn."

Deti looked up, dropped Hent's feet in the grass and ran back into the stable. She coughed and hacked, dodging places where the straw was already on fire. She grabbed the baby hard against her body and raced for the door. Quinn reached his arms back over Deti's shoulder, screaming his sister's name.

Fighting her fears and struggling to breathe in the thick air, Ruby climbed back up the ladder. Ambe was sitting against the wall, still not fully conscious. The smoke reached nearly to the loft by then and Ruby fought her claustrophobia, the heat and the smoke. Sweat ran down between her breasts. Ruby grabbed baby Crimson. The baby put her arms around Ruby's neck and linked her little legs around her rescuer's waist.

"Hold on tight," Ruby managed between coughs. Slowly she climbed back down into smoke so thick it looked solid. "Ambe, climb down after me," she shrieked. Half-way to the bottom, she screamed for Deti who stood in the doorway, fear making her features into a mask.

"I am going to drop the baby to you. Catch her now."

Ruby's voice broke Deti's flesh-lock and she ran to stand at the base of the ladder. Ruby peeled little Crimson away from her body and held her in the air above Deti's head. Deti raised her arms up.

"Fly down, little one," Ruby murmured and felt the weight of the small warm body fall away. Deti grabbed the baby out of the air and ran screaming from the stable, her hair on fire.

Ruby climbed back up for Ambe. She was sitting at the edge of the loft, her legs hanging over into the smoke. She seemed only partly conscious, watching the smoke climb up to Ruby's waist.

"Ambe, you have to climb down behind me." The woman just looked at her, eyes wide in horror. "Ambe, if you can't climb down the babies will die. You are the only one who has milk for them."

Ambe coughed and slowly turned around, lowering her feet to the top rungs of the ladder.

"I have you now," Ruby told her, linking her arms around Ambe's waist, "I won't let you go."

Slowly the women made it to the bottom. Ruby turned on the last rung and reached her foot out into dark air, feeling for the floor. Flame jumped onto her boot. Both of them were coughing.

"Follow me, Ambe," she cried and dropped into the flaming straw. Ambe screamed behind her. The heat was ferocious. Something deep inside Ruby, some basic instinct for life would not let her turn back. She dropped into a crawl and fought her way desperately toward the stable door. Something soft bumped against her. It was Deti.

"I'm going back in for Ambe," Deti said.

# Chapter 18
## After the Fire

It was a sober group that greeted a cool windy morning at Halfhigh. Both Ruby and Deti had burns on their legs and feet. Hent had been severely mauled by the leopard and was unconscious. Ambe had inhaled a lot of smoke and struggled for each breath, coming in and out of consciousness. Quinn and Crimson were in the best shape, but bewildered and frightened by the injuries of the adults. Ruby propped Ambe up against the outside of the stone house and put Quinn to her breast. He latched on lustily, but Ambe was too weak to hold him and he rolled off her lap. Deti knelt beside them, lifting Quinn up to take nourishment. Baby Crimson was crawling in the grass, talking to herself.

Ruby walked over to the baby and sat down beside her. "The big cat is gone now, little one," she told her. "You don't need to be afraid."

"Man-ee," Crimson said looking piercingly at her.

Ruby didn't know what she was saying. "Yes. He was a very bad manee-cat, but we are fine now."

"Man-ee," she said again, louder. She looked intently at Ruby.

Ruby picked her up and held her in her lap, checking her over carefully. She seemed fine, except for some small red spots. Ruby stood up and carried the baby to see Star in the paddock.

"Man-ee," Crimson called out, holding her arms back toward the edge of the mesa.

"Star, come here," Ruby called and the pony trotted over to the boma fence. Hent and Ambe's ponies followed. Ruby gave them both water from her leather waterskin and the baby petted them. Star's body looked round as a barrel. She certainly hadn't been that round when they left Namché, Ruby thought. *Could she be pregnant*, she wondered.

"Crimson, can you say, Star," Ruby asked.

"No. Man-ee," Crimson said, looking at her penetratingly.

"Star," Ruby said.

The child shook her head saying, "No, no, no."

"Ruby," Deti called out. "Come over here will you? We have to get some nourishment into Ambe, or she won't make it.

"She doesn't seem to have much milk left. Quinn kept squirming away and sitting up instead of nursing."

"I'll check all their supplies," Ruby said, putting Crimson down in the grass beside Deti. "See if you can figure out what Crimson is saying, will you?"

Looking through Hent's pannier packs, Ruby found some dried chanry meat and fruit. Walking to the Aid station created in the black dweli, she looked through the medicines. One container had three white pills. She put them in her pocket. She found some bandaging and took that as well.

"What are these, Deti?" Ruby asked, pulling the white pills from her pocket.

"They are poppy pearls. Give one to Hent. It will ease his pain."

"Man-ee," Crimson said again louder. The girls were confused by the word she kept saying and ignored her.

Feeling a bit squeamish, Ruby opened Hent's mouth and put a pearl inside. She held his jaw closed until he swallowed. He was semi-conscious and babbled words about the panther attack. "Should I give him another poppy pearl?" Ruby asked.

"Let's chance it," Deti said.

A few minutes later, Hent opened his eyes. "What happened," he asked.

"A panther attacked you. Ambe is alive, but ill from smoke inhalation."

"Where is she?" he asked. Helping him to his feet the girls managed to support him until he reached Ambe. He sat down heavily beside her, groaned in pain and sank into unconsciousness again.

Ruby poured some water into Ambe's mouth. She blinked, coughed and tried to speak.

"Manny?" she asked.

"Oh Goddess, no," Deti cried, "That's what Crimson has been saying. Hent and Ambe have a two-year-old. His name is Manny."Deti and Ruby looked at each other in shock. They hadn't seen any sign of the toddler.

"Ambe," Deti kept yelling until the woman opened her eyes. Her eyelids fluttered, wanting to close. "Where did you see Manny last?"

"Dweli," Ambe managed.

Deti and Ruby grabbed the babies and ran to the aid station, praying the little child was still alive. Just as she was entering the First Aid Dweli, Ruby stopped. An enormous warrior on a horse rode into the arroyo below them.

"Deti, look," she whispered.

It was a mounted Kosi warrior. He was headed directly toward the Halfhigh trail. The girls stood frozen; terrified it was one of Hozro's allies that had not sworn allegiance to Ghang. As the warrior reached the base of the trail, he looked up.

Deti stood as if made of iron, holding Quinn in her arms as the warrior thundered up the trail on his warhorse. Ruby grabbed Crimson and crawled beneath the shelter of a shrub. She curled up in a tiny circle with her arms protecting the baby.

When the warrior reached the top of the butte, he yanked his horse to a stop. The horse reared in the air and screamed. The Kosi warrior controlled him and dismounted. His feet were heavy and the earth quivered as he strode toward the girls. Deti's face was white, but Quinn began to smile. The baby held out his little arms toward the Kosi.

"I am Lord Sta'g, now First Blood Arrow," the Kosi said. Looking over at the brush Ruby had cowered under, he frowned. "Sab-ra, raise yourself. You know have nothing to fear from me." Ruby looked up and a confused expression crossed the man's face. "Who are you?" he asked.

Trembling, Ruby stood up. "I am Ruby, sister to Sab-ra," she said, her voice quavering. "This is Deti, and this is Quinn, Sab-ra's son."

The warrior began to smile. "Small Kosi Prince, I salute you," he said and went down on his knees before the small one. Then he took the baby in his arms. Little Quinn wrapped his arms tightly around the warrior's neck.

"Lord Sta'g, we have survived a leopard attack and a fire here," Deti told him. "There are two adults who are badly injured and a toddler missing. We need your help."

"Manny," Crimson said again.

"The two-year-old is named Manny," Ruby told him. "We are searching for him."

They found him an hour later, lying unconscious in a crevice in the rocks. Deti pulled his little body out and he made a small sound.

"He lives," the warrior said complacently and carried him to his mother.

Ambe made a soft whisper of gratitude as the warrior placed the little boy in her lap.

"Can you carry Hent and Ambe into the dweli?" Deti asked Lord Sta'g. Lifting them easily as he had little Quinn, Lord Sta'g placed them both on the soft bedstraw. He came back to get Manny but stopped short when he saw Crimson in Ruby's arms.

"Whose child is this?" he asked, scowling.

"Sab-ra had two Babas," Ruby told him, "But the only milk we have is Ambe's and she is so ill. I fear for their lives."

"Fear kills," Lord Sta'g told her. "Cease to fear. I will go for Wirri-Won." He mounted his stallion, nodded to the girls and thundered down off the mesa.

Knowing the great Kosi Medicine Woman would come, Ruby heaved a sigh of relief.

Deti and Ruby spent all afternoon fetching water from the spring and feeding it spoonful by spoonful to Ambe and Hent. Although Manny remained unconscious, Deti forced his mouth open and poured water down his throat. He coughed and opened his eyes. Ruby had found some dried chanry meat in the dweli and cut it in small pieces. "Eat this, Manny. You must be hungry," Ruby said. He would not take it and started to cry.

Ruby filled her water skin and tried to get Quinn and Crimson to drink, but most of it dripped down the front of their little chests. They grew weaker by the hour. Their eyes were enormous. By late afternoon, they couldn't even sit up. Both lay huge-eyed and silent on the straw.

As the sun fell slowly behind the mountains, Deti heard one of the horses grunting. She ran over to the boma to see Star lying on the ground.

"Ruby, come and help me. I think Star is having a foal. It seems stuck inside her."

"There's nothing we can do," Ruby said, repelled by the thought.

"I will hold her while you try to pull the baby out," Deti said.

"No. How disgusting. I'm not going to do that."

"Then she will die and the colt will die. Once the foal is born, Star will nurse him and we will be able to get her milk for Quinn and Crimson. Come over here."

"I can't," Ruby kept backing away.

Deti ran over and dragged Ruby back by her hair. "You will help me, or I will tell the Kosi Warrior you refused to help the King's son. Do you want to face Lord Sta'g if Quinn dies?"

"Oh my God, no. He terrifies me."

"Then grab the baby's hooves. They are just visible, sticking out of the mother. Pull as hard as you can."

Although Ruby's face was a mask of distaste, she grabbed the tiny hooves of the foal and slowly the colt emerged from his mother's body. When his back legs emerged with a popping sound, Ruby fell backwards and the foal landed on her chest.

"I did it, Deti," Ruby cried from under the foal. Her voice was elated. "He's alive." The little colt struggled to his feet. He was wet all over. The setting sun lit his translucent ears from behind.

"Why he's beautiful," Ruby murmured. The baby's mother lurched to a standing position and as her son nursed, she licked him dry.

Deti cautiously moved close to the mother's side. She opened her water skin and stripped the mare's teats watching drops fall into the water bladder. Star didn't have much milk yet but the babies were growing weaker. Even a little would help.

"Wirri-won needs to come soon, or the babies, Ambe and Manny, you and me—we will all die."

# Chapter 19
## Healing

The next two days were the longest of Ruby and Deti's lives. They tried every medicine in the dweli. They cut up chanry pemmican for Manny but he refused it. He would only drink water. Hent's injuries were badly infected and although he fought bravely, he succumbed to a fever before Lord Sta'g returned. The girls could not bury him. They dragged his body to the edge of the cliff and rolled him over the edge. Deti prayed for his spirit. Ruby asked God to bless him.

Ambe continued to sink lower. The girls feared she walked the dying road. She had no milk left and the babies were silent. They hardly moved any more. Quinn and Crimson's little bodies began wasting away. Their eyes were filled with fear.

Deti tried repeatedly to get Star to let down her milk, but the horse kept moving away. She kicked Deti and nipped at her. By the end of the second day, both girls had given up. They too were sleeping more and more.

In the darkest part of the second night, Ruby woke. She heard singing. The melody was hauntingly beautiful. She shook Deti's shoulder. "It's Wirri-won. She's here," Ruby said. They struggled weakly to their feet and stumbled to the edge of the mesa. Looking down they saw the white egg shaped head of the medicine woman riding a silver mare. Lord Sta'g rode behind her.

When Wirri-won walked into the dweli. Seeing Ambe unconscious and the twins in a stupor, she shrieked in rage. She whirled toward Lord Sta'g and sent him racing from the dweli, screaming for him to hunt—to bring meat to the injured ones.

Lord Sta'g returned as dawn lit the mountains with four chanry birds hanging around his neck. He started a fire and cooked them over a spit. When he reached out to cut a wing away for himself. Wirri-won slapped his hand saying, "Kosi Warrior, you eat last," and pushed a small vessel under the dripping meat. She caught the juice as the bird cooked. The scent of the meat floated deliciously over the camp at Halfhigh. The Healer poured the meat juice into her water skin. She walked back into the dweli and sat across the tent from Quinn.

"Future King of the Kosi," she said. "Come here."

Quinn tried desperately to stand, but fell again and again in weakness. Ruby reached for him, but Wirri-won pushed her away. Deti cried, seeing him so weak.

"Do not help him. He must do this himself," Wirri-Won said. "Kings must be strong. Small Kosi Prince, come to me."

The girls clung to each other trying to keep from rescuing Quinn as he fell repeatedly, but at last, dragging himself on his belly, he reached the Healer. Wirri Won gathered him into her lap and he sucked the juice down. His little body relaxed in the comfort of a full belly.

"Useless Iztar girls, you will chew this chanry meat, but you will not swallow it. When it is a paste, spit it into a bowl and feed it to Ambe and her son. Take none for yourselves. You will not eat until tomorrow."

Both girls quailed before the Healer. She watched their chewing carefully and once hit Deti when she saw her swallow. They took turns spooning the meat paste into Ambe and Manny's mouths and rubbing their throats to make them swallow.

"Blood Arrow," Wirri-won called out for Lord Sta'g, "Get mare's milk for the Kosi Princess."

"I have tried and tried," Deti told her desperately. "The mare only kicks and bites."

"You are no warrior," Wirri-won said disparagingly. She turned a gimlet gaze on the Kosi. Lord Sta'g leapt up to do her bidding.

By morning, Ambe could sit up. Manny had improved miraculously and was walking around the dweli and asking to go outside.

"Where is my husband?" Ambe managed to ask.

"He rides the skies, Ambe," Deti told her with tears in her eyes. "I am sorry, but his injuries took his life."

Ambe started to cry and reached for her toddler. Manny came and sat in her lap. Ruby sat beside Ambe, putting her arm around the woman's shoulders, comforting her.

Over the next few days, the sparkle came back into Quinn's eyes. Baby Crimson was still terribly weak, but she swallowed the mare's milk every time they brought it to her and slowly began to talk again.

"Lord Sta'g, how did you get Star to give you her milk?" Deti asked. "I tried hard. Wirri-won called me lazy, but I tried in every way I knew."

"It is good I came here," Lord Sta'g said patronizingly. "You are only small weak girls. The mare required convincing. I crippled her foal to get her attention."

"What? How could you do such a thing?"

Lord Sta'g shrugged. "The children of the King needed milk. The foal will live. He will be lame, but the mare will stand still now to nurse him and we can take her milk."

Slowly the little band at Halfhigh recovered. Lord Sta'g hunted each day and brought back chanry. The children struggled back to life. Ambe's eyes were lifeless, although she took some comfort from the fact that her son lived. Deti noticed Lord Sta'g sitting beside Ambe often by the evening campfire. Once Ruby surprised them and saw the Kosi's arm around Ambe's shoulders. After a time, whenever Lord Sta'g came to sit beside her, Ambe smiled shyly.

The Kosi warrior made a tiny bow for Manny and short stubby arrows. As Ambe gazed on, still too weak to stand, the Blood Arrow taught Manny how to shoot. "He will make a good Kosi Warrior one day," Lord Sta'g told Wirri-won.

"And his mother will make a good Kosi mate," Wirri-won said, pursing her lips to hide a smile. Lord Sta'g grinned.

Late the following day, Ruby spotted the band of Kosi Warriors. A huge wave of men on horseback and behind them another group of men on foot were headed toward Halfhigh. They were an hour away from the mesa. The largest Kosi warrior and a white woman were in the lead. The woman's red hair caught the rays of the setting sun.

"It is my sister," Deti said aloud.

# REUNITED
## Sab-ra's Story

# Dedication

For my late husband, Bill, who knew me well & loved me
anyway. His personality inspired the character of
Lord Rohr

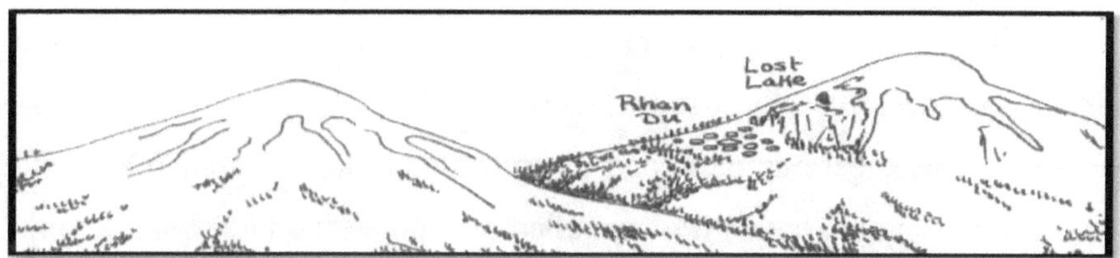

# Chapter 1
## Moon of Snows, January

The Moon of Snows had buried the high country in white by the time Lord Rohr, First of the Kosi Blood Arrows and I, Sab-ra of Talin, reached the great circular caldera within which lay the castle of the King of the Twelve Valleys. Lord Rohr left me at its rim and plunged straight down through snowdrifts that reached his stallion's shoulders. We had travelled for many months and by then I was so weak I could not stand. I sank to the earth beside my brave pony Yellowmane's feet and slept on the windswept ridge with nothing to cover me but blowing snow. Oddly, the cold did not fully penetrate my bones. Even lying on the caldera's rim, a small sun seemed to shine inside me. I could feel its feathery movements.

It was getting dark and I must have slept. I remember only someone lifting me onto a travois pulled by a horse and then waking to the benison of warm furs and my best friend Conquin's voice. When I woke fully, she was sleeping near me in a chair. We were in my apartment in the castle.

"Say'f?" I said, waking Conquin. Her eyes flew open.

"Thank the Goddess, you can speak," Conquin said. "Now you must eat and grow strong again."

"Is Say'f here," I asked her, pleading with my eyes.

"No, he is not," her voice was sad.

"If he is dead, then I want to die. I will take my own life."

"No you won't," my friend said, bluntly. "It is your duty to keep the seed alive."

"What do you mean?"

"Sab-ra, my friend, don't you know? Your death would mean two would die."

"What are you saying, Conquin?"

"My dear Idiot Lakt, I speak of the child of the Kosi, the babe you carry."

I sank back on the furs. I had never sensed I was pregnant all those days on the trail. My baby had kept me warm. The tight band of anguish, which wrapped around my chest, melted a little, a part of the King had come with me after all.

When I learned my husband was not in the Valley of the King, I cried until my eyes were dry as the upland salt flats. When Conquin told me I carried his child, grief took me into a different world. I watched myself through what seemed an impenetrable glass window as I stumbled through the days—looking alive but feeling dead. My pragmatic dark-haired friend told me the baby would absorb my feelings and be sad his whole life unless I raised my spirits. She asked me if I had seen the King's revenant, his spirit, riding his stallion among the clouds. I told her I had not.

"Then he may yet live, Sab-ra," she said. "A Warrior always keeps his word. He said he would meet you here. I believe he will come."

I forced the dark cloud in my mind to lift a little and went to work serving others in the Kingdom as a Physician, wearing the red Healer's cord I had earned at Maidenstone. The back kitchen of the castle became the clinic where patients came for me to look at their skin, their throats and listen to their bellies. Some of the children even came without their parents. They stood silently waiting until I came to look at them. Most of them had nothing at all wrong with them, except a yearning to be the center of attention. They giggled when I felt their tummies and backs. Thus, as huge snowflakes fell on the flanks of the Blue Mountains, I fought against despair while my son grew strong inside me.

I was walking down the hall of windows one bright blue day when I glimpsed two dark-skinned Kosi Warriors plunge down the vertical cliff into Natil. They were shouting war whoops of victory, high-pitched keening cries of triumph as the stomping feet of their warhorses churned the sparkling snow. I leaned against the window breathing deeply and closed my eyes in joy. Just as he had promised, my King had come.

But, when I opened my eyes I could see it wasn't Say'f. Two Blood Arrows, nobles who guarded the King of the Kosi, and a young child riding a pony had come to the Kingdom. I felt the wave of grief grind me, cold as the remnants of melting snow.

The Blood Arrows dismounted and King Ruisenor strode out to greet them. They stood together on the stone forecourt and locked arms reinforcing their status as allies. Then the King turned to the child. He lifted her from her pony and she knelt on the stone forecourt. He raised her face and I could see her golden skin. Her features were small and fine. She was the child I had seen at the Citadel—the girl who learned to ride on my spy partner's pony. A second warrior came up, carrying a toddler. I hadn't seen the little one riding with the other Blood Arrow.

"Welcome to my Kingdom," King Ruisenor's voice resonated, "Please come in."

The men walked through the great doors of the castle with the slender older child running beside them. King Ruisenor, who longed for an heir to his Kingdom, carried the smaller one.

I turned my face away from the scene, tears wetting my eyes.

All winter I had scrutinized the towering cumulus clouds, gray and heavy with snow, drift over the Valley of the King. I watched to see if Say'f, the King of the Kosi, rode the thunderheads. Although I didn't see his face in the skies, each day that went by my hope that he lived grew weaker. I felt blood pound in my temples. I dreaded the news brought by the Blood Arrows. I feared they brought word of my husband's death.

The next morning a servant came to my apartment. "Lord Sta'g, Blood Arrow to the Kosi King, wishes to speak with you. He is in the Throne room with the two children."

"He will have to wait," I said and spent an hour trying to compose myself. Outside the palace windows the winter winds stirred the tops of drifted snow banks. I trembled like the dead leaves of the Rholam tree, wondering what news Lord Sta'g had of my husband.

When I finally went down to the Throne room, I brought Conquin with me. Lord Sta'g rose when we entered the room, holding the two little girls by their hands. "Wife of the King," he said, "I bring you the King's daughters. Their mother, Martyn, rides the skies. They are yours now."

The silence rang as he finished speaking. The oldest of the little girls walked forward and knelt at my feet. The little one toddled after her sister. I was shattered. I lifted their little faces up with a finger. The eldest had her father's beautiful golden eyes. The baby was pudgy and bewildered looking. She started to cry.

"What are their names?" I managed to whisper.

"They are Kim-li and Kensing."

"Thank you for your gift, Lord Sta'g, but such young children need a family. I am a Healer and Far-Seer. I am no family for the daughters of the King."

"It was the King's command. If he didn't return from the War, his daughters were to be given to you." Sta'g met my eyes unyieldingly.

I hesitated, feeling tears sting my cheeks. If I took the children, it would be like accepting that Say'f was dead.

"Lord Sta'g," Conquin said, after giving me a scorching glare, "It would be my privilege to care for the Kosi King's daughters until Sab-ra is ready." She turned toward me and whispered fiercely, "Do not say another word." Her dark eyes snapped in anger.

The Blood Arrow went down on one knee to the children and the oldest girl made a circle blessing above him in the air. He kissed the smaller child on her head.

"Have you any news of the King?" I begged.

"Nothing since the day of the Avalanche," Lord Sta'g replied. "Soon the choosing of a new King will commence."

I felt dizzy and the room swayed around me. No other man should serve as King of the Kosi. That honor belonged to my husband alone. Lord Sta'g drew a black fur cape around his shoulders and strode from the room, taking all my hopes with him.

Conquin took Kim-li by the hand and picked up little Kensing holding her tight against her own pregnant belly. Once inside her home, Conquin set a kettle boiling, called the girls to the table and gave them Ghat milk and sapritet fruit. They were not used to sitting at a table to eat, at the Citadel everyone ate together on the soft white sand around the fire. The girls took their food and sat on the floor by the window. Kim-li sang quietly to her baby sister.

"I can't believe you would tell Lord Sta'g you didn't want the children," Conquin hissed. "I wonder what Brother Jun would have said." Her voice was disgusted.

Brother Jun, my compassionate Empath teacher, had taught me to read the minds of others and ways to ease their sorrows. How I wished I could ease my own sorrows—how I wished I could heal myself.

"Truly, I am appalled, Sab-ra." Conquin shook her head.

"I didn't say I didn't want the children, but I am a Healer, Conquin, not a mother. I don't know how to take care of these children, especially without their father."

"Well it looks to me like you better figure it out soon," she said, glancing at my belly. The corners of her mouth tightened in aggravation. "Sab-ra, these children are Kosi royalty. If you don't have a son, Kim-li will become Queen of the Kosi. She will marry the new King when she comes of age, and I remind you," she scowled, "they are the sisters of the babe you carry. I don't understand you sometimes, but I will keep them until you come to your senses."

# Chapter 2

## Hunger Moon, February

At the beginning of the Hunger Moon, I woke from a deep sleep to hear Conquin calling my name. "Sab-ra, help me." I sat bolt upright in bed and looked around. It was the middle of the night. There was no one else in my palace apartment, but Conquin's voice woke me as clearly as if she stood beside me. I knew instantly she was in labor. I dressed quickly, pulled on my coat, grabbed my Healer bag and ran through snow drifts to Conquin's home.

Pushing through the door, I called out, "Conquin, it is Sab-ra. I am with you. You will bring this baby into the world alive, warm and whole."

"Sab-ra?" Conquin's voice was terribly weak. I whirled toward her women in a cold fury.

"How long has she been in labor?"

"Nearly ten hours, Healer."

I was enraged, "How could you let her get into this state without calling me? Where is Thron, her husband?" They wouldn't look at me, but one finally admitted he had been there, but they had sent him away. My mouth tightened in displeasure.

"One of you go and find him," I ordered. Turning back to Conquin, I lowered my voice. "Together we will bring this baby to the light. The Goddess called and woke me, Conquin. She spoke to me with your voice." Conquin managed a tired smile.

I sent the other attendant for broth for Conquin to drink, warm water, towels and the beautiful clothes Conquin had made for her child. My dearest friend labored until morning, but my certainty she would have a healthy baby bore her up from the depths of watery pain, to the surface of the warm sunlit world and the child was born. She came to us with her eyes wide open. She looked directly at me and I gazed back at her. Thron had returned by then and was standing shyly at the back of the room. His eyes pleaded with me for reassurance.

"Your child is strong and your wife will live to bring you more children," I told him, smiling as I handed him his daughter. I looked at the little mite cuddled in her father's arms, knowing I would give birth myself soon. *Goddess of the Winds*, I prayed, *let Say'f be here to hold his son.*

"We will call her Sab-ri," Thron said, his voice heavy with emotion.

It meant "little Sab-ra." She smiled at only three days. The Goddess had used me for her purposes, but for that one moment in time I was content. I had received a gift beyond price. I felt born to do her bidding.

The following day, a servant came to my rooms to tell me King Ruisenor wished me to attend him in the Throne room. I pulled on my fur coat and hide boots. It was icy-cold outside as I walked from my apartment to the wing of the palace where the King received petitioners. When I entered the room, I saw the King and young Queen Ion'li sitting on their thrones. Ion'li sat at his right hand now.

Before I went to the war, there were two Queens of the Twelve Valleys. Queen Verde, as first Queen, sat on the King's right in those days, but I sent her from the Kingdom when I discovered she planned to murder Ion'li. I came forward seeing Queen Ion'li smile radiantly.

"I have told the King that I am with child," her face was pink with pleasure.

"I am so pleased," I said. "Queen Ion'li, I wish to know this baby you carry. May I place my hands upon you?" She nodded and I put my hand on her stomach and called out, "She will bear you a healthy son by the end of the year, my Lord."

"So you know already," the King said. His voice was deep with pleasure. 'Truly you can see the time-coming-to-be. Tell me, Sab-ra, will my son be born alive and well?"

Ion'li had lost two babes before I told her to stop riding her horse and bathing in the hot springs in early pregnancy—advice from the jealous Queen Verde who could not conceive the King's child. "My Lord, unless the life of his mother is taken, you and I will help Queen Ion'li bring him into the world. It will be my pleasure to lay him in your arms."

The King smiled and Ion'li's fears evaporated like the dawn-mist rising over the mountains at sunrise. I turned to leave the Throne Room, but the King stopped me with a gesture.

"There is another reason I called you here, Sab-ra, I wish to award you the cords that are mine alone to grant," he said.

When women get married or become mothers in the Twelve Valley's country, they are given beautiful braided cords to wear around their waists. One of Queen Ion'li's serving women entered and laid a small gem-encrusted chest in the King's hands. He opened the container and pulled out the golden Cord of Marriage. I felt my heart race. *Had he heard something? Was there any news? Could my Warrior have lived through this brutal winter?*

I knelt before them.

"There is no need to kneel, Sab-ra," he told me. "Rise. I will thread the Marriage Cord around your waist. When you have your child, you may return and I will grant you the silver Cord of Motherhood."

"I have no husband," I murmured softly. "It wrong for me to wear the Marriage Cord."

"He will come," the King, pronounced. "If he is not here before your child is born, I believe he will be here before mine enters the world."

He and Ion'li looked at each other, holding hands. Their happiness and love wrenched my heart.

I walked from the Throne room back toward my own apartment gazing down at all the threaded Cords around my waist—red for the Healer and ivory for the Far Reader—cords I had earned at Maidenstone when I was a novice there. Superstitiously, I unthreaded the golden Cord of Marriage from the other two. I placed it on my windowsill where the moonlight would glaze its satin surface. I would not wear it again until I knew my warrior's fate.

Two weeks after baby Sab-ri was born, one of the Bearer people who carry messages throughout the twelve valleys, brought me a message. It was a drawing etched into the bark of a lily tree, showing a body wrapped in the shroud of the dead. A second sketch showed a woman holding the hands of many children. In the background, I saw a small building, a river and a waterfall. I felt a frightened tingling across my shoulders and my belly tightened. The message bore the sign of the ancient Kosi Healer woman, Wirri-won. I took it to Lord Rohr, the Blood-Arrow who brought me safely to the King's Valley after the Avalanche.

"I think this message is from Wirri-won," I told him. He nodded. "Do you know where I can find her, Lord Rohr?"

"In the Blue Mountains above the ninth valley. She lives in the river."

"What do you mean, *in* the river?" I touched the base of my throat, feeling anxiety rise.

"On the Island of the Eaten," he said, ominously. Despite all my questions, he would say nothing more.

Perplexed, I took Wirri-won's message to Conquin. "This is a message from the powerful medicine woman for the Kosi. She came to me during the War at Halfhigh, the way station between Talin and the high range. Wirri-won tended the wounded there so I could go to the front. I asked if I could study with her when the war was over. She said I should come to her when I was pregnant, if I survived the final battle."

Conquin was nursing baby Sab-ri. They made such a lovely picture, with the sun lighting Conquin's hair as she held out a finger for baby Sab-ri to grasp. "I am not sure the King will permit you to go, now that Ion'li is pregnant. Perhaps you should wait until the son of Queen Ion'li is born. Or at least until you deliver."

I feared losing the opportunity to study with Wirri-won, but knew Conquin was right. I could not leave the Kingdom without the King's permission.

# Chapter 3
## Vernal Moon

Waiting for my turn to kneel before King Ruisenor, I vividly recalled standing before him when I suffered from the drumbeat and terrible migraines. It had been a year since I begged the King to let me go to war. I was addicted to opium then, with dull eyes and lifeless hair. Now I was in perfect health, glowing with the gloss pregnancy gives a woman. When I reached the front of the line of petitioners and knelt to ask for permission to leave the Kingdom, he immediately denied my request.

"Sab-ra, I must have you here as Queen Ion'li's physician," he said. "You may not leave."

"I know my duty lies with Queen Ion'li," I told him, "I would never fail her. However, she will not give birth until summer and I promise to return soon. I would remind you, King Ruisenor, that it is Wirri-won who asked for me."

After hearing that I was responding to Wirri-won's summons, the King reluctantly granted my request. Wirri-won's fame as a Healer was known even in Natil. For the first time since I arrived in the King's Valley, except for the night Conquin delivered, I felt needed. Wirri-won, the ancient Healer with white hair that flowed down below her waist had called for me. I felt a tiny breeze of relief wave across me, insulating me from the dark sadness of my husband's loss. The Wind Goddess, my totem spirit had brought me a message of hope and duty.

I went to the Clinic and gathered all the medical supplies I could fit in two saddlebags. I took pearls of the poppy, feverfew and boneset. I took Deep-sleep leaves and Lethal Sleep. I grabbed long white bandage rolls and soap grasses. Then I went to the kitchen and asked the cooks for extra food. When I told them I was travelling to work with Wirri-won, they raised their arms and crossed them over their faces, backing away. They practically threw the food at me, running from the kitchen. I found it baffling.

Lord Rohr was grooming his stallion in the stables. When I told him the King had ordered him to take me to Wirri-won, his dark features blanched. "You will not go," he said fiercely.

This Warrior had led me safely across the top of the Blue Mountains in winter. Why would a short trip to the ninth valley in spring scare him so badly? It was baffling, but I was unmoved. Wirri-won had called me. Like the time I felt called to war, I would erase whatever barriers stood in my way to heed her summons.

We left for the Island of the Eaten on a cool spring morning several days later. I could hardly mount Yellowmane. I had to try several times, vastly amusing Lord Rohr. I was almost six months pregnant and already very large. Conquin kept teasing me, saying I carried more than one baby. I told her she wasn't funny. When I turned back to wave farewell, I saw Conquin's husband encircling her with his arms. She had collapsed against him, sobbing. My dearest friend didn't have the ability to see the future, but she was highly empathic. I feared what she might sense.

We rode through lands dripping with spring rain. Yellowmane was excited to be on the trail and pulled hard on her reins. Lord Rohr kept a relatively slow pace beside me, but it was obvious he was deeply unhappy. He kept pointing at my belly and shaking his head.

Two days later, we reached the valley of Tinsen, where Justyn's grandparents lived. Justyn, my dearest friend, had begged me repeatedly to marry him, but I had chosen the Kosi King, against all the mores of my culture. I hoped for a welcome, perhaps even an invitation to stay overnight. When I knocked on the door, Justyn's Grandmother came out on the stoop.

"I greet you, Grandmother of Justyn," I said, smiling. The muscles in her face tightened when she saw my pregnant belly. The lines around her mouth deepened.

"Do you carry Justyn's child?" she asked, looking at my belly.

"No Honorary Grandmother, I carry the son of the King of the Kosi. We were married before the Avalanche destroyed the Skygrass valley."

After the Kosi King and I were married, I sent Justyn a letter telling him of my decision. I wondered if he ever received the message. Now he would hear the news from his bitter grandmother. She took a deep breath and then turned around, gently closing the door between us. At first, I was dismayed, then angry. I could understand her disappointment, but it hurt that she didn't even invite me to come in the house.

Lord Rohr and I spent a cold, wet night sleeping on the ground as the wind rose. The warrior asked me to stop the rain, but I shook my head. Since becoming pregnant, I had not been able to command the Wind Goddess. Pregnancy had taken away my gift.


First Blood Arrow Lord Rohr and I arrived at the White River the following day. It was evening and the rain had finally ceased. The trees were dripping, but the afternoon sun lit the leaves and nature shone around us. We looked north at a great waterfall cascading down the Blue Mountains. At the very pinnacle of the falls amid wild roaring waters, tall trees walked across the rapid churning river. I could see no land up there at all.

"Island of the Eaten," Lord Rohr said, pointing to the walking trees.

"How do I get up there?" I asked him, starting to realize why Lord Rohr was frightened, why the cooks warded off evil spirits and Conquin shook in her husband's arms.

"We wait," he said and so we did.

The following morning, I saw three riderless donkeys pick their way slowly down the steep walls of the Dhali Ra. The Dhali Ra is the most sacred peak within the Blue Mountain range. My People believe it is the home of the Great Mountain Goddess. When the donkeys reached us, out of breath and wet with sweat, they stopped. Their small bulbous knees, ears like furry brown arum lilies and huge dark eyes captivated me. I scratched them between the eyes. Only one wore a saddle. The other two had empty pannier packs on their backs.

"Am I supposed to ride this donkey?" I asked Lord Rohr. "Up that vertical cliff?"

He eyed me in dismay. "Don't go," he said. He reached out his hand to touch my belly. "I beg you, Wife of the King, please don't do this."

I felt his fears and my own flare inside me. My heart quickened as I slowly put my supplies in the donkeys' packs and clumsily mounted the lead donkey.

"Lord Rohr, my Guardian, Wirri-won had asked for me. I cannot deny her summons."

"Then I will wait here to claim your body," Lord Rohr said and turned his back on me. It was a chilling farewell. When he and I left Skygrass after the Avalanche, Say'f had commanded Lord Rohr to protect me. He told Lord Rohr his life was forfeit if he failed to bring me living to the Valley of the King. Lord Rohr clearly believed this foolhardy venture would mean my death. If that happened and Say'f returned, Lord Rohr would have failed and would pay with his life. I felt a ghost shiver-walk across my shoulders.

The ascent was almost vertical. The path was narrow as a snake, filled with slippery shale. The lead donkey picked her way carefully, but I could feel her fears. I tried desperately to calm myself, knowing donkeys could feel human panic. Afraid to look down I studied the cliff face, seeing lovely air orchids that bedecked the stunted pine trees. Tiny blue dipper birds dashed in and out of the falling waters, catching caddis flies under splashing blue water. In the trees I saw many birds. They were green with long beaks and curving tails, a species I didn't recognize. I saw one returning to her nest. She carried a small furred body in her mouth. It was an ominous sign. The birds were carnivorous and lived by the trail, waiting to eat the bodies of those who perished.

About twenty thent below the top, we reached a landing carved out of the mountain. The donkeys were breathing hard. I let them rest and gave them water from my water skin. When my donkey's breathing slowed, we began the final ascent. She got a running start and plowed straight up. I leaned as far forward as I could with my belly in the way. My heart rose in my throat as the donkey slipped, clambered to her feet and dashed upwards again. Behind us, the other two donkeys waited patiently until we reached the second landing when they began the ascent.

Two small men emerged from the shadows of a stable made out of green branches and moss. Both wore dark scarves across their lower faces. Between the scarves and their long hair, I could see nothing but their eyes. In this land of water and mist, I wondered why they needed such protection from snow-blindness. Neither man spoke. They took my donkey, leaving me standing beside a vast sheet of moving water. The men unloaded the leather packs from the other two donkeys who carried my supplies.

I looked across the wide river for a better view of this island that so threatened a Kosi Warrior. Now that I had reached the summit, I felt calmer, more in control of my fears. It was only an island, nothing that frightening. A small building made of white stone stood in a grove of Rholam trees toward the rear of the island, but I saw no bridge leading from the landing where I stood to the island.

Then I noticed a floating platform, a barge made of tree trunks lashed together with leather lacings, tied to a nearby tree. I motioned to one of the men in the stable. He walked over and I reached for his hand to read his thoughts. He yanked his whole body away from me, looking terrified. He pointed at my belly. I was confused, wondering if he was worried about my baby. He gestured for me to step on to the barge. I touched it with my toe, but the roaring river rocked it precariously. Terrified, I leapt back on to the bank. The donkey-minder and I looked at each other in silence.

"I can't ride on this barge," I told him, my heart pounded so hard I shook.

He pointed up into the trees where I saw a small woven seat attached to a liana cable hanging above the foaming water. The cable was tied to the stable on our side and to one of the trees on the island. The donkey man pulled the seat down and indicated I should sit on it. The little seat looked old and had started to fray. I looked down a thousand thent to see Lord Rohr standing on the riverbank below me. We were so high above him; he looked like a black beetle—a black beetle who waited to eat my dead body.

"Wirri-won?" I asked the donkey man. He nodded. "Help me," I said and the donkey man helped load medicines, bandages, food and soap grasses onto the barge, but he would not touch me, nor lift me into the seat. Holding my terror at bay, I climbed very carefully into the small rocking seat. It was not wide enough for a pregnant woman. The wind grew stronger. The man pulled on the cable, hoisting me jerkily high above the river. I screamed in fear and clung desperately to the seat as he propelled me furiously across the roaring water. It seemed forever, but in truth took only moments until he lowered me down on the island.

Dozens of people ran toward me, screaming, greeting me with high-pitched cries. A roaring horror took my mind. They had no faces. Their hoods covered nothing but skulls made of skin. I held my arms up, screaming for them not to touch me.

"Wirri-Won," I shrieked. "Help!"

# Chapter 4
## The Island of the Eaten

An Mali, the Healer from Maidenstone, had taught me about Leprosy when I studied with her in Namché. She said it began by consuming the nose and mouth. Then it ate the fingers and toes. These people had no features at all, only holes in their heads. They were nightmares wrapped in white rags. They circled me screaming in a demented dance and I remembered Lord Rohr waiting patiently a thousand thent below. Dread coursed through my heart. He had been right. I had put my life in jeopardy. I had risked the King's son. I reached up desperately for the swing, but donkey man had already raised it high above the waters, pulling it back to his side of the river. I was trapped. The non-humans would eat me alive.

"Wirri-won," I screamed frantically.

The door to the white building opened and the ancient Healer came walking out. She was wearing a yellow dress decorated with beads forming shining suns and red flowers. The sun hit the bald top of her head making it look as if she wore a halo. Pride and pleasure suffused her features. Walking toward me, she stopped several times speaking to the eaten and touching their wasted bodies. When she reached me, she raised both arms in the air saying, "Welcome, Wife of the Kosi King."

Remembering my manners, I knelt and murmured, "I greet you, Great Healer. I came because you sent for me." But when she reached her hands toward me, some innate memory made me flinch. I wrapped my arms around my belly, my skin crawling. "Don't touch me," I cried. Wirri-won looked at me with deep compassion in her eyes. Her empathy reached all the way to the bottom of her soul. When she turned back toward the white building, she called over her shoulder to me.

"Maidenstone Healer," she said. "Your babies will never have Terosi." It was the People's word for leprosy.

I stood there breathing deeply. I wiped the sweat from my brow and prayed to the Wind Goddess, asking her if I should enter the building. A trace of Lobelia perfume washed the island, the sign and blessing of the Wind Goddess. Straightening my shoulders, I followed Wirri-won into the Clinic, fearing I would never see my Grandparents, my husband Say'f or my dearest friend Conquin again.

When Wirri-won opened the door to the next room, a barrage of happy voices called out. To my immense surprise, I saw many children. Some were babies, standing up in tiny hanging beds. Others were older, a few were adolescents on the verge of adulthood. I dreaded seeing their tiny noses and ears eaten, but when I looked closely, all of them were perfect. Not a single blemish marked their brimming vitality.

I realized then what Wirri-won had done. This amazing woman was not a Healer. This woman was a Goddess. Alone, on this island at the top of the waterfall, she had somehow placed a healing membrane around each child. The evil tentacles of leprosy hadn't touched a single one. She had not cured the flesh-eating disease: she had prevented it.

Wirri-won led the way toward the back of the building. All the children followed, speaking a mix of Kosi words and those of the People. Some were laughing; others sang. We reached a kitchen filled with enough tables for all the children. A young woman came out of a doorway bringing trays of food. I thought she was also whole, but then noticed that she had only two fingers on one hand. I wondered if she was the first person Wirri-won had tried to cure. We took the food trays over to the tables for the children. All of them took their places cheerfully. Wirri-won lifted the smallest ones up into high chairs.

I looked out through the windows. The terrible people with no faces hovered around looking inside. I knew they were the parents of these children. Even with no features, I could feel their longing and love. I wondered if Wirri-won permitted them to touch their infants even once, before she took them away for the inoculation she had developed.

Later the Healer took me to a small room at the back of the white clinic. "This is where you will sleep," Wirri-won informed me. I put my things in the room, noticing the sleeping hammock sway and hearing the tumbling waters rushing by. The sound was an ominous sign of the river's power. I looked out the window at the grass verge where the land met the river. The constant thrust of the water tore another hunk of the sod away.

At night the Isle shakes," Wirri Won said, "The White River is strong. Blanda must leave soon." Blanda was the Kosi word for children.

My fears roared across my spirit again, fearing the cold muscularity of the river. I felt the beginnings of a migraine headache, something I hadn't had for many months.

"Walk with me," she said.

We left the building and walked to the end of the island. She pointed down at the rear bank. The fierce current battered against the earth, sharply undercutting the land. Wirri-won pointed to the trees in the river above us. Some still stood, although the water level reached their leafy crowns. The river had tipped over others—their roots jutted up. If the island was once large enough to hold all those trees, the White River had eaten half of it already.

I thought I would never again experience the paralyzing fear I felt when Captain Grieg captured me and took me inside the Great Dhali Ra Mountain, but I was wrong. I had risked everything to be here and now I would die and so would my son. Wirri-won and the beautiful Blanda she had saved—all of us would fall victim to the White river. I should have insisted on leaving right then, but it was already dark. In the morning I would inform Wirri-won I had to go. I would not risk my child a moment longer. I spent a horrible night, lying in a hammock that seemed to rest only inches above the wild waters. The White River growled beneath me. In the morning, I helped Wirri-won give the children their breakfast.

"It is good you came," she said. "You can help the Blanda escape. It is time."

I shivered, wondering when she planned to get us off the island. After they ate, she led the children singing to the barge. She lined them up, two by two. Each older child held a younger child by the hand. She gestured for them to sit down on the wooden platform. We strapped them together with long leather harnesses. The cracks between the boards were wide enough for a person's hand to reach into the frothing waters. She told the children to huddle close together in the center.

"What if they fall off?" I asked her, terrified for them.

"The Island dies tomorrow," she said, ominously. "I can do nothing else."

As the day passed, Wirri-won and I continued to ready the children for evacuation from the Island of the Eaten. Seven children were able to sit on the barge in the first crossing. When the raft started to move, they screamed, clutching each other desperately. Three fell into the river, gone before a hand could reach for them. I could hardly watch. My stomach heaved. I retched into the reeds. When they reached the landing, the men put the babies in the donkey packs to begin the vertical descent. With only three animals to carry the children down, it would take many hours to evacuate everyone.

We assembled the next group of children, putting fewer on the raft this time. All of them made the other side and took their places waiting for the donkeys. When all the children stood on the other side of the river, Wirri-won and I began packing her medicines and supplies. The whole island was shaking by then, several trees creaked as they came crashing down. The wind lashed the trees. I tried desperately to hurry the Medicine woman, but she calmly made trip after trip until at last she stepped on the barge, surrounded by her medicines. I tried to step onto the barge with her, but she pushed me back on the island. She beckoned to the kitchen woman indicating she could board the barge.

"Maidenstone Healer," she said pointing to the woven seat floundering in the air high above us. "You ride the air."

I looked back at the ghostly parents standing behind me. They were all huddled together, sobbing. Tears streamed from empty eye sockets. The donkey men levered the seat across the water to me. I jumped into the air repeatedly, trying to grab it. It was my one chance to reach safety. The Island throbbed. Once I touched the seat, but it slipped from my wet hand and I fell in the mud. I tried again and again. Several of the Eaten came forward. I waved them back shrieking, afraid to have them touch me. Clumsily, I got to my feet. One of the Eaten managed to pull the seat down for me. He held it, careful not to touch me in the roaring wind, as I climbed awkwardly in. I heard a horrific snap and the donkey man yanked the seat high in the air.

The sound increased and I saw the whole island begin to move. I sat in the air, buffeted by the screaming wind, high above the tragedy. More trees fell. One crashed beside me, its limbs nearly ripping me from the seat. The white building crumbled. Time slowed and I saw the Eaten parents tip over, one by one into the water. Those who still had hands not yet eaten by leprosy held them together in prayer. The whole island disappeared over the verge and the waters closed over the heads of the last swimmers.

Not one of the Eaten had tried to board the barge. Not one tried to board the flying seat. They chose to save their children: they chose to save me. For themselves, they chose death by water. Although my People believed those who died in water could never walk the sky worlds, I said the prayer for the valiant dead. I asked the Mountain Goddess to take their souls to the skies.


All the children who reached the riverbank alive, made it to the bottom of the mountain over the next two days—before the last donkey died. I grieved for him. He had saved so many children, only to lose his own life. I swallowed hard, honoring the flame of his steadfast courage.

Wirri-Won, the girl from the kitchen and I were still waiting at the top when Lord Rohr sent my pony, Yellowmane, running, falling, slipping and breathing as if her heart would break, up the vertical slope. When she reached the enormous flat stone, I held her quivering until her heartbeat slowed. I took her into the stable for food and water.

Wirri-won handed me a small packet containing a powdery substance. "For you and the babies," she told me, pointing at my stomach, "When they are one year old." She held up one finger.

"Thank you Great Healer," I said. "I honor your achievement with the Blanda." We stood in the pounding rain looking at each other, drenched. I shook from the cold and the emotion of our escape. We were hardly able to believe that we had lost so few and saved so many.

"I must go now, Wirri-won. Will you descend with me?"

She shook her head. "Maidenstone Healer takes the Blanda. Find them families."

"I have to find homes for all these children?" I asked, wanting to be sure I understood.

"It was for this task that I called you," Wirri-won replied. She made the Kosi sign of farewell and entered the dark stable. She and the kitchen helper weren't going with me. I felt a lurch of despair in my chest. *How in the world was I to find families for all these children of the feared and despised lepers?*

It was a desperate descent, Yellowmane fell several times, once pinning me beneath her. I was terrified for my baby. When we reached the bottom at last, I was exhausted and filthy. I looked at the children standing quietly in the rain. They were hungry and afraid. I didn't know if it would work, but I called on the Wind Goddess. Raising my arms into the air, I begged her to stop the rain. Blessedly, she did so.

We started out walking to the Valley of Tinsen in the morning. It had been an awful night. Lord Rohr had constructed a brush arbor for the children, but they all had to sleep on the ground. In the morning, I put one young girl on Yellowmane's back and gave her a baby to hold. I put another baby in Yellowmane's saddlebag. I put one larger boy on Lord Rohr's horse and bade him hold the littlest infant in front of him. To his disgust, I made Lord Rohr walk. I gave my shoes to an older child who had none. His toes were white with cold. So were mine.

We trekked up and down the folded earth. Many of the younger children couldn't keep up and stragglers made the line longer and longer. I ordered Lord Rohr to return for them and carry them up to the front. He did so repeatedly, but was furious. It was no work for a warrior, he said.

We reached the house of Justyn's Grandmother at evening the next day. I decided I would not tell her where the children came from. The prejudice was very strong against anyone with leprosy. Wirri-Won had inoculated the children against the disease, but I wasn't sure a non-Healer would understand.

"I greet you Grandmother of Justyn," I said when she opened the door. "I have ten children who need families and five more that are old enough to help the Fur Trappers. I beg you in the name of the Mountain Goddess. Will you help me?"

She looked at me; wet, bedraggled, pregnant and barefoot. She hesitated and I fell to my knees. "For Justyn," I said.

"Come in," she answered

I hugged her so hard she could hardly breathe.

In three days, we had homes for all ten of the smallest children. The remaining five who ranged from nine to sixteen, followed us out of Tinsen on foot. I was grateful to have my shoes back. The valley of Royenal needed laborers in the salt flats and took three children. The last two came with Lord Rohr and me—a boy around ten, whose name was Bumpy, and a girl of nine. Her name was Belaro. We were fortunate that Justyn's Grandfather had given us a dweli, the warm folding shelters we use in the mountains. It would keep the rain off the children while they slept.

# Chapter 5
## The Settlement of Rhan Du

When I came out of the dweli tent the next morning, Lord Rohr was loading the horses. Seeing the profile of the mountains, I realized that we were very close to the settlement at Rhan Du, a village near the entrance to the Lost Lake. I had been inside the Lost Lake valley only once, when the evil Captain Grieg kidnapped me and held me prisoner, but since then its unearthly splendor came to me often in my dreams.

"Lord Rohr," I called to him, "I wish to go to the Lost Lake. Rhan Du is nearby and there might be an entrance near the village."

Lord Rohr glowered. "You have only a short time until you are delivered of the King's son. It is not safe. The Avalanche destroyed your precious Skygrass valley that cost the Kosi so many warriors during the war. There is nothing left for you there."

I felt determination rise in my blood, strong as the White River.

"If the King is alive, Lord Rohr, he could be waiting for us inside that valley unable to get out. Would you deny the Far Seer? Would you fail to obey the call of the King for your service?"

"Do you know he lives? Have you seen him?" Lord Rohr asked me. Although the Kosi Warriors prayed to a God of War, they honored and believed in the Far Seer gift.

"In my dreams have seen the Lost Lake where Grieg held me prisoner. In every dream, I see the King's face. He looks sad."

"Then the King is dead. You have seen his revenant," Lord Rohr's voice was adamant.

"You may be correct, Lord Blood Arrow, but I must be sure. I beg you to take me there."

I heard a stirring inside the dweli and Bumpy and Belaro's sleepy voices.

"What will you do with these children?"

"Take them with us. They are forest adepts and could help us find our way."

Lord Rohr grunted and looked at the ground. "Sab-ra, the King is dead. You risk the life of the King's son. I will go alone and kill this soldier, Captain Grieg, who hurt you inside the mountain. This I will do for you, my Queen."

It was the first time he had called me his Queen and it warmed me. My mouth curled in a smile. I remembered Hodi and the two of us, hardly more than children, arguing about which of us would kill the Kosi who had abducted his mother. Hodi thought the honor should be his, but I said I would go with him and the two of us would take the life of the Kosi abductor. I felt the same way now.

"I cannot let you take this obligation from me. Lord Blood-Arrow. We are bound together to the will of the Kosi King."

Lord Rohr glowered, but turned the horses west.


Three hard days ride later, we came to the outskirts of Rhan Du, a small wool market village on the western side of the Dhali Ra. The entire settlement was wet, bedraggled and had been mostly destroyed by the Avalanche. There were only a few homes, all inhabited by Bearer families. The women and children ran into their houses when they saw us. One man came outside and recognizing a Kosi Warrior, nodded his head. The three of us had a fractured conversation, ending with me taking a Skygrass stone from my pouch and holding it up to the skies, pointing in the direction of the Lost Lake. I asked if would take us there.

The Bearer shook his head. I felt a desperate pain pierce me. If the Bearer people, who would take anyone into the Blue Mountains in the worst winters, would not take us into the high range, the Lost Lake valley was closed forever.

A woman invited us into her small house. We entered a kitchen where a woman served us a meal of chanry meat and vegetables. The children devoured the food. After we ate, the woman showed us beds for the night. She was not from the Bearer tribe and looked like the women of the Twelve Valleys. I tried to talk with her in my language.

"My name is Sab-ra," I said, "I am from Talin on the other side of the mountain range. Do you know my People?"

She hesitated, but then in a stuttering fashion began to speak my language. It was obvious she had not spoken our tongue in many years. She asked about the children.

"If I gave you two silver parthats, would you keep them until I return?" She nodded and the children looked relieved, but what she said next made my blood run cold.

"Army man, yellow hair. He came here last year. My husband saw him," she said.

My old enemy Captain Grieg who threatened my life in the city of Namché and later tortured and tried to kill me inside the mountain had been in Rhan Du.

"When?" I asked her, my heart frozen.

"Before the Crystal Mountain shattered," she said, making a smashing motion with her hands.

What the Bearers call the Crystal Mountain and we call the Dhali Ra, has the shape of a giant pyramid. The four great rivers of the world begin at its summit. The Green River flows south and brings the blessing of water to my land. The Yellow River flows east to a land of mystery and magic. The Blue River flows from the north side. The Bearers say it travels to the top of the world. The Red River flows west, but it disappeared inside the mountain after the Avalanche.

"Who guided him?" I asked.

"En Sun."

"En Sun is your husband?" I asked. She nodded. "Have you seen the man since then? Captain Grieg?" I trembled as I said his name.

When she shook her head, I told myself that he must have died in the Lost Lake valley, but I could feel him coming—the face of the dire wolf stalked me. Sweat broke out on my forehead.

"Lord Rohr and I want to enter the Lost Lake valley. We will pay a man of the village to guide us."

She didn't answer my request, but refilled our water containers and gave us bread and Ghat cheese to take with us. As we were finishing the meal, En Sun walked in. I remembered him from the time Captain Grieg held me prisoner. He seemed turned to stone when he saw me.

"You," he said, quivering in fear, "Red hair spirit. You died in mountain."

"No, I lived," I said and looked at him. He was shaking like the waters in the Scry bowl. "You gave me water. You fixed my dislocated shoulder. I do not blame you for what happened." As I said these words, I could feel him start to relax.

He reached out to touch me, still wondering if I was a ghost, and Lord Rohr growled at him.

"I am not a ghost," I said. En Sun touched me gingerly, as if I might burn his fingers. The Bearer thought I blamed him for my kidnapping, but I did not. The evil Captain Grieg alone was responsible for that horror.

Once he had calmed, Lord Rohr asked if he would guide us up the mountain.

En sun became extremely agitated and spoke so fast we could understand little. I caught, "Red River, blood, fire," but nothing else. I took some silver parthats from my leather bag and laid them on the table one by one, making a curving silver road. En Sun's wife kept pointing to the silver, pleading with her husband to give us what we wanted. At last he nodded. He left the house, motioning for us to follow him. When we reached our horses, he pointed to the black dweli packed on Lord Rohr's warhorse. Using sign language, he showed me that he wanted the dweli in payment for his services.

"If I give you this, will you take us?" He nodded. "Once we arrive at the entrance to the Lost Lake valley, you can have the dweli tent. Not until then."

Later that evening, En Sun brought us circles of leather and long laces, showing us how to tie them to make little boots to protect our horses' feet. The terrain above Rhan Du was rough with broken lava from the volcanic eruption that followed the Avalanche.

We left the village the next morning, after buying an additional pony from the Bearers, a bright roan named Jemma. If we found the King living in the Lost Lake valley he would need a mount. We left the children with En Sun's wife. I kissed them good-by, relieved they would be safe and well-fed while we were gone. We followed En Sun up the mountain, stopping now and then to check the horses' leather boot covers. By late afternoon, we reached the bottom of the "bite," the huge chunk of white quartz the Avalanche ripped out of the Crystal Mountain. At its base I saw a spring of red water. It was the start of the Red River that flowed down the white quartz cliffs. It seemed menacing, as if red blood flowed across a pure white skeleton. En Sun, visibly shaken, kept raising his clasped hands to the skies, pleading with his gods to keep him safe.

As the sun went down, I noticed Yellowmane was limping. We had been riding continuously for many hours by then and I thought she might be going lame. Then I saw her step into a hole, heard a horrible cracking sound and my pony went down on her knees. I feared the sound was the crack of a bullet. I looked around in every direction, but saw no glint of metal, no bushes moving. Then I jumped from her back and tried desperately to find out what was wrong. Lord Rohr came over and together we felt along her right front leg. I saw no external injury, but she wouldn't put any weight on it. Her leg was broken.

En Sun found a small depression nearby and set up the black dweli tent. He helped me get Yellowmane's saddle off her back. She was moaning continuously in terrible pain. I held her beautiful face in my hands and crooned to her, making the sounds I made to women in hard labor. I tried to enter her mind, but forests of pain blocked my way. With En Sun's help, I found some long straight tree branches. Using the leather from her shoes as a bandage, I made a splint by tying the sticks tightly along her broken leg. It seemed to help and her cries quieted. We managed to walk her slowly on three legs to the area where we planned to spend the night.

Lord Rohr he pulled out his long knife. He made a cutting motion near Yellowmane's neck, wanting to slit her throat. I burst into tears and begged him not to. I knew it was foolish—ponies with broken legs must always die. The men could continue up the mountain on foot, seeking an entrance to the Lost Lake, but I would not take another step. Yellowmane's injury told me to go no further on this trip of fools.

I searched the area around our camp for willow bark. It grew along the watercourses but there were few springs in this arid area. With the help of the Goddess, I finally located a seeping spring with a willow bush and cut some branches. Ground willow bark was a pain reliever. Lord Rohr helped me grind the wood into a powder and I fed it to Yellowmane. The clouds hung low above the earth and lightning forked from them. Thunder roared in the distance.

En Sun and Lord Rohr left the next morning on foot. They said they would ascend the trail and return soon to tell me what they had found. After they departed, I searched for food for Yellowmane and the other horses. I carried back armfuls of the yellow sedge grasses. The horses whinnied when they saw my approach and ate eagerly. With some trepidation, I took Lord Rohr's horse and Jemma, the roan pony from Rhan Du to the blood water spring. They swallowed the water immediately. It didn't seem to bother them, but I did not give any of the red water to Yellowmane. I feared it might take away the power of the willow branch powder. I gave her water from my water skin.

For a day and a night, I sat near Yellowmane as she rested and put my hands on the break in her leg. I prayed for the healing power to come, but felt only a small tingle. Sitting near her warm body, I drowsed and dreamed of Angelion, the white mooncat of my visions. I had not heard his voice since I escaped Captain Grieg on that fateful day inside the Mountain, but in my dreams I saw the mooncat limping.

On the third night, my pony seemed more comfortable. I decided I could leave her outside and sleep in the black dweli. In the middle of the night, I heard a horrible rending cry. I stuck my head out of the flap. Moonlight bathed the camp and I saw Yellowmane rear into the air. As I watched in horror, an enormous spotted leopard attacked her. He sank his teeth into her throat. She fell to the ground and struggled. He roared and she made fearful high-pitched cries. I screamed and ran out of the dweli.

The leopard jumped on Yellowmane's back biting into her neck repeatedly. I grabbed a stick and poked at his glowing eyes. He gripped her throat more tightly with his teeth but then suddenly released her body and ran away.

As I screamed in rage and despair, my pony breathed her last. I went to her body and sat weeping for a long time, remembering sweet Yellowmane and all the times she had carried me—on black cutting lava and grassy plains—from the golden fields of Talin to the dreaming spires of Namché. The next day, weeping continuously, I said the blessing for the dead over her still form. The sand was soft and I buried her in its warmth. I sang the Kosi farewell song and asked the Goddess to take her spirit to the skies so she could run among the clouds. On the day I entered the sky world, I knew she would be waiting.

# Chapter 6
## The Crystal Steppe

Ever since Lord Rohr and En Sun departed trying to find an entrance into the Lost Lake, I had felt stabbing pains in my lower back. I didn't know if the pains were early labor, but they frightened me. I lay inside the dweli, afraid even standing up might bring the baby from my womb. In late afternoon, I heard the men returning.

"Come inside the dweli," I called to Lord Rohr. When he came in and saw me lying in my bedroll, he grimaced and looked worried.

"Tell me what you and En Sun found?"

"We found a passageway we believe leads into the Lost Lake, but it is hidden in a cleft behind an enormous wall of fallen stones. We worked at removing the stones for a full day, but it would take many moons to move the rock fall. We would need the help of all the Bearers in Rhan Du and they would demand many silver parthats in payment. Even then, I fear it would be impossible. Where is Yellowmane?" he asked me.

"Gone to the belly of a Mountain leopard," I said, my voice low with sorrow. Tears quickened in my eyes. I sought control and said, "I believe I am in labor, Lord Rohr." He blanched. "But it is too early for the babe to come."

"You became pregnant the night you married the King," Lord Rohr murmured. "Now the Vernal Moon is ending. The child comes soon. "

"No, Lord Rohr. The baby should not come for three more moons. He will come during the Flowering Moon. The People's women carry their children for nine moons."

"Kosi women deliver after six moons," he told me.

A feeling of doom came across my shoulders. I had not realized Kosi pregnancies were only six months long. The father of my child was Kosi. It could mean my pregnancy would be shorter.

"The Blended ones at the Citadel, the children with mothers from the People and Kosi fathers, how long did the women carry those babes?"

"Seven moons, sometimes a week or two more."

I felt a little surge of relief. The pain was probably what An Mali called false labor.

"Then I am not in labor," I told him, but fear still showed on Lord Rohr's face and echoed in my heart.

"If the baby is very large, sometimes even the Blended ones arrive in six moons," he told me. We looked at each other in dismay.

I looked down at my belly moving as the infant kicked. I pulled my shirt up to just below my breasts. "Do you think this baby is a large one?"

Lord Rohr's eyes opened wide. "Cover yourself, Wife of the King. No man can look upon the womb of a pregnant woman, save the man who put the seed inside her." His eyes snapped. He was furious at my careless revealing of my body.

"Lord Rohr, you and I have travelled many days and nights together. On the way to the King's Valley after the Avalanche, we slept together in caves of snow. We ate hulion in frigid winter winds. Once you made me eat a worm because you knew I was pregnant, even though I did not know it then. You have been my friend since I met you, but on this day, I do not need a friend. I need a midwife."

Lord Rohr looked as horrified as if I had asked him to give birth. "Wife of the King, I cannot do this." He shook his head backing out of the dweli.

"Would you risk the life of the King's son?" I called. "Lord Rohr, I order you to obey me. Bring the candle lamp so you can see clearly between my legs."

"If I look upon you like that, I will be unmanned. I will no longer be a Warrior." He was trembling.

"Then I will make En Sun look," I told him.

"No," he said fiercely, "En Sun is not from the People and he is not Kosi. He is only a meager Bearer person, not worthy to touch the foot of the wife of the King."

"What shall we do, Lord Rohr?" I asked him in despair. "If the babe comes tonight, you will have to deliver him."

Lord Rohr called out to En Sun. There was a high tense note in his voice. When En Sun came inside and saw me lying on my sleeping robe, he frowned, looking troubled.

"En Sun, I fear the child comes soon. Do the men of the Bearer Tribe help their wives deliver their children?"

"Never," he said, his eyes opened wide in fright. "If you want your child to breathe the air of the mountains, we must return to Rhan Du."

I lay all night alone in the dweli, fighting the pain and begging the Wind Goddess for her protection. On toward morning, the rain stopped and my pains eased. I walked outside to the fire and woke Lord Rohr.

"We will descend, Lord Blood Arrow. You were correct. I should never have come on this trip."

We reached Rhan Du by evening. My pains had not resumed. We spent a comfortable night and I felt much refreshed. En Sun's wife had taken good care of Bumpy and Belaro, they looked happy and well fed. I asked her if she and her husband would adopt them, but she told me they could not. She was pregnant herself and the living they made from the messages her husband carried from valley to valley was insufficient to feed that many.

After dinner, I asked En Sun for some information. "Have you seen Captain Grieg since the Avalanche?"

"No, but I have heard he still lives. He is an evil spirit, a djinn that appears and disappears at will."

"Who told you he lives?"

"A member of the Hakan tribe. They serve as hunters for the white men who climb the great mountain."

"Where did this Hakan see Captain Grieg?"

"Near the Lost Lake valley during the Hunger Moon last winter."

A tidal wave of fear paralyzed me. My nemesis and implacable enemy, Captain Grieg, had made it through the winter alive. "Have you had reports of Bearers seeing the Kosi King?"

"None of the Bearers have seen him."

I closed my eyes in pain.

Lord Rohr and I started back toward the Valley of the King at dawn the next day with Belaro and Bumpy riding behind us. As we rode down the Mountain, despair coated me in anguish. How could the Goddess have let Captain Grieg live and taken the life of my King? What kind of deity would permit such horror?

We were two days east of Natil when I felt a warm gush of fluid run down my leg. My heart sank. There was no question this time. My labor had begun.

"Stop," I called to him. "Lord Rohr, I need Wirri-won. The King's son is coming." Sheer terror struck me down like an axe. The baby was coming two months early and I stood in the middle of an open plain with nobody to help me. All the color leached from Lord Rohr's copper face. If he rode straight to the White River, he said, he could make it less than a day, but it would be another day before Wirri-won could return to me. I felt a hard grinding pain in my lower back. I had no idea how long I would be in labor. Lord Rohr and I looked at each other, calculating the time it would take him to reach Wirri-won.

"Would it be faster for you to get my Grandmother in Talin or Wirri-won?"

"If you were not the Wife of the King, I would leave you here to die," he told me, harshly. "You have been foolish. Such arrogant resolve is not the way of the Kosi or their Queens."

"You can either ride for help or you can deliver this baby," I threatened him.

"I will get help." His face filled with panic and he whirled his stallion back down the trail.

Because we left the dweli behind with En Sun, the children and I would have to sleep out in the open. I looked around at the nearly barren area we had reached. There was only one small grove of trees lying to the south. I walked slowly toward it with the children following me. It was late afternoon and I had only one slice of bread and two curds of cheese for the three of us. I had counted on Lord Rohr shooting a chanry bird for dinner.

By the time we reached the grove, the pains were much stronger. I asked the children to make a small shelter by bending birch branches over in an arc and tying them to low shrubs. I pulled my sleeping roll off the pony and cursed my own stupidity for leaving nearly all my medicines and supplies with Wirri Won.

In my pocket, I had the small knife Mistress Falcon gave me when I left Maidenstone. I would need it if a mountain lion found us, but could not use it to cut the cord binding baby to mother. Poison could still coat the blade. A single touch would bring the Yellow Water Fever. All night I lay in that small bower as the pain took my lower body in its teeth and shook it as a large cat shakes a mouse. I knew better than to make any noise. If I cried out, the sound would draw a predator, and I had to protect the children who lay just outside my branched shelter.

By early morning, I could stifle my cries no longer. I cried for my mother, the mother who abandoned me, the mother I had never seen. In one brief lucid moment, I promised the Goddess if she let me live to hold my son in my arms, I would never fail him. But as I prayed, I feared I would not live to see the face of my child.

# Chapter 7
## Return to the Valley of the King

The pain of labor was appalling. I had seen many women in labor, but the intensity of the pain stunned me. Most women experience intermittent pain, with pauses giving them time to catch their breath, but I knew only one continuous screaming agony. I wanted desperately to escape this body which held me prisoner to the earth. I found myself losing consciousness.

Abruptly, I felt myself rising and floating. I seemed to lay spread out in the air, arms and legs stretched in a star, looking down at the small shelter. The two children sat in the dark, leaning against each other as cries of anguish came from beneath the arched branches. I watched my superfluous body begin to bleed. The red stain spread relentlessly across the sleeping roll, but I felt nothing but a kind of flying peace. At that moment, I knew I could choose to escape. I only wanted to fly away from the discarded husk on the bed below me. Brother Jun once told me such choices come to everyone who walks the dying road. I felt my body and spirit begin to separate.

"I call you to return," I heard the Angelion speak in strong ringing tones.

In an instant, I was back in the brutal pain, but the voice of the Angelion calmed me. Then the pain stopped abruptly. I had never seen this happen before and feared my son was dead. If he were dead, labor would start again, but hours could pass before that happened. I crawled out of the shelter. It was morning. The children, Bumpy and Belaro, were hungry, tired and dirty. During my labor, I had forgotten to give them any food. I gave Bumpy my knife and a simple snare from my pocket.

"Try to trap a ne-ne," I told him. His dark eyes were grave. "We need food, Bumpy. I need food or I will not be able to make milk for the baby."

His face darkened with the importance of the task I set him. He ran off silently in the early morning light, almost a shadow.

"Belaro, will you get water?" I asked, handing her my water skin. She flashed away like a sprite. Forest-adepts could move so silently among the trees, they seemed made from magic. Belaro returned an hour later with water. We managed to wash the blood from my sleeping robe, and I enlarged the shelter so all of us could lie down inside its shade. I tried to reach my son in my mind. I felt nothing. Dread made me quiver deep inside.

Bumpy returned in late afternoon with two hulion he had trapped. Together we skinned them and stretched their bodies over the fire. Warm after the meal, we cuddled together in the shelter. Eventually, the children slept. My conscience lashed me that I had disregarded Lord Rohr's counsel to return to Natil after we found families for the Blanda. Had my stubbornness killed my baby?

The pain began again at dawn. The fearsome labor-cat bit my lower body relentlessly. I sent the children outside, not wanting them to see a dead baby born. Hours passed and I prayed to the Wind Goddess for the return of Lord Rohr and for Wirri-won.


In late afternoon, I heard the sounds of hoof beats. Lord Rohr had returned with Wirri-won. I was teary-eyed with gratitude. I got shakily to my feet and hugged him. He looked down at me, still pregnant and smiled. He was immensely pleased with himself. They had brought a dweli and I laid down on my bedroll, relieved to be out of the elements.

The Healer expertly tended me. She had brought a plant mixture she said would open my womb and bring the child. A few hours later, I felt the crowning and in a rush of pleasure, my child emerged. I looked down to see a tiny girl, alive and well. I thanked all the Goddesses in the pantheon as I examined her strong golden body. Her feathery hair was red. She breathed well. A wave of intense love struck me as I looked at her. She opened her eyes and knew me. I felt we had known each other for a thousand years.

Conquin told me I carried a son. She was rarely wrong, but she had been wrong this time. Wirri-won examined the infant carefully and nodded her head in satisfaction. She had brought a blanket, baby clothing and nappies with her. We dressed the small one as she slept. Wirri-won pulled me to my feet. She wrapped her arms around me and together we sang the Kosi Victory song, a lullaby for the birth of a Warrior's child.

But late that night my pains resumed. I wondered if the placenta was still inside me. I lay in silence between the Bumpy and Belaro as the pain rose and rose again. Several hours later, I gave a soft cry. Wirri-won, who slept outside our door near the campfire entered the dweli and knelt beside me.

"I'm sorry, Wirri-won," I whispered. "It's probably just the afterbirth."

"No," she said. "Another."

I had no idea what she meant, but when the labor beast seized me again, I knew. I had been pregnant with twins. I remembered Grandmother telling me I had a twin sister and Conquin teasing me that I carried two. I gritted my teeth against the pain and fear. I forced myself to stay inside my body. The thought of a second baby gave me strength. Wirri-won held my hand and sang to me. At dawn, I felt myself open. There was no birth fluid left and this one didn't want to leave my body. Every inch was agony. At last, Wirri-won lifted the miniature baby from between my legs. It was a boy, but he was bright blue. Wirri-won turned away, holding the baby so I couldn't see him. I heard her slap him repeatedly. I cringed, feeling his pain.

"Is he dead?" I cried, agonized, but then I heard the harsh cry of the newborn.

"He lives. You have a son," Wirri-won said proudly and laid my baby beside his sleeping twin. As he breathed, he turned a golden pink. I closed my eyes in pride as the tears of joy came down. The Healer took my water skin out to the fire. She returned with warmed water and washed the tiny child. She wrapped him tightly in a blanket and showed me his face. He blinked and I saw my husband's golden eyes. My daughter's red hair was already dried and curly. Her skin was lighter than her brother's and her eyes were a shining gray.

"I will name my daughter Crimson," I said. "The boy I shall name Quinn, for my dearest friend Conquin, who knew all along that he was coming." I hardly said the last sentence aloud. I was already falling asleep. Outside by the fire, Wirri-won and Lord Rohr were singing the cadenced rhythms of the song for the birth of a Kosi prince.

Wirri-won departed on her small silver mare in the morning. She took Bumpy and Belaro with her saying she could easily find a family for both of them. Lord Rohr and I set off for the King's Valley with tiny Quinn sleeping in a sling around my body and Lord Rohr carrying Crimson in his arms on his stallion. Every time he looked at the babes, he couldn't stop smiling. He was as proud as if he had birthed the twins himself.

It took us three days to reach the King's Valley. When she heard our horses, Conquin came running out, screaming in happiness. Thron walked behind her, carrying baby Sab-ri. I felt a sense of profound relief as the fears of the trip washed away. Everything would be all right now. I was with Conquin again.

# Chapter 8
## Justyn Returns to Natil

Every day I could see my babies growing stronger. They were both astonishing in their physical abilities. Quinn could sit up at only three months. Crimson could speak in words by then. At four months, both of them could crawl. They knew Conquin's name, baby Sab-ri's, Kim-li's and Kensing's. The babies' coordination and skills clearly came from their Kosi father. I missed him dreadfully, but my children's amazing spirit and total lack of fear entranced me. Late one evening I heard the jingling of a horse's harness and a man's voice. I walked out to the door step. My dear friend Justyn had returned.

"Sab-ra," he said and took me in his arms. "I have come to ask you again to marry me. My Grandmother said you married the Kosi King in the Skygrass valley and that you were expecting a child. I am sorry to give you this news, but the Bearer people tell me the Kosi King rides the skies. Your child needs a father. I would be that man." His declaration brought tears to my eyes. He confirmed the fears I had about Say'f but his generosity of spirit gave me a wondrous gift, his willingness to serve as father to my children.

"I had twins," I told him and his openhearted smile warmed me, reminding me of my lost spy partner, Hodi. He took my hand and we walked into my apartment. He looked down on Quinn and Crimson, sleeping so quietly. They lay curled around each other. Sometimes at night, they even sucked each other's thumbs.

"Sab-ra, they are perfect," he said, "Absolutely flawless."

Tears stung my eyes as I reached for Justyn's embrace.

Over the next few weeks, Justyn stayed in rooms near us. He took little Quinn's hands and held him as he learned to stand. He told Crimson stories of the People. Soon Quinn called him "Soama," a word for father in the language of the People. If Justyn became the twins' father, I knew their Kosi heritage would die. Still, I treasured Justyn's love for my children. I told myself I should marry him.

One sunny afternoon, Justyn and I sat together watching Quinn and Crimson crawling through the lilies in the King's garden.

"Sab-ra, we have become a family," Justyn said, his eyes crinkled with warmth, "Marry me, sweetheart, be my wife and my love," his voice was plangent with adoration.

I looked down at the grass, trying to gather my thoughts. I didn't want to hurt this wonderful man, but I knew I could not marry him. "I cannot, Justyn." I felt my stomach clench. "I love you, but not as I love the Kosi King."

"Is it something I've done, Sab-ra?" The wrinkles around his eyes deepened and his voice was sorrowful.

I took a deep breath. "When I entered the Kosi King's chamber at the Citadel and saw Say'f for the first time, I felt my body had joined the warm waters of a running river. The current of his life pulled me toward him irrevocably saying we were destined to be together. I am sorry, Justyn," I held out my hand to him, but he would not take it. His face was dark with pain. His lips tightened with anger.

"I remember when Say'f named you Wind Woman, and called you wayward. He was right. Even now, when I know he is dead, you vacillate between us," anger tinged Justyn's voice.

"Against my culture, against a years of Kosi predation on Talin's woman, against all of nature it seems, I long for the Kosi King. Living or dead, I want him still," my voice was bleak.

"But he is gone," Justyn said gently. I reached for his hand and felt him tremble.

"Dear friend, I must have proof. Until I see for myself that he no longer walks the earth, I am a married woman. I cannot have another." My voice filled with unshed tears.

"Then I will be Quinn and Crimson's father until their mother is ready," Justyn said reaching out his arms for me. We embraced and I felt my sorrows ease.

"If Say'f is still alive, what will you do, Justyn?"

"I will return to Namché and wait for you."

"But I don't plan to ever return to the city."

"Someday you will return to Maidenstone and I will be waiting." When he said those words I wondered if Justyn too had the ability to see the future.


On a beautiful evening several weeks later, as the fireflies danced in the trees, I carried my children to visit Conquin. Her husband Thron greeted me warmly. Kim-li and Kensing, Say's two daughters from his marriage to Martyn, lived with them. I played with the girls a little while and they asked to hold their baby brother and sister. Crimson said their names quietly. Conquin brought me tea and cookies warm from the oven, scented with cinnamon.

"I have been thinking about my future," I told her. "It seems to me that I have three choices. I could stay here in the King's Valley. If I stayed, Quinn and Crimson would grow up with their sisters, Kim-li and Kensing.

Little Sab-ri could become my daughter's best friend. I would be able to be with you," I smiled at her.

"What else have you considered?" Conquin asked.

"If Say'f is dead, I could marry Justyn. If we returned to Namché as a family, I could become midwife to the women of the city. Or I could return to my own valley of Talin. My grandparents have never seen my children."

"Do you believe Say'f gone?" she asked. Her eyes probed mine.

"I see him often in dreams, fighting with someone in the blue snows. It could be the fight I see is his last." I looked down, blinking away my tears.

"What about your children's Kosi heritage?"

"I think about it often," I told her. "They carry the blood of the People, the blood of my red-haired mother and the blood of the Kosi. I want them to know their whole lineage."

"If Say'f is gone, you realize that Quinn is King of the Kosi," she said thoughtfully.

Struck by Conquin's insight, I felt a stab of guilt. Since arriving back in the King's Valley, I had not thought of Quinn as a future King. The night Say'f and I were married, he told everyone that our son would be the next King. I should have remembered.

"What do you think I should do, Conquin?"

"Well, I want you here, but I think you should first visit Talin. Then, perhaps you and Justyn might go to the Kosi Citadel at the Springs of Natrun. Didn't Lord Sta'g tell you it was time for the Kosi to choose a new King? It wouldn't hurt for the Kosi to see that the son of the Kosi King lives. If you go, would you want to take Kim-li and Kensing with you?"

I hesitated. Kensing was still just a baby, less than three. I thought a long time about Kim-li. She was nearly seven. She missed the Citadel and described it to me often. She needed her Kosi heritage too, especially if both her parents were dead, but I finally decided I would leave them with Conquin. I explained to Kim-li that I was taking Quinn and Crimson only because they were still nursing. I promised to return soon with news of her father. I had hoped Lord Rohr would come with us, but when I asked him, he said his duty had been fulfilled. He was returning to the Citadel. I bade him farewell on a bright windy morning, tears brimming. We had not been apart since we escaped together after the Avalanche took the People's Skygrass valley.

"Farewell, my friend. I hope we will meet again in this life."

"I will await the day," he said confidently, "But I told you before, Warriors are not allowed to have women as friends."

"Then farewell, my Hero and my Guardian," I told him and the corners of his mouth lifted up in a smile. When he cantered out of the King's Valley, he raised his arm in a Kosi salute and I returned to pack for my long delayed visit to Talin, my childhood home.

In Lord Rohr's absence, Conquin's husband Thron, and Norgay, the King's Horse Captain, were assigned to escort me and my children to Talin. Justyn was coming with us and would then he would continue on to Namché. The King had his carpenters make a small wagon for the babies. The leather workers made a harness to attach the wagon to Jemma, the roan mare I bought in Rhan Du. Conquin and I padded the bottom and sides of the wagon with pashmina wool. We put Quinn and Crimson in the wagon and had Jemma pull them around the castle garden, accustoming them to riding in it.

The morning was bright with sunshine and the small ones were bouncing happily in the cart the day we rode straight up and out of the caldera that encircles the Valley of the King. Less than an hour later I heard Quinn call his sister saying, "Crim-mee, Crim-mee." He sounded worried. I turned around to see that somehow my daughter had managed to climb out of the wagon. She fell, landing on the road. She scraped her knee and at the sight of her blood, Quinn wept. I had noticed this before. Whenever Crimson got hurt, which was often, Quinn cried. When Quinn injured himself, he had the stoicism of a tiny warrior.

"Stop the wagon, Justyn," I said. I dismounted, grabbed my intrepid small daughter and sat her in front of my saddle. Enthralled by everything she saw, she was completely still, her eyes wide open. There was no fear in my daughter's heart. Holding her was like having a small falcon in your hand or a lion cub in your lap.

Less than half an hour later, Crimson cried out, "Q-Whin, Q-Whin." It was her baby name for her brother. We stopped. Looking back, I saw Quinn hanging on the outside of the wagon, about to let go. I handed Crimson to Justyn, dismounted and grabbed my son.

As we rode east, I pointed out some flying raptors, telling my son their burning eyes sought the nest of the ne-ne. He seemed compelled by the sight of them and raised his little voice calling, "Sky Dog, down." I remembered the feathers of enormous eagle in the King's sleeping space at the Citadel. If Say'f were dead, that eagle would belong to Quinn.


At the King's command, Justyn and I announced the Peace Accord to the Elders in each of the Valleys as we rode across the folded earth. The King's scribe had made twelve copies of the treaty between the Kosi and the People. The Accord had been drafted at my instigation and bound the Kosi to take no more women against their will. Kosi women, to their unending sorrow, were infertile. Kosi men who desired a wife who could conceive a child, could come and court one of the People's women as was the old practice. A marriage could not take place without the woman's consent.

We were welcomed everywhere, although many of the men asked difficult questions. We met at evening around the Communal Flame. I spoke as an Elder then, a married woman with children. I told them about the importance of the Accord. I brought Quinn and Crimson with me to the Flame. My son sat beside me unmoving, held rapt by the night, the flames and the stars. When the men asked to hold him, he shook his head, holding my fingers tightly. Crimson had no such reservations. The men passed her from hand to hand. She sat so quietly, erect and proud.

I spoke of Quinn as the future for our People. He became the honorary son or grandson of everyone there. Crimson had many offers of marriage before the night was over. I obtained the names of the People's women the Shunned took from each valley. I had Say'f's promise they would have a choice about whether to return to their home valleys.

Although they welcomed my visit, most of the Elders looked at me with doubt in their eyes and shook their heads. They said Say'f was dead and doubted a piece of paper would control murderous Kosi warriors with no one to enforce their obedience. My heart sank, knowing they were right. Without Say'f, I could never bridge our cultures and ensure peace for the high country. I lay awake a long time each night, trying to reach my husband with my mind, across the hills and valleys of the pleated land.

We rode into Talin in the early evening. The news that we were coming preceded us. The People had erected festival tents, were cooking food and the scents of Talin rode out to meet us. I smelled fragrant herbs, warm tsampa bread and Ghat cheeses. Grandfather and Uncle Hent rode down toward us, calling out welcoming greetings.

I remembered the first time I rode into Talin with the Say'f, it seemed an eternity ago. That day Grandfather had been irate and ordered the Kosi King and his warriors away. Only by invoking the Wind Goddess, was I able to convince grandfather to let Say'f speak to the Elders. This time the air resounded with songs and happy cries.

"How beautiful they are," Grandmother said, taking Quinn in her arms. Grandfather took Crimson and showed her to everyone in the village.

"They both are amazing," I told them, "Quinn can already take a few steps on his own and Crimson is talking so much. I am so proud of my children."

"Sab-ra," Quinn said, looking at me and laughing. He already knew how to tease me. He knew I didn't like him to call me by my first name.

"You must not call me Sab-ra, Quinn," I said for the hundredth time. You should call me Bah-ma," the Kosi word for mother.

"He probably should call you Queen, you know," Grandfather said quietly. "Quinn is the future King, but you are Queen of the Kosi now."

Shaken by my responsibilities that hit me like a hailstorm, I realized this trip was about far more than presenting Quinn to the Kosi at the Citadel. I felt the crux of time and the absolute necessity of reaching the stronghold of the Kosi. I trembled, fearing the remaining Kosi Warriors would despise me, but dampened my fears, praying I would be welcomed at their Queen.

# Chapter 9
## The Citadel

"I must leave here soon and go to the Kosi Citadel, Justyn," I told him after spending a few days with my grandparents in Talin.

"I don't think you should," Justyn said. "As the wife of the dead King, they will not want you there. And you are a mother now. You must think of your children before yourself."

I felt a wash of shame, but it didn't stop my burning intent to visit the Kosi stronghold. I begged Justyn to accompany me to the Citadel, hoping against hope that Say'f would be there. Grandmother cried and urged me to stay longer, but dried her tears when I said I would leave Quinn and Crimson in Talin. One of the young mothers in Talin who had just lost her child, could nurse mine. I would be back in a few weeks, I told her.

Justyn shook his head in despair at my stubbornness. "Why can't we all go to Namché? We could be married there. Since the Harn Army is gone now, I could get a position translating for the Headman of the city. You could resume your Healer work. We would be a real family." Justyn's eyes pleaded for my consent.

My heart crunched a bit for Justyn and in truth for myself, although I found my mind turning away from the vision of the four of us living in Namché. I could not stop thinking about the Kosi. What would I be to the Warriors? Would I be their Queen, as Grandmother said? Or, would I be a threat, a problem to be disposed of, as Justyn feared. My old dread of the Kosi woke inside me as Justyn and I rode south on the Wool Road toward the great Kosi grasslands.

We entered the side trail leading to the Springs of Natrun at evening four days later. We travelled among tall green bamboo that caught the evening light. The Citadel was several hours ride east of the springs. I began to feel terribly vulnerable. I was angry with myself for allowing Norgay and Thron to return to the King's Valley after they left us in Talin. I brought my old knife from Maidenstone, its blade still coated with the deadly poison. I could use it to defend myself, but then I felt a shock. I couldn't use a poison knife on a Kosi, they were my People now.

Justyn and I camped near the Springs of Natrun, in a valley filled with tall green grasses and white windflowers. The springs were full of turquoise water, warm as summer sun. I soaked my tired body in its warmth. Later, we lay on our sleeping bags on the grass floor, looking up at the skies through a frame of waving bamboo. The grasshoppers flew high that night and the lightening bees looked like stars. For the first time, I seemed to see my twin sister's face. I wondered if she had come to my land from the far place that was her home. She seemed very close and I sent her my love on the wings of bees.

"We should talk about what you are going to say to the Warriors at the Citadel," Justyn said. I smiled at him, thinking how much he really was like Hodi.

"I brought a white gown with me, made of the finest pashmina wool. I plan to enter the Citadel dressed as their Queen. I will claim the right to sleep in the King's Alcove."

"You might find someone else has taken that place," Justyn said, looking at me from narrowed eyes in an anxious countenance.

"Who would have the temerity to do such a thing?"

"Sab-ra, sweetheart, the Bearers told me the Kosi King was dead. They probably told the Kosi that also. All the Kosi who survived the war have by now returned to the Citadel. They will pledge loyalty to the strongest warrior. I suspect many battles have taken place since you left there, battles over who is King now."

This whole trip seemed perilous and despite the beautiful evening, I felt dread inside me. Without the King, what would happen to the Accord? How would I accomplish my goals of healing the wounds that still festered between the People and the Kosi? I had been so proud presenting the velum copies of the Accord to each Headman in the Twelve Valleys. Now my dream of peace between the People and the Kosi could die. *Goddess of the Winds, please guide me,* I prayed, but a cold breeze swept us that night as we slept by the fire—the night before the onset of the death mission.

We rode into the Citadel at midday. Everything seemed too quiet. I heard a crow calling and a dog fox bark in the distance. No one came out of the Citadel to greet us. We dismounted and tethered our mounts. I walked to a nearby grove, dressed myself in my white gown and combed my hair in the high braided Kosi style. Justyn and I walked to the sliding rock that concealed the main door to the stronghold. It seemed to swing open of its own accord and we strode into revulsion. The stench was overwhelming. I turned aside and vomited in the nearby grasses. When I could make myself stand upright, I peered into the Citadel. In the dim light, we could see dozens of bodies of men and women stabbed, beaten, killed. We saw two children and one pregnant woman among the corpses. I knelt by each body and took pulses. I found no one alive. The dark metal colored feathers of the King's golden eagle lay on the ground. I prayed he had escaped the charnel house.

We found a young female gazehound hiding in the bedchamber of the King. She was starving and desperately thirsty. She made the sound of the feral lynx when she heard us. I picked her up, crooning to her. Justyn searched the area around the Citadel and located a cold spring. At the bottom, he saw a leather container, partially covered by waterweed and rocks. He pulled it to the surface and we were elated to find good chanry meat inside. The little gazehound shared our meat rapturously.

The next morning, working like slaves in the hot sun, Justyn and I began burying all the Kosi. There were thirty-one men, three women and two children. It took us many days. The earth was hard as granite. We had no choice but to cover their bodies with rocks and pronounce the blessing for the dead. I had learned the Kosi song for those who had passed away from little Kim-li and sang it. The notes rang in the evening darkness. I didn't know what the words meant, but it was an eerie lament to the lost beauty and glowing warmth of the Citadel. The ancestral home of the Kosi was gone, like the great Skygrass valley. Darkness filled my soul. I found it hard to breathe.

Once every Kosi body was buried, we opened all the doors, every smoke hole and each hidden exit to the stronghold. We rode back and forth to the Springs of Natrun, returning with many containers of hot water. I scrubbed the stone floor of the fortress on my hands and knees using soap grass. I was determined to leave the bastion empty and clean, in case any Kosi who escaped might return. I left the beautiful furs of the King untouched, adorned with the bright feathers of his eagle. If I stopped working for any reason, the little gazehound came and sat directly at my feet. She looked intensely at me and crooned a high-pitched anxious sound. She was trying to tell me something, but I brushed her away. I was too busy to listen.

Justyn and I began to argue about what we should do next. He wanted to proceed directly to Namché, saying Grandfather could bring Quinn and Crimson to us when he came to the city during the Harvest Moon to sell his wool. He feared if I returned to Talin, I would want to stay there permanently. My own intent grew slowly during those days. I did not want to return to Namché. I did not intend to return to Talin either, but I missed my children desperately. Before I could do anything else, I needed to see them again.

"We must return to Talin. The little ones wait for both of us," I told him. At last, Justyn agreed. He hoped we could marry there, but I had made another plan. I would go north from Talin to the Lost Lake valley. Since I had been at the Citadel, I found myself believing my King still lived. There had to be a reason he hadn't returned. It was my duty and destiny to find him.

# Chapter 10
## The Last Kosi

Late in the day, desperate to wash the dust from my body, I sought a nearby hot spring. I took the little gazehound with me. As we walked, I noticed whenever I glanced down, her intense eyes locked on mine. When I found a small warmed pool, I stripped off my clothes and dove in. After I finished my bath and sat on a sun-warmed boulder combing my hair, the little gazehound closed her teeth on my comb and pulled on my hand. She wanted to take me somewhere. I finally had time to heed her wishes.

We walked through several meadows until I heard the Lakt. It was a huge swarm of the half-bird half-serpent creatures buzzing in excitement. A dark cloud of them circled overhead. The gazehound led me up a high ridge. When I looked down at the fallen rocks below, I saw hundreds of Lakt feeding on more dark bodies. I felt faint with the terrible smell, but the gazehound kept urging me on. Then I heard a scream of rage. Below us I saw a Kosi warrior. He was alive and throwing stones to keep the Lakt from ripping skin off his dark companions.

Stepping carefully down through sand and rocks, I made it to the bottom. The warrior called out to me. I ran to his side and was elated to find my dear friend and guardian, Lord Rohr. Beside him lay the unconscious body of Ghang, my guard when I left Maidenstone. I didn't recognize the other man, but the female was the Kosi woman named Niffa who brought me soup when I first came to the Citadel.

Lord Rohr could hardly speak. His body stank from shed blood and the infection from his wounds. He leaned heavily on me as we walked to a creek nearby where he drank his fill. I refilled my water skin and left it with him. I said I would get help and return. The gazehound, gratified at finally getting her message through to me, trotted at my heels, obedient as the rest of her kind.

When I reached the Citadel, Justyn stood up, holding out his hands.

"Sab-ra, I've been so worried about you. You were gone a long time. The spirits of the Kosi call out for justice. I can hear them. This is no place to linger. We should leave for Talin now."

I was out of breath, but managed to say I had found Ghang and Lord Rohr alive as well as two other Kosi who might yet live. Justyn was clearly disheartened at the thought of additional delays before leaving for Talin, but we mounted our ponies and returned to the stream. Lord Rohr had washed himself in the creek.

"Queen of the Kosi, I salute you," he called out when he saw me.

I felt a shiver, a soft stroke upon my face, as if a feather waved across my forehead. The crown of a regent had descended on me.

Justyn managed to get Ghang on his pony and I lifted Niffa on to sturdy Jemma. Lord Rohr was well enough to walk. We left the last man called Argo with more water, telling him we would come back for him. Justyn made a rapid round trip and brought Argo to the Citadel. When they reached the stronghold, I tended his wounds. Lord Rohr roasted the rest of the chanry. Like the gazehound, all the Kosi were grateful for the hot meat.

Lord Rohr spoke my language well and told us that it had been Hozro, the leader of the Shunned, who had attacked the Citadel. He had waited until all the Kosi returned after the Avalanche struck Skygrass. He killed any Kosi who would not swear allegiance to him. The few who would swear fealty, all women and children, he took with him. They travelled to the camp by the Green River. He and Ghang escaped just before the end of the battle. They had been trying to reach me.

I was enormously grateful to both of them. I didn't need to extract an oath of loyalty from Lord Rohr, First of the Blood Arrows. He had saved me after the Avalanche. Ghang had demonstrated his devotion to me on the trip from Maidenstone to Talin. Both these men were steadfast to the bone. Niffa immediately swore to be my servant.

I was leery of the last man, Argo. Lord Rohr told me he was the tribe's assassin. His eyes were proud and he had a haughty look. He appraised me disdainfully, narrowing his light gray eyes. I took out my knife and with Justyn's help we forced him to kneel. We probably could not have overcome his resistance, but he was weak from his time in the Lakt feeding grounds. I put my knife to his throat telling him even a single prick would give him the Yellow Water fever.

"I am wife to Say'f, King of the Kosi. I am your Queen," I told him fiercely.

"You are not a Queen," he hissed. "Among the Kosi, there can be no Queen without a King."

"You will obey me," I commanded him fiercely. "Say it now or I will have Justyn cut you. You will die the death of a loathsome serpent. You will not be able to piss. At the end you will drown in your own fluids."

He looked at me a long time, but finally bent his head in submission saying, "I will obey," but I caught his murmured words later whispering, "While I live, you will never be Queen of the Kosi."

I glared at him, knowing I would have to watch him carefully.


I slept in the King's alcove on our final night. The Citadel smelled warm and clean by then. Justyn walked me down the long hall. When I said I would sleep alone, he blinked back tears.

"What is it, Justyn?" I asked. My voice was low in pity. My heart clenched for what I had done to this loyal friend.

"Sab-ra, I sense you have come to a decision. You have chosen a life I can't be part of, haven't you? You have decided to reign as Queen of the Kosi. I don't understand what could make you give up a life of love and comfort in Namché with your children and me, for these few remaining warriors." Justyn's eyes were dark with pain and I felt my heart clench. How I hated hurting him.

"It is because there are so few Kosi that they need me, Justyn," I pleaded, wanting him to understand. The small number of Kosi still alive had hit me with a terrible force. The Warrior King said I cost him his Kingdom in the fight to save Skygrass. I owed him the lives of these last few warriors. It was the same fierce intensity I experienced when I realized my own People were going extinct from losing so many women to Kosi kidnappings. The Kosi now faced the same fate.

"Sab-ra, you are no warrior," Justyn shook his head. "If you try to lure the rest of the Kosi from the leader of the Shunned, he will take you as his slave queen or kill you."

I remained stubbornly silent, but the Goddess of Fear crept into my heart.

"Sab-ra, if you cannot speak the truth to me, at least don't lie to yourself. You are risking your life and probably the lives of your children as well in this quixotic task. What you want could be the death of them. If you lost Quinn, it would be like Hodi all over again. I cannot imagine your pain if you lost Crimson."

Fear slid down inside me, cold and wet. Justyn was right. Both children needed protection, but I knew what I owed the King of the Kosi, even if he rode his stallion in the clouds. For me, there was no turning back. I was in the grip of the Goddess. I hated saying farewell to Justyn, but I had become one with my adopted Kosi. Despite Argo's disdainful assertion that I was not the Kosi Queen, I felt the dark mantle of a regent descend around my shoulders.

Looking at my face, Justyn grimaced. "There is no need for me to return with you to Talin now. Lord Rohr will take you." Pain crossed his features. "Do you plan to try to look for the Kosi King's body?" he asked, struggling for control.

"Yes, I do. Justyn, when you heard Say'f was dead, what made you believe it?"

"One of the Bearers found his boot," he said. "Say'f had carved twelve arrows tipped with red stones, into the leather. A large predator had chewed on it, but there was no doubt. It was his. It was found on a ledge high in the Blue Mountains."

I felt cold despair and my jaw clenched. When a man in the high range begins to shed his clothing, there is no hope. The People do not know the reason, but when a person begins to die in the heights, the thin air tells them to remove all their garments. The Wind Goddess takes them naked into the skies. Finding his boot was a terrible sign. Say'f would never remove his boots unless he walked the dying road.

"The life of a warrior is uncertain," Justyn called back to me as he walked down the central hall of the Kosi Citadel. I looked at his slender body and felt his pain. "Your children may still need a father. When you find the Kosi King's body, remember I will be waiting for all of you in Namché."

"I'm sorry, Justyn," I called out to him, but he didn't turn around and left early the next morning without speaking to me again. I shivered, wondering if the path I had chosen would mean my death, or that of my children.

# Chapter 11
## Returning to Talin

After Justyn left, I walked the length of the Citadel, calling Ghang and Argo. I stood tall before them. "I command you both to go the Green River Camp and find Hozro. I want him captured and brought alive to Talin."

Hozro had killed nearly thirty Kosi when he raided the Citadel. I would make him stand trial for his crimes. The Elder Council in Talin would determine his guilt. Although the People had walked the path of peace for a thousand years, after the War, the Guildmasters passed a law permitting a death penalty in the case of mass killings. At Hozro's trial I would argue for his beheading. I would see the demon slain. I wondered as these thoughts crossed my mind and where the gentle girl I had been once had gone.

"Don't kill you dare kill Hozro, Argo," I told him sternly. "I want to see his face when the Guildmasters sentence him to death." Argo nodded, but his sly eyes still mocked me. "Do as I say," I commanded him. "Do not fail me."

Turning to Ghang, I said, "Lord Rohr and I are going north to Talin and from there on to Halfhigh, the mid-point between Talin and the entrance to the Lost Lake. Once you have taken Hozro captive, bring him and any Kosi warriors who would swear allegiance to King Say'f to Halfhigh. If any refuse, say I banish them and their descendants forever from the Twelve Valley's country." I was the Queen Incarnate then, and she wore a dark crown.

I said a silent good-bye to the Citadel, remembering its glowing presence when I first arrived from Maidenstone, trying to banish the memories of the slaughter. The Shunned had left no horses behind. We had only little Jemma, the roan pony I bought from the Bearers in Rhan Du and Lord Rohr was far too heavy for her. He and Niffa, the Kosi woman, walked beside me as I rode. I named the little gazehound, Dusk. She ran beside us for hours, never winded. Watching her, I missed Cloudheart terribly.

Three days later the sounds of screams and whip-cracks rose from the great grass plains. Lord Rohr scouted ahead while Niffa and I hid in the deep grass. When he returned his face was dark with rage.

"It is some of Hozro's Shunned Warriors. They are Kosi by blood, but have no honor. They are driving a stolen group of women and children ahead of them," Lord Rohr said.

"Women and children? Is that the sound of their cries we heard?"

He nodded.

"How many were there?" I asked him, trying to still my horror.

"About a dozen women and a few children. The man are On horseback, but the women are walking, carrying the young children."

"Which way are they going?"

"They are headed in the direction of the Green River."

My heart filled up with despair, like a cup of hemlock. I knew that camp. It was the place where the Kosi Wolf took the life of my spy partner, Hodi. I still felt a stabbing pain in my heart remembering the night Hodi made the dire wolf's cry to lure the Kosi's eyes away from me. In that moment, Hodi saved my life but lost his own. I shuddered at the fate of anyone who defied the white-eyed Kosi Wolf.

Lord Rohr, Niffa and I came upon a small spring late that evening. Its waters were cold and pure. We set up camp near the bubbling artesian well. When the ringed moon rose, I stopped to fill my scry bowl and walked to the nearest hill. I tipped the bowl to catch the moonlight and watched while the waters pleated, folding over repeatedly. Nausea gripped me, but I held on. The bowl itself grew hot. It almost burned my hands, but I would not let go. At last, the waters cleared and I saw the face of a woman with long red hair. I thought at first I had seen myself, but when I looked more carefully, I knew it was my sister. My twin rode in front of a large Kosi Warrior on a dark horse. The man had a red feather in his hair. Time swept around in a great circle and I keened, shrieking my rage to the heavens. The Shunned had killed Hodi and now they had captured my sister.

Then the waters rolled again and I saw the Lost Lake valley. In that place of transcendent beauty, I saw a Kosi Warrior. He climbed the massif toward a beautiful Angelion who lay bleeding among broken stones. I closed my eyes, shaking. Did the image mean Say'f lived? Would I find him only to discover an Angelion lying dead in splintered rocks?

Two days later, we spotted a herd of wild horses. A stallion stood in front of his group of mares on the top of a hill. Seeing him, Lord Rohr quivered like a gazehound on point. He whistled through two fingers and the stallion lifted his head abruptly. The stallion saw us and charged. I backed my mount, Jemma, away and gestured to Niffa to stand back. The stallion came on like a screaming hurricane. When he reached Lord Rohr he reared, his front feet striking the air. Lord Rohr gave an enormous cry and darted underneath the upraised stallion. He grabbed him around the chest and they stood together for a moment. Then the horse slowly lowered his body and Lord Rohr slipped from under him. The stallion's bridle was gone, but he knew his master and Lord Rohr mounted him with ease. He offered a hand to Niffa and swung her up behind him.

We reached the rising road to Talin at dusk. Although we were allies now, I knew the People might fear the Kosi who rode with me. I asked Lord Rohr and Niffa to wait at the bottom of the trail for my signal. Riding Jemma, I galloped at top speed to the village. She reared in the air suddenly, as a small white furry ball hurtled toward me. Total joy flooded my body. Cloudheart had somehow come to Talin. He pelted toward me like an arrow from the bow, flung himself into my arms, and I staggered backward with the force of his love. I held him in my arms, laughing down at his shining eyes, our hearts beating in the same rhythm.

A slim young girl emerged from the stable. Seeing me, she dropped the reins of the pony she was leading and dashed toward us.

"Deti?" I asked, astonished as she came to a dusty stop before me. "How did you come here?"

"With Ten Singh," she blurted out. "Sab-ra, something terrible has happened. Your twin sister, Ruby, came to Maidenstone to find you. We were on our way here, but a Kosi Scout kidnapped her."

"I saw her with the Shunned in the Scry." My voice was choked with pain. We walked to the stable. I refused to set Cloudheart down. I kept hugging him and looking into his happy eyes. I felt enormous relief he was alive. It clashed against my despair about my sister's fate and my ever-present despair about Say'f.

"Let's go to the house and you can tell me everything, Deti."

Grandmother opened the door and reached to hug me. "I am so relieved you are back, Sab-ra."

After hearing all Deti could recall, I told my grandparents that only four people were alive when Justyn and I reached the Kosi stronghold.

"Your husband was not at the Citadel then?" Grandmother asked.

"No. Neither the living King nor his body were there," I said and tears came into my eyes. Grandmother reached out to touch me gently on the shoulder.

"Where is Justyn?"

"He returned to Namché when I told him again that I would not marry him." My chest got tight and pain stabbed me behind my eyes.

"Should you not have waited until you knew the King's fate?" Grandmother asked softly. "Justyn loves you so much, Sab-ra." Her eyes were sad.

"I know, but when I learned Hozro had killed most of the Kosi, the Goddess called me. I must make one more attempt to reach the Lost Lake. If Say'f survived the winter, I believe he will be there. Seeking Say'f would mean travelling north, but my sister is at the Green River camp, due east of here. I don't know which way I should go."

"Ten-Singh already left to rescue your sister," Grandmother said. "I think you should wait until you know the outcome of his efforts."

"Perhaps you are right, Grandmother. Ghang and Argo are also going to the camp of the Shunned. I'm confident the three of them will bring my sister to Talin."

Turning toward Grandfather I said, "Please go to the edge of the plateau and welcome the Kosi woman who rode here with me. She is called Niffa. Lord Rohr is also waiting at the base of the mesa. You remember Lord Rohr, I'm sure, Grandfather. He brought me safely to the valley of the King after the Avalanche. Both these Kosi are trustworthy. They have a gazehound with them and Rohr's warhorse."

"While your grandfather sees to the Kosi, let's go and see your babies," Grandmother smiled and the spirit of the Goddess of the Great Dhali Ra descended upon me, bringing joy.

# Chapter 12
## Going to Halfhigh

A week went by before I told the Elders that I planned to go to the Lost Lake valley with Lord Rohr. They unanimously opposed the idea. They said Say'f was dead and thought if I stayed in Talin, I could protect them from marauding Kosi. I reminded them gently that I didn't need their permission any longer. I was an Elder myself and sought only the blessing of the Wind Goddess. Lord Rohr, first of the Kosi Blood Arrows, would be more than enough protection from the evil deeds of men. It had been a difficult decision. I longed to remain in Talin with the babies. I ached to know my sister's fate, but the image of the Lost Lake from the scry bowl pulled me north. The vision had given me hope that Say'f still lived. I would ride north in search of my King.

Although I missed them terribly while Justyn and I were at the Citadel, I couldn't take my babies with me. Quinn had already progressed from taking steps while holding my hand to running. Grandmother didn't think he ever walked. Crimson was chattering continuously, most of which I couldn't understand, but she was so serious and intent I knew it was important.

When I brought the little gazehound, Dusk, to see my children, they were captivated. Quinn ran to the pup and Crimson began to cry. She couldn't walk yet and was jealous of Quinn's skill. Quinn wept whenever he heard her cry. He stood on his toes to pull on the gazehound's ears. The dog followed Quinn and lay down at Crimson's feet. She used her chubby little hands to wipe away her tears. She whispered her intense serious words to Dusk. He lifted his almond shaped eyes to hers. The gazehound was a good listener.

Quinn was empathic, I realized. His body looked exactly like his father's, but his mind belonged to me. I remembered him calling to the eagles with their flaming eyes and wondered if he could hear the thoughts of humans. *This will be the last trip*, I promised myself. With or without my husband, I would rule in the Citadel until Quinn became King and Crimson found her destiny.

If there was any disobedient prideful child left in me, the birth of the twins erased her. I cared only that the twins would grow up alive and well, so when it was time, Quinn could assume his Kingship. If they lived to reach adulthood, I would be satisfied I told myself, but I lied. Goddess forgive me, I lied. Having the twins reach adulthood was not enough. I wanted the man who made them. All my hopes for the Kosi, who were now my People, and for peace between our cultures would turn to dust without him.

Lord Rohr and I left Talin a few days later for Halfhigh. Halfhigh stands atop a large butte and is a semi-permanent camp on the way to the Skygrass Valley. Until the evil Captain Grieg dragged me into the tunnel that connected Skygrass with the Lost Lake, the People hadn't known of its existence. When the Avalanche descended, it severed the connection between the two valleys and closed the blue diamond mine forever. I kept alive a faint hope that Say'f was alive there, cut off from escape.

I had sent a message to En Sun asking him to meet us at Halfhigh and to bring a guide to take us into the Lost Lake valley. A wall of rocks blocked the original entrance, but I hoped En Sun would know a different route. When we stopped for the night, Lord Rohr vanished into the trees. He was hunting. He would return triumphant and I would be grateful. It was still cold in the high range and hot food would raise my spirits. After roasting the chanry on a split over the campfire, Lord Rohr spoke.

"Have you seen the King in the Scry, Queen of the Kosi?"

"Only brief scenes of him fighting in the blue snows, but whether he lives or rides the skies, I must know."

He nodded, grunting in agreement. "Wife of the King, I will find him without you. Return to Talin. The King's children need a mother."

"This is an old argument between us, my friend. I will not go back. We must find him together."

"You should not call me friend. A Warrior may not have female friends," he said, frowning. "I have told you this before. A Warrior is bound to his fellow Blood Arrows, owes fealty to his King and loves only his wife and children. He may not have a woman who is not his wife too near him, or he will be tempted to take her for himself."

"Lord Rohr," I cried out delighted, "Do you desire me for yourself?"

"Any man but a Blood-Arrow, sworn to the King, would have taken you long ago," he told me gruffly.

"Even if the King lies dead, I will never marry Justyn," I told him, suddenly aware that my ambivalence had vanished. "I know my destiny now. I will raise the twins. I will rule the Kosi."

"If the King lies dead, by our tradition the Queen of the Kosi must name a new King from among the Blood Arrows. A Queen may not rule Warriors alone. If that day comes, I will stand and offer myself to you."

"In the time coming to be, if I must name a new King, I would be honored to choose you, Lord Rohr."

His gaze rested passionately upon me. I felt its warmth like the sun, but when I reached out to touch his hand, he pulled it away, as if my touch seared.

"Do not touch me, my Queen," Lord Rohr said, "Lest I be tempted beyond my ability to resist."

When we reached Halfhigh, I first checked the Aid Station we used during the war as a clinic. It was still standing, as were the two buildings. One was used as a stable and had a haymow. The second was reserved for any travelers needing shelter. After we ate, I made myself a bed of the soft plants called bedstraw. I carried the plants into the Aid Station, lay down and drifted off to sleep, fragrant hay for my pillow.

The next morning, I heard the jingling of horse harnesses and looking over the rim saw En Sun riding up the butte with a male companion.

"En Sun," I cried when they reached the top. "I am happy to see you."

He smiled and told me his friend's name was Kilby.

"I greet you, Kilby," I said. "What tribe do you come from?" He was a short, squat man with a proud carriage. His eyes were sly and furtive. Something about him reminded me of Argo, the Kosi assassin who swore I would never rule his tribe.

"He is from the Hakan, Mistress," En Sun told me. "He doesn't understand your language.

"Ask him if the Hakan have a new Queen."

The men exchanged a few words.

"Yes, they do. Her name is Verde."

I felt satisfaction, remembering the night I sought the future in the scry bowl for Queen Verde and saw her wearing the crown of the Hakan queen. I had banished her from the King's Valley that night, telling her to go to the Hakan.

"Tomorrow we must find a way into the Lost Lake," I told the men.

"It will not be easy," En Sun warned. "Many have died seeking that paradise."

"It is not my time to die," I told him confidently.

"Nor is it mine," Rohr said and we smiled at each other.

En Sun and Kilby talked for a while. Then En Sun turned to me. "An enormous fall of rocks blocks the old route to the Lost Lake. Kilby knows another way into the hidden vale."

The Hakan would tell us nothing more. He turned away when I pressed En Sun for details. I regarded Kilby with caution. The Hakan had long been enemies of all who lived in the high country.

"Why won't Kilby tell us where we are going?" I asked, bothered by the man's silence.

"He says the White Snake will kill him if he does."

"What is this White Snake he fears? Is it a true snake?"

"He says it is a man, but immortal. Humans cannot kill him. He saw marks on his body, marks of stones, snakebites, cuts from a knife. Yet still he lives."

"What does this man look like?" I asked, panic filling my mind.

"He is tall with yellow hair."

"Lord Rohr, the Hakan is describing Captain Grieg." I could hardly speak the words. The Army Garrison Commander was my mortal enemy, the man who sought my death in the depths of the mountain. I felt dread rise inside me. My stomach lurched, wanting to bring up my dinner. I ran from the campfire, retching into the brush. When I had regained some composure and washed the sick taste from my mouth, I returned to the men.

"When we find the Kosi King, he will tear the guts from inside the body of the White Snake," I told them fiercely, but none of the men would meet my eyes.

## Chapter 13
### The Crystal Steppes

Lord Rohr and I left Halfhigh the next morning following En Sun and Kilby. For the first few hours we rode the flat plains below the mesas but by afternoon we entered the middle reaches of the Blue Mountains, a region called the Crystal Steppes. Feeling the small body of Jemma beneath me, I missed Yellowmane terribly. Jemma was a strong plodder but lacked the smooth gait of Yellowmane. In the days when Yellowmane and I were comrades, I rode the winds. Now she paced the clouds without me. My heart was low with grief as Kilby led us up and down on tiny mountain paths. Most were only as wide as my arm. The enormous massif of the Dhali Ra, the mountain home of the Great Goddess, rose like a giant thunderhead beyond the Crystal Steppe.

Despite all my efforts to dig information out of Kilby, he continued silent as a captured prisoner. I hated not knowing where we were headed, trusting a man I didn't know. I sensed that he might be a traitor, leading me straight to Captain Grieg.

"Lord Rohr," I whispered at one point when we were able to ride side by side, "Do you trust this man?"

Lord Rohr looked at me. "No," he said, with a thoughtful glance, but still we followed the Hakan.

In late afternoon, we entered a narrow valley leading deep into the Blue Mountains. The area was heavily wooded, crowded with sentinel pines and the yellow trunks of syce trees. Their scent lay across us, practically visible in its intensity. I felt uneasy in this deep forest. It awoke memories of my capture by Captain Grieg and my imprisonment in the mountain. En Sun and Kilby talked together in whispers. I kept my eyes on

Lord Rohr. He was as irritated as I was fearful. Both of us felt Kilby was leading us into a bad situation.

"Where are we, En Sun?" I asked.

"This is near where the Hakan found the Kosi King's boot," he responded. I felt my spirits sink lower.

"Show me," I commanded.

The Hakan led me over to an area at the end of a box canyon, directly below a ledge high on the mountain's face.

"He says he found the boot on that outcropping," En Sun said, pointing up to the ledge.

"Did he leave it there?" I asked En Sun. He said something and Kilby nodded.

I turned back to the Blood Arrow. "Lord Rohr, can you climb up to that ledge and see if the King's boot is still there?"

Lord Rohr surveyed the terrain and pulled a rope from his saddle packs. He tied a loop at the end of the rope and threw it upwards. It landed near a yellow syce tree that grew nearly straight out of the rock. He threw the rope again and again until it caught. Using his phenomenal strength and pulling against the rope, he climbed upward through the trees. When he reached the ledge, I saw him peer into a large dark hole.

"What do you see?" I called up to him.

"The lair of a cave leopard," he called down. He entered the cave and after a few tense moments, during which I worried that En sun and Kilby might take the opportunity to run off or take me prisoner, Lord Rohr came out again. He held something in his hands.

He descended slowly—hand over hand. My breath caught as I watched. Although Lord Rohr would not name himself as my friend, I cared deeply about him. If he fell and hit his head, I feared I could do nothing to help. At last, he reached my side and pulled the King's boot from under his chest strap. I remembered the boot. It had belonged to Say'f and seemed further proof that he was dead. Tears pricked my eyes.

It was wrong that Captain Grieg still lived. I had willed a snake to bite him, I had stabbed him with my poisoned knife, and I had pelted him with rocks. *Goddess of the Winds, how had I failed?* A superstitious fear made my heart shudder. I worried that Kilby was right when he called Grieg immortal. Perhaps no living person could kill the fiend. Lord Rohr took my arm and led me to an area where we could not be overheard.

"If the White Snake once lived in that cave, he has not occupied it for a long time," his voice was low, "I saw no campfire or supplies. If he is still alive, he has probably gone deeper into the mountain." Lord Rohr looked apprehensive saying this. He feared the dark tunnels that riddled the Dhali Ra, as did I.

"What do you think we should do?" I asked.

"I think the Hakan will desert us soon," Lord Rohr said philosophically. "En Sun may leave too. He has the look of fear on his face. I would go deeper into the mountain, but I didn't want to leave you alone with them for very long. I sense treachery."

A rising tide of blood lust rose in me, fierce as the burning frenzy I felt seeing all the dead Kosi at the Citadel. Like Hozro, Grieg's deeds demanded his life in payment. I glimpsed Brother Jun's gentle face in my mind, but pushed away his counsel. Captain Grieg's life was mine to end.

"If the King lives no longer, I demand the blood right to avenge him. If we come upon Captain Grieg in the tunnels, you must stay your hand, Lord Rohr. Hold back, I beg you and permit me to deliver the final blow."

We were silent for a moment, considering our next steps.

"I would ride the rope with you Lord Rohr," I said. He started to protest, but seeing the look on my face, he nodded.

We walked together to the trailing rope. Lord Rohr tied it around his waist and began to climb with me on his back. His tremendous strength was tested to the limit but we rose, hand over hand to a narrow ledge. We stopped then, although the ledge we stood on was only as wide as my foot. While Lord Rohr's breathing returned to normal and he threw the rope again upwards to the ledge outside the cave leopard's lair, I said I would climb the last part by myself.

He didn't respond, looking down a hundred thent to the men at the bottom.

"They ride," he said and I saw En sun and Kilby on their ponies, pulling Jemma behind them. They fled the canyon as if the dogs of hell pursued them. As Lord Rohr screamed all the things he would do to them if they took our supplies, I grabbed the rope and began to walk straight up the mountain.

"No," Lord Rohr yelled, but I was already above his reach.

It was far more difficult than it looked. My shoulder began to hurt. It had never completely healed since Grieg dislocated it when he held me prisoner. My breath came faster and my heart thudded in my ears. Twenty feet below the upper ledge, I felt my shoulder give way and I screamed as I dove down. With tremendous force, Lord Rohr grabbed me from the skies and hauled me back onto the tiny landing.

"You will stay here," he said fiercely, breathing hard, "Or I will beat you—Queen of the Kosi or not. You shame yourself." He climbed upward to the ledge, looking down from time to time to see me sitting meekly beside the syce tree. Then he vanished into the darkness.

Once Lord Rohr entered the tunnel, I looked about to see if there was any other way to reach the upper ledge. Finally, I spotted a possible approach through the sentinel pines. I crawled hanging on to trees that grew straight out of the mountain. It was difficult and I poured all my concentration into not falling. Lord Rohr had entered the cave. When I finally pulled myself on to the ledge, the pain from my arm was intense. My foot was hurting too, and I sat down and pulled off my suede boot. There was a hole in the leather. A stone had worked its way inside. I leaned back against the warm rock, resting my sore shoulder. I looked up at the clouds seeing the pink of late afternoon gild their undersides. I closed my eyes and drifted into the world of sleep.

In my dream, I mended my leather slippers with a silver needle. The world grew dark and an enormous weight pinned me to the mountain. I heard the voice of my nightmares.

"You returned to me," Grieg said and laughed aloud.

I screamed, twisting with all my might, trying to escape. I opened my eyes and saw his eyes bore into mine. With all my strength, I forced my dream needle into his eye. He screamed and vanished. I opened my eyes and saw Lord Rohr's amused face above me.

"It was a dream, my Queen," he told me gently, "I only wished to wake you. You tried to kill a dream."

"No, no it was Grieg. I forced a needle into his eye," my voice trailed off.

"There is no one here except the two of us," Lord Rohr told me. "It was your knife that stabbed the air, although I had to dodge a little to keep you from injuring me. Of course, it would take more than a small white woman's knife to kill a Kosi Warrior." He was clearly enjoying my embarrassment.

I kept shaking for a long time. My chest felt so tight I could hardly breathe. At last, I was able to ask, "What else did you find in the cave?"

"The cave ends in a wall. There is no way in, save from the front. It is the lair of a man-killing leopard, the stalking kind. It was the leopard that brought the King's boot there—a totem of his kill."

I took a deep quivering breath. My voice when it came from my throat was resonant with grief. "Then I fear the King lives no more," I said, as if pronouncing a blessing on the dead.

"If the King is dead, so is Captain Grieg," Lord Rohr said, trying to comfort me. "The Warrior King would not succumb to his wounds until he first took the life of your enemy."

I nodded.

"It is almost sundown. We must descend my Queen."

He strapped me to him, breast to breast, heartbeat to heartbeat.

"Put your arms around my neck," he told me, "And wrap your legs around my waist."

"If we fall, we will both die," I warned him.

"Then we will both ride with the King," he said, smiling.

It was a brutal, terrifying trip. We bumped and lurched down the cliff-face, but arrived finally at the bottom, bruised and cut from rocks, but alive.

Wrapped so tightly against Lord Rohr, I felt his great heart beat with mine. I saw the two of us ruling as King and Queen of the Kosi. His body and his loyalty warmed me. Then guilt stabbed me. It was wrong, thinking of naming Lord Rohr as the Kosi King. Even if Say'f rode the clouds, allowing myself to have such feelings for another man, I had betrayed my husband.

When we stood on level ground, I told him, "We must return to the great rock wall. It is possible that Say'f escaped. Perhaps the leopard took Grieg's life. The King could still live."

"My Queen, you see what you want to see. This is a foolish chanry's errand," Lord Rohr told me softly, his eyes warm.

"He might still be alive," I said fiercely and burned Lord Rohr's eyes with mine. "I must know, Lord Rohr. When we conquer the rock wall that hides the Lost Lake, we will walk into the valley shoulder to shoulder," I told him.

"As you command, Queen of the Kosi," Lord Rohr said, but I saw a tiny twitch of bemusement on his lips.

# Chapter 14

## The Lost Lake

Lord Rohr and I rode the trails of the Crystal Steppe all the next day. We were headed to the enormous rock wall that sealed off the Lost Lake valley after the Avalanche. It was cold and misty. Kilby and En Sun had taken Jemma, so I sat behind the Blood Arrow on his warhorse, Kys, who seemed undeterred by walking along the extremely narrow trails cut into the mountainside. Even dense fog didn't seem to bother him. On my right, the mountain fell a thousand thent straight down into a misty nothingness.

In the afternoon of the second day, the fog lifted and we entered an area of the mountainside covered in trees. We walked through dappled light that fell on us in a tapestry of shadows. Limbs of trees made a delicious shaded canopy over our heads. I asked Rohr to stop so I could dismount. I wanted to walk for a bit and to stretch my legs. Rohr said he would scout the trail ahead. The trail jogged to the right and I lost sight of him.

Hiking around the bend, I heard an animal scream so terrifying for a second I could not move. Then I ran in the direction of the scream. I saw a spotted yellow and black streak propel itself from a large branch and fall on top of Rohr and his horse. The warhorse bucked and yelped in pain. The mountain leopard clung to the horse's side. Rohr kicked at it, desperate to save his mount. The leopard fell to the rocky trail. Rohr jumped from the horse's back and pulled out his knife, slashing at the leopard who roared again. The enraged leopard struck—a blur in the dying light. Rohr fell to the ground. I ran to him, my small poisoned knife in my hand.

The leopard whirled around and stood up on its back legs. He was twice my size. He had injured my Blood Arrow, and I felt a rage of blood lust. I stuck him deeply again and again in the belly. He fell down on top of me. His weight crushed my lungs. I smelled the stench of death. Then he struggled to his feet and disappeared into the higher range.

"Lord Rohr," I called as I managed to stand. The leopard had clawed me and I was bleeding in several places. "Lord Rohr, can you speak?" He didn't answer. I walked closer to his fallen body. "Lord Rohr," I whispered.

"My Queen," he murmured and closed his eyes again.

"Don't sleep," I told him. I managed to pull him to a sitting position. He lolled forward. His horse had run down the trail, but I called him back. Obedient as the gazehound, I heard him returning. I checked Kys over carefully, seeing several deep puncture wounds in his chest and withers. I tied him to a small tree and pulled Brin from Rohr's saddlebags. I forced Rohr's mouth open and dribbled the Brin down his throat. He struggled, pushing my hand away.

"Wake up," I demanded fiercely.

"Stop," he managed. His eyes cleared and for a moment he was fully conscious. "Give Brin to the horse," he managed. Then his eyes rolled back and he returned to the land of unconsciousness. I sat beside him, resting on the trail, our backs to the warmed mountain. We faced a desperate situation. Spotted mountain leopards prey on Lakt. When they sink their talons into the Lakt, their claws pick up filth and disease. I had nothing with which to clean the deep punctures on the horse or Lord Rohr's body, except a few swallows of Brin. There was no water this high in the range.

"Lord Rohr, can you ride?" I asked, poking him awake.

"No," he told me and fell asleep again.

Both of us were feverish the next morning. Lord Rohr was raving in delirium. His horse stood to the side of the trail, head hanging, breathing hard. I was in the best shape of the three of us and knew I would have to go for help soon. I used the last of the Brin on my puncture wounds, cursing mountain leopards in every language I knew. *I am such a stupid girl*, I thought suddenly. Although the Wind Goddess rarely came to me while I was pregnant, I was not pregnant now.

"Rain," I begged her. "Send rain to the least of your worshippers. Send rain to the Kosi and his horse. Send rain to the mountain country." Late that afternoon, I heard the crackle of lightening. The aptly named Thunder Moon gave us its blessing. Lightening split the clouds that boomed back together. I smiled to myself as I fell asleep. The rain was coming.

Towards morning, I woke to Rohr bending over me in the dark. "The mountain burns," he said. I looked up and saw a finger of fire racing down the mountain. A high wind whipped the fire into frenzy. The deep roaring sound of the fire terrified me.

"We have to leave," I said. It was horridly difficult for Rohr to mount his horse, but we finally managed, leaving everything behind. The horse ran straight down the mountain, away from the searing, burning, throat-closing heat. When we stopped to rest, the rain began in earnest. I caught as much water as I could in my leather canteen, found soap grasses and washed Rohr's wounds. I poured more into my punctured sores and used the rest on the horse. I touched Rohr's chest to see how far the infection had spread. My heart fell when I saw red streaks running from the punctures toward his heart. He had blood poisoning.

"Your skin is warm, Lord Rohr," I told him. "The infection is spreading."

"Today is not my day to die," he said gruffly and despite our desperate situation, I found myself warmed by Rohr's unstinting confidence.

"Nor is it mine," I said unhesitatingly.

Our interchange raised my spirits, but we were far from any settlement and had a long way to go for help.


When I woke the following morning, I felt better, although my sores were stiff. Rohr was sleeping. I checked on his horse who seemed better. I had kept about half the water from the rainstorm the previous night, and I gave Kys a drink. Then I led him down the mountain, looking for a meadow where he might graze. I found one about an hour later, spread like an embroidered carpet between rising pale gray peaks. One small tree stood on the edge of the meadow. I tied the horse there and returned to Rohr.

"Lord Rohr, you need to wake." I pulled him to sitting position. He shook his head and bared his teeth at me, growling. I poured water into his mouth. He shook his head and sputtered. His eyes cleared and he knew me.

"Your horse is better and I took him to an area where he could graze. We need to leave here so I can get help for you," I touched his forehead. His eyes were already closing. "Stay awake," I ordered him fiercely. "You are my Guardian and I need your counsel."

He murmured some blurry words, nothing I could understand. I looked around to see where we were in relation to the sun and the mountain. It had been dark the night before when we stopped our headlong flight down the mountain. Looking up into the fastness, I saw a huge swath of blackened trees. Tendrils of smoke rose from it still, curling. We were only about a day's ride from the settlement at Rhan Du but before I could go for help, I had to make sure the fire was completely out.

I climbed back up the mountain. Only one or two limbs stuck out from the sides of blackened trunks. They seemed to hold out their fire-blistered arms for rain. When I reached the devastated area, some embers were still smoldering. One little burning coal rolled out of the ashes and hit some dead leaves. They caught fire lazily. Rohr lay a hundred thent directly below me. I couldn't leave him in the path of the near-dead fire, but he was twice as heavy as I was. We were out of food and water. I was a poor shot with a bow and already felt the rumble of hunger. Fear rode my mind, whipping it into a blaze brighter than the forest fire.

Descending, I tried again to wake Rohr. He had slipped into a fever coma. I went down to the field where the horse was grazing. It was a beautiful day, with high blue skies and a light warm breeze. The meadow itself was a floor of flowers, some pink, some purple. I took the horse's tether and led him back up to Lord Rohr. I was going to try to get the Kosi on his horse.

After struggling with Rohr's limp heavy body for several hours, I wept with despair and frustration. I could not lift him. He was far too heavy. I was going to have to ride to Rhan Du by myself. I managed to roll Lord Rohr under a rocky shelf beside a sheltering tree. I left the rest of the water in his water skin. I pulled his bow from the leather strap across his back, removed the arrow points from his belt and mounted them on the shafts. I pulled his knife from his pants pocket and laid it carefully in his right hand. I would not leave my Guardian unarmed.

"Lord Rohr," I told his recumbent form. "I am riding to Rhan Du. I will be back as soon as I can." He did not respond. His skin was darker than ever and he lay so still. I was deeply afraid. I knelt beside him, leaned forward and kissed him gently on the lips. His eyes opened just a crack. "Do you know who I am?" I asked him, low and quiet.

"I could never forget you, my Queen," he whispered and said no more.

"Farewell dear Guardian and friend," I called as I mounted Kys. The stallion was huge, much bigger than anything I had ever ridden. I hoped I would be able to control him.

"Run," I told the horse and although I'm sure he thought my accent funny, he bolted forward. We raced down the mountain, far too fast for the little trail. I leaned forward on his enormous neck and whispered encouragement to him. "We must save Lord Rohr. Run to Rhan Du!"

## Chapter 15
## At Rhan Du

I thundered into Rhan Du in late afternoon, leapt from my saddle and ran toward En Sun's house. I thundered my fists on his door. When he came cautiously to the door and opened it, fury ran down my arms. He turned pale. He was clearly appalled to see me.

"You are a liar and a cheat," I told him furiously. "You promised to take me to the Lost Lake, but you and the traitorous Hakan waited until you could steal all our supplies. You ran from the box canyon. You are a yellow coward."

En Sun backed away as my rage flamed over him. "I am sorry, Mistress," he said. "The Hakan made me leave you. He said the White Snake was coming. He threatened to kill my wife and unborn child if I would not go with him. When we reached the lower mountain, he left and I rode home. My wife was near to her time. She delivered the baby the day I returned. I wanted to come back for you, but dared not leave her."

"Your betrayal may have caused Lord Rohr's death," I told him, coldly. "We were attacked by the spotted leopard on the way down. The Blood Arrow lies on the trail in a fever coma. You and two more men will come with me to bring him down the mountain." When he hesitated, wavering, I screamed at him, "Now you idiot, now!"

While they assembled their gear for the ride, I searched the area for plants with medicinal properties. No feverfew grows in the high range. Nor do poppies grow there. Luckily, En Sun's wife had poppy pearls and dried feverfew. She gave me what she could spare. I found osier wands growing by the creek and took several dozen. I smashed them with a rock until they opened and I cut their marrow out. Osier takes fever away.

We rode from Rhan Du at a furious pace as the sun set. Lord Rohr's horse easily outpaced the Bearers' small ponies, anxious to return to his master. We rode most of the night as the moon rose. We reached Rohr's resting place as the sun came up. I dismounted, feeling a horrid trepidation. My heart pounded so loud I felt it in my temples. The First of the Blood Arrows lay where I had left him. I fell to my knees. Beside him was the dead body of a huge spotted leopard. Rohr's knife was imbedded in the beast's chest. Desperate to find a pulse, I checked Rohr's throat, wrists and ankles, but the Guardian of my body, the Defender of my King rode the sky worlds.

I led Kys over to see his master's body. He sniffed him tentatively, shying away from the leopard's reek. I knew he was afraid. Dying Kosi Warriors kill their stallions so they would have their mounts with them to ride the clouds, but I could not take this beautiful animal's life.

"Lord Rohr lies dead," I told En Sun and the Bearers, coldly. "Place his body gently on the travois. We are taking him down the mountain until we find a cave large enough to contain his great spirit."

"Please Mistress," En Sun pleaded. "Lord Rohr is huge. We won't be able to lift him. We will cover his body with rocks and leave him here."

"It was because of your treachery that he died," I told him viciously. "Even in his death throes, the valiant Blood Arrow took the life of a mountain leopard larger than himself. His courage shames you all. How dare you plead and whine that he is too large a man for you three weaklings to lift." I clenched my jaw together to control my fury. I wanted to sink my teeth into the cowards.

It took all three of them, but they finally managed to get Rohr's body on the travois. While they struggled and cursed, I sat down on the trail beside the leopard's dead body. I sought some appropriate way to honor the memory of Lord Rohr. Taking out my knife, I began cutting off the leopard's head. It took a long time. When I held the great head in my hands, I put it in the horse's pack. The stallion shied away, fearful of the smell. I stripped the leopard's organs from his spotted pelt, threw them into the brush and rolled his skin into a cylinder. Kys reared and protested at the scent but I forced him to stillness while I tied it to the back of his saddle.

"Now we will descend," I told them, my voice chilled with the contempt I felt for their spinelessness.

None of the Bearers' ponies was strong enough to pull the travois with Lord Rohr's body on it for very long. One after the other the ponies began to wheeze and cough. Finally I acceded to En Sun's request and we made camp. We would rest for a few hours.

Later, we transferred the travois harness to Kys. He had difficulty standing still for the harnessing, but ultimately it was accomplished. As we descended the mountain, I sang the song for the Death of a Blood Arrow, blessing Kim-li for teaching me so many Kosi songs before I left Natil. Finally we reached a tiny mountain valley lying right up next to the high peaks where I saw a cave opening.

"We have reached the Crystal Cave," En Sun told me.

"You will bring Lord Rohr's body here," I ordered them, "And we will seal the opening with rocks. No leopard will ever mutilate his body." They grumbled, but did it. Once they almost let him fall and I pulled my knife. I had to scream at them before they would try again. By the time the light left, Lord Rohr's body was lying peacefully on the white sands inside Crystal Cave.

"You," I ordered pointing my finger at each of them in turn, "You find food. You start a campfire. You find water." They fled from my wrath.

I walked into the cave carrying the head of the leopard. I placed its head on my Guardian's chest. The screaming leopard in full roar faced my

Blood Arrow whose face was contorted in a grimace. I was in the grip of a dark passion, as if I walked in waist-deep water. Trembling, I took my knife and made a long slice in my arm. Then I took one of Rohr's arrows and dipped the feathers in my blood until every pinion was scarlet. I pushed the point of the arrow deep into one of Rohr's wounds and then forced myself to stick the point deep into my palm, screaming in pain. I closed Rohr's cold fingers over the arrow that dripped red with my blood and his.

"From this moment, I take your place as First Blood Arrow for the King," I said. The finality of his death hit me and I began to shudder. I wailed my sorrow across the mountain valley in a harsh ululation. When my sobs slowly quieted, I knelt and kissed his forehead. "I have buried you with honor, Lord Rohr. We are one blood now. I would have named you King of the Kosi, lain with you and conceived strong sons for you, had I not believed the true King still lives. I will always grieve for you. Even in death, you were the Heart of the Leopard."

No one spoke to me when I came to the flame. They handed me food and water but averted their eyes from my despair.

The next morning I told the morose Bearers they had to find enough rocks to brick up the entrance to the cave. One had already deserted. I could tell En Sun and the last Bearer felt unequal to the task and sliced their faces with my eyes.

"We are already very tired, Mistress," En Sun told me.

"En Sun of the Bearer People, unless you close the door of the Blood Arrow's Crystal Cave, I will have the Kosi Assassin cut off your feet when he returns."

Without feet, no Bearer could make a living carrying messages throughout the mountains. En Sun straightened his shoulders, signaled to the other laborer and they began to build a wall of rocks at the cave's entrance. I worked with them.

When the sun set and the world cooled, I pulled the leopard skin from Kys's saddle and wrapped it around my shoulders. In the fading light, I murmured through a crack in the rocks, "I will carry the skin of the leopard to the King of the Kosi. I will tell him of your faultless courage, Lord Rohr. I will tell him of our epic journey across the high range in winter. I will tell him how you brought Wirri-Won to coax our babies from my womb. I cannot take the life of your stallion, but I will groom and exercise him each day until Quinn is old enough to ride him into battle."

After a night in Rhan Du, I called for all the male Bearers in the village to come to En Sun's house to hear my plea for laborers. Even the death of my Guardian, Lord Rohr, had not dissuaded me from trying to enter the Lost Lake valley. I stood on En Sun's raised porch looking toward the little straggle of houses clinging to life on the flanks of the Great Dhali Ra. Eight men assembled grudgingly below me.

"Do you all know the great fall of rocks that separates your village from the lands inside the mountain?"

There were murmurs of assent and several nods.

"I want the wall removed." The men turned to each other and I saw them shaking their heads. "I see eight strong men here, but I also see your women and children. They are thin and weak. The village needs money to buy food. Winter is coming."

The men looked at each other uneasily. One of the women came out of the house with two little children.

"If you will remove the rocks that block the passage into the Lost Lake, I will give you three parthats for every day you work." At the word "parthats," I saw the woman's face light up. She took her husband by the sleeve and talked with him earnestly. Several more women came outside, including En Sun's wife who carried their newborn.

"I ask for your help, Bearers of Rhan Du. Who among you is willing to work for silver parthats to save your women and children from the winter wolves of starvation?"

When no one responded, I called "Women of Rhan Du, for the sake of your children, compel your men to work for me. The white men who need guides to take them up the mountain will not return until spring. If your men will not work for me, who will feed the hungry mouths of Rhan Du?"

At his wife's pleading one man walked forward. Slowly, all the rest joined him.

"We begin tomorrow. Bring wagons and carts to haul the stones away from the bottom of the rock fall. Each man who comes must work a full day from sunrise to sunset. Only then will I give him the promised silver."

As the gathering began to break up, I pulled En Sun aside. "What have you heard about the White Snake? Tell me," I ordered. "I must know what we face on the other side of the rock wall."

"A Bearer told a man of my village he saw the White Snake earlier this moon. He stood on the mountain face not far from the blocked entrance to the old blue diamond mine."

I felt the earth sway under my feet and my fears rose into my throat choking my breathing. Captain Grieg was still alive. It took me a few moments to get myself under control.

"Have any of the Bearers reported seeing a Kosi Warrior on the mountain?"

"One man saw a Kosi warrior, but it was last winter and he was on foot in the high range."

# Chapter 16
## The Lost Lake Valley

The next day all the men, ponies and wagons from Rhan Du trekked across the lower grasslands until we came to the rock fall. I felt a dreadful qualm when I saw it. The fall of stones was enormous, almost as big as Maidenstone. The Bearers stood quietly as I gazed upwards. When I looked at them, I saw a look of shock on their faces.

"Make camp," I ordered. I couldn't let the men know how afraid I was that the rock wall would prove too much for us. The men assembled the one black dweli I had given En Sun. Other men set up small leather flap tents. En Sun's wife and several of the other women had sent stew with us in olla pots. We started a fire and put the pots on the flames. The air was soon redolent with the scent of chanry meat and root vegetables.

Around the campfire that night, I asked if any of them had climbed the rock fall. One man, a short Bearer who resembled the Hakan traitor Kilby, said he had.

"What did you find?" I asked him.

"An opening, Queen of the Kosi. It was only as large as a dog, but I looked inside and it went on forever."

"That is a good sign," I told him. "What is your name, Bearer of Rhan Du?"

"My name is Ra Khat," he told me.

"Before we begin to carry away the rocks, you will climb up again, Ra Khat," I told him. "A Hakan traitor told me he had seen the White Snake on the Mountain. Have you seen him also?"

"He came out of the opening one moon ago," he told me. "I was riding my pony below and saw his yellow hair when he emerged."

"Tomorrow, you will see if you can wiggle into the White Snake's lair."

Ra Khat shuddered and looked away. I had to do something to compel his obedience.

"Five extra parthats to enter the Snake's hole," I said, forcing myself to be calm. The fact that Grieg was still alive had shaken me badly, but I could not let them see my fears.

"One hundred," he said softly. A fine tremor shook his hands. "It would take a hundred parthats to tempt me into the Serpent's nest, Mistress," he said. I saw sweat on his forehead.

"Twenty," I said calmly, looking off in the distance.

"Fifty," he said, but I saw the corners of his mouth twitch. He was starting to enjoy the bargaining. The rest of the men began laughing, shoving each other and placing bets on the final price.

"I will crawl into the hole myself, before I give even forty parthats of the People to a cowardly Bearer who is afraid of tiny white snakes," I said, narrowing my eyes. His eyes sparkled, knowing I was teasing him.

"Thirty," he said. "And not a parthat less will I take."

"Twenty-five," I said, grinning at him.

"What is money, when we are all family?" he asked, laughing.

"That is right, little brother, I need pay you nothing. Family obligation should compel you to do my bidding for free."

"No true sister would endanger her brother's life in such a quest," he told me. "Only twenty-five parthats and we are forever blood."

I stood and walked to him, held out my hand and he took it.

"Twenty-five," he said.

"Blood," I agreed.

Smiling, we each pricked the tips of our fingers with knives and pressed them together.

"Now I would see these twenty-five parthats," he said, still amused.

"And I would see your bottom enter the snake's nest before I show them to you," I said and neither of us could stop laughing.

The next morning, he climbed the Crystal Steppe and entered the black hole. It was so small from the ground it looked like the pupil in the eye of the Great Goddess.


Ra Khat had still not returned by the next morning and I feared for his safety. The men emerged from their tents and walked around me. They prepared a simple breakfast and ate silently. I stood and looked at their gloomy faces. En Sun stood beside me. I looked up at the thousand thent of rocks guarding the secrets of the great Goddess.

"This attempt of yours to oppose the will of the Great Dhali Ra is wrong," En Sun said. "I see a frown upon the face of the Goddess."

I felt a wave of fear thinking that the Goddess had cursed this venture. My knees gave way and I collapsed on the ground, breathing hard.

"It will be the darkest day of a hundred year-long winter before all these rocks are moved away," En Sun told the Bearers solemnly. "Those rocks belong where the Goddess placed them. I am going back to Rhan Du. Any of you who wish to ride with me, let us go." They filed silently from our makeshift camp. As they walked past me, I handed each man his silver parthats. As they were mounting up, I called, "I will pay anyone who will stay here with me double the promised parthats. Six per day."

Two men looked slightly interested.

"We will not enter the snake's hole," one of them said warningly.

"Agreed."

Two men dismounted and after talking with each other for a moment or two began loading rocks into the carts. It was like emptying the ocean with a child's water pail.

"Cowards," I yelled after the rest of the retreating Bearers as they rode down the mountain. I went to work carrying rocks to the wagons. My shoulder ached by afternoon and my hands were bleeding from granite cuts. The two last Bearers worked steadily, but the rock fall had defeated us. It stretched from our level almost to the top of the great mountain and was a hundred thent wide at the base.

I walked over to Lord Rohr's horse and led him to a grassy area where I found a small spring, bubbling out of the ground, bright and cold. I knelt and drank with him. I filled my water skin. The sparkling water drew my eyes like metal to a magnet. I gazed at the liquid beauty, envisioning my little ones and their father. How I missed them all.

*Sun on the water*, I thought and instantly I saw my husband's revenant stand before me. Tall and very dark, his eyes looked down into my soul. "I have sought you long, my husband," I told him.

His golden eyes flashed. He held out his arms. I stood to enter his embrace, but the image wavered and was gone. My heart lifted up. Say'f was still alive. Alive! All I had to do was reach him. Leading Lord Rohr's stallion by his reins, I brought a full water skin to the two Bearers who stood wiping their foreheads with rags in the hot sun.

"I have been a foolish Lakt. En Sun was right. This rock fall is the work of the Goddess. It belongs here. I will enter the Lost Lake through the snake's black hole. Will you climb with me?" I asked. "I don't ask you to go inside, only to wait for me."

"And if you do not return, Mistress?"

"If I don't return in three days, then you will ride to Rhan Du and take Ra Khat's share of the parthats to his family. Give him twice what I promised him. Tell En Sun to ride to the village of Talin. He must tell my Grandparents the news of my death and give them the remaining parthats for my children."

I had no thought of success. But something deep inside me drove me to try. Like the day of the final battle, I would make one desperate last stand.


The Bearers and I began the climb early the next morning. It was a bright day and the sunshine raised my spirits. I caught the scent of the Lobelia flower and felt some relief. The Wind Goddess had sent me a blessing. The men climbed behind me, looking apprehensively up toward the black pupil-like hole near the top of the mountain. When we reached the landing, all of us breathing hard, the tallest Bearer handed me his knife.

"For the White Snake who took Ra Khat's life," he said.

I thanked him, handed him my small leather sack filled with silver parthats, adjusted my water skin and feeling for my own small knife with its poisoned tip in my pocket, I bade them good-bye. The opening was slender, not quite as wide as my shoulders. I had to turn sidewise to make my way forward. What little light penetrated the dimness quickly vanished. I groped my way into the mountain, holding my right arm up so I would know if the ceiling lowered. I found my anxiety rising and fought the panic of claustrophobia.

"I will not fear," I told myself. "I am in the arms of the Great Dhali Ra. She will protect me." I began humming a Kosi battle song. Hours went by in the dense stifling darkness, then my foot bumped into something soft. A horror seized my heart. I bent down to feel a softness. It was a body. I shook all over, but forced myself to kneel and search for a pulse. I found an arm and trailing my fingers toward the hand found the wrist at last. Did I feel warmth? Was there a faint pulse? I worked my fingers back up the arm, across the shoulder and toward the neck. It was faint, but it was there—the beautiful sacred throb of life. It was Ra Khat. He had been coming back out of the dark slit toward the light.

"Ra Khat," I whispered to him and heard a very faint sigh. He lay on his belly, wedged into a crevice. I backed away, careful not to step on him. He was very heavy but I had been walking uphill since I entered the hole. Pulling him back might be possible since I would be dragging him downhill. I grabbed his hands and began to pull. It took a long time. When I felt my strength fail, I turned and walked toward the light, calling the Bearers.

When I emerged, blinking, they raced forward with their water skins. I drank and then told them I had found Ra Khat.

"He is injured, but alive. I can drag him no further, I need you to go in and pull him out." They looked at each warily and I felt my rage rise. "Would you let your comrade die? If you will not help him, I tell your wives their gutless husbands refused to help one of their own. He lives, I tell you. He is only twenty thent inside. Go."

They disappeared into the hole and emerged a short while later, dragging Ra Khat. We carried him down the mountain to the camp and gave him water. He was not fully conscious, but in a few hours began to moan and twitch. I examined him carefully. There was a large blood patch on his right leg. I cut aside his pants and found a bullet hole in his thigh. A bullet had gone straight through his leg. Someone had shot him. I cleaned and bandaged his wound, packing it tight with feverfew.

"You will live," I whispered to him. "Take heart and tell us what happened inside the mountain?" I gave him more water. He coughed and cleared his throat. I pulled him to a sitting position. He opened his eyes.

"I made it through to the Lost Lake," he croaked. "The tunnel goes all the way through."

"Did you see the White Snake? Did he shoot you? Did you see a Kosi warrior?"

He took a deep breath. "I hid among the yellow trees watching a long time. When the moon rose, I saw the White Snake. The moon hit his hair. He saw me. He raised his long gun and shot me. The pain knocked me down."

"Did you see a Kosi?"

"No, Mistress, I am sorry, I knew I should search further, but it took everything I had to crawl back into the slice."

The next morning one of the last Bearers from Rhan Du and I climbed again to the ledge by the black hole. The other Bearer stayed in the camp with Ra Khat and the horses. I lit a burning brand from the campfire as a torch. I was going in. I nodded a farewell to the terrified man, asked him to wait three days for me and walked into the cleft.

This time I had a light and rapidly reached the area where I found Ra Khat. The torch was still burning when I saw the large blood patch. Suddenly, I felt a draft of wind and heard a huge whopping sound, as if large wings beat the air. The torch went out. Terror seized me again and it took me some time to regain my breathing. The ceiling of the slit was lower, and I had to crouch and then to crawl. I quietly hummed the Kosi song for the Day of the Final Battle remembering our victory at Armageddon. After what seemed like hours, I saw the tunnel grow lighter. I hugged myself in happiness. I was almost to the other end—to the entrance into the Lost Lake.

The egress of the slice was partially blocked with rocks but my fear was gone by then. Seeing the light gave me strength. I doused my torch and quietly moved the rocks away, setting them to the side silently, as if they would break. I would not alert Grieg to my presence with sound.

At last the whole basin lay before me. Superbly matchless it lay before me—a gift from the Great Goddess of the Dhali Ra. The water in the mountain basin was an unbelievable azure blue color, so clear and bright, I had to shut my eyes. It looked like an enormous blue diamond, large enough to have adorned a ring on the finger of the Great Goddess. Blue green grasses and trees with white bark surrounded the sapphire water, like the setting for a wedding band.

Nothing had changed since the last time I looked upon the Lost Lake after Grieg sealed me into the tunnels of the mountain. Then I had made it to the Lost Lake by following the sound of Grieg's footsteps. We battled there, almost to the death, yet I survived. I left his body cut and bleeding. I caused a rockslide to trap him in the valley where I didn't think he could survive the winter. Yet the white snake lived.

Carefully surveying the entire basin, I saw a crude shelter made from tree trunks. It had not been made by a Kosi. The Kosi make woven shelters of grass on the trail, graceful rounded golden nests. This was Grieg's house. My breath came fast and my heart thundered in my chest. Then I found the fury that lived in me when I sought Grieg's death. How dared this demon, this denizen of hell, live when my Say'f was still missing? This time there would be no mistake. This time I would take his life or join my King in the world that lies beside our own, invisible to the living.

I darted silently to some nearby sentinel pines and sat down on red pine needles that had fallen around their trunks, breathing their wonderful scent and drinking water from my water skin. When the sun went down, I made my way carefully to a spot above Grieg's shelter. When night came and Grieg lay sleeping, I would murder the repulsive worm. My eyes narrowed and my teeth clenched as I saw myself dance in victory around his dead body.

# Chapter 17
## Battle of the Rivals

At midnight, with all my spy skills on fire, I stepped silently from my hiding place. I cursed the moon as I crept from the sentinel pines, fearing the light would hit my hair and alert Grieg. Stripping off my dark shirt, I used it as a hat, tying the sleeves under my chin hoping to keep the moon from lighting my hair. I kept my eyes on the ground beneath the trees, fearful I would step on a fallen branch and it would snap. Slow as a glacier I crept, until I was directly above Grieg's shelter. I tried desperately to keep my breathing silent.

In the bathing moonlight, I saw a moving white glow on the mountain ridge above the Lost Lake on the other side of the valley. It had to be Sumulus, the mystic Angelion of the high range. His white coat glowed in the moonlight, soft as snow. A second Angelion padded behind him. Then I heard a tiny cry as if from a baby mooncat and the second lion turned back. Sumulus descended the mountain like melting ice, inevitable as the coming of winter.

"Come to me, great mooncat of the high range," I whispered in my mind. "Join me in the hunt."

The Lost Lake was alive with the scents of the wind and I sensed the presence of another person. On the western side of the valley, a second shadow flowed down the slope, dark as the mountain panther, moving fluidly as water sliding over stones. It was a Kosi warrior. I felt my heart pound loud as the Elders' staves on the stones around the communal flame at Talin. The scent of Lobelia filled my senses and I swam in its pale aura. My King lived. He and Sumulus sought Captain Grieg's death together.

I forced myself to stay among the trees. I gave the Kosi King my unbounded passion, sending it flying to his heart and mind. He stopped moving for a fraction of a second and looked toward the trees where I hid. His eyes flashed. How I wanted to join him on the death hunt, but kept my feet in flesh-lock. The King sought Grieg's death. It was his right as my Warrior and Protector. I would not take that honor from him. Sumulus kept pace with Say'f on the opposing flank of the mountain. Black and white, they flowed down the mountain toward my enemy.

Grieg's door swung open. He stood with his back to his shelter, his long army rifle in his arms. Both the Warrior and Sumulus stopped moving.

"Goddess of the Winds, cover the moon with clouds," I prayed. She did my bidding, but far too slowly. Grieg had spotted the mooncat. He raised his rifle in slow motion, took aim and fired. The bullet raced through the air. Sumulus screamed in cat rage and lay where he fell. The shadowed Kosi pulled his knife and the metal caught the moonlight. He roared down the mountain like an avalanche. Sumulus screamed again. The Angelion was injured, I had to go to him.

To reach the Angelion, I had to circle around the Lake and climb up the mountain. Grieg spotted me as soon as I moved and took shot after shot at me, but that night I was invincible. The bullets screamed by my head and chunked into trees. When I reached the opposite edge of the lake, I looked back. The Kosi was charging like a bull toward Grieg. He swung his gun around, pointing it at the Warrior.

"No," I screamed. "Kosi King save yourself."

The bullets flew. I heard a cry of wrath. I sank into reeds by the Lake, panting in fear. Looking back I saw the Warrior unhurt, still running toward Grieg. Their bodies collided like stars. It had to be Say'f. I saw my lover's knife slash and slash again. I heard Grieg grunt in pain. They were on the ground, rolling, fighting and bellowing like animals. I heard the Kosi death roar but I did not fear. My lover would prevail.

While they fought, I climbed up to Angelion. Every muscle in my body bent to the task of reaching him. Stabs of pain crossed my chest. I dislodged rocks that tumbled down. I grabbed for a tree and hung for a moment, dangling in the air. I shot a quick glance across the lake. The two men were still locked in mortal combat.

Slowly, hand over hand, I dragged myself to the ledge where the great white lion lay. He was so still. My heart stopped as I fell to my knees beside his great recumbent form. I whispered, "Don't go, great one. Please don't leave me." I felt for a pulse in his soft white throat. It was there, slow and powerful, like the sound of a muffled drumbeat.

I looked down at the scene of mortal combat. The moon came out from behind the clouds and I could tell the Kosi King was injured. I saw blood drip from his body and bit my lips in fear. He raised his knife again. The scene slowed down. Grieg battled against the Warrior's strength, forcing the knife away. The clash went on and on. I heard the Kosi battle cry and I saw my Warrior's dark hands around the throat of the White Snake. I heard my enemy's death rattle.

Quietly at first, and then louder, I sang the Kosi song for Victory at Armageddon. The victorious Kosi warrior raised his head and saw me. I raised my arm in a salute. A beautiful white smile lit his dark face. It was Say'f, but when he started to walk, his stride was very different. He had injured himself.

I pulled my water skin from my belt and opened Sumulus' mouth. I poured the liquid over his great tongue. Trying to determine where the bullet entered his body, I felt his ribs. Under my touch, I saw a red spreading stain. Using my small knife, I cut into the wound. I reached inside and pulled the bullet from his flesh. Then I lifted the great white lion's head and gazed into his half-closed silver eyes.

"I must go now," I told him. "Sleep my Champion, I will return with feverfew. You will live to raise your family." I held his great head in my hands and whispered, "My mother sends her unending love to you." I kissed his brow and began to climb down again to the floor of the valley. When I reached the tumbled rocks at the base of the mountain, I ran toward the place where the two dire enemies had battled. I stopped for a moment and looked down. Grieg's body lay dead. I felt his pulse to be certain, but he was a corpse. A shudder, a paroxysm, a *grand mal* of relief flooded my soul.

"Goddess, take this one to the bottom of the earth," I prayed. "The belly of the White Snake must never ride his war horse in the sky worlds."

Say'f was walking away. "Kosi Warrior stop!" I called. The moonlight was bright enough that I could see a slick blood trail. Heart pounding, I followed the red road. Was it him? The footprints in blood did not look like his. My palms grew sweaty as I saw the trail grow wider. "Wait" I screamed. He raised his amber eyes, turned and saw me.

"Spirit of Sab-ra, cease to follow me. You are dead. I cannot come to you."

By the time I caught up with him, he was hunched over at the edge of the Lake. He drank like a lion from the waters. His gaze saw my shirt, still tied on my head and my bare breasts. He reached to touch me and was startled.

"Is it really you, my bare breasted Kosi wife?" he asked and I caught a glimpse of a grin. He held out his hand for mine. "Did I marry a Kosi woman after all?"

He reached for me and we embraced. A huge flower of joy opened in my heart. I had found him. I helped him stand and examined him as best

I could by moonlight. He was cut and bleeding in a dozen places. "My Warrior, I can hardly believe we are together again. I feared the Captain might have injured you fatally, but you took his life," I felt triumphant. Nothing could keep us apart now. "I have sought you long, my husband. My heart rises in joy to find you alive."

"The White Snake could not injure me in a hundred fights," he answered, calmly. We sat together on the sand at the edge of the lake while his breathing returned to normal, watching the moon gild the mountain. "It is a miracle you appeared on the very night I chose to take the White Snake's life. I have seen your spirit a thousand times since I have been in this valley." He bent to kiss me and I felt my body respond.

"Tell me what happened after the Avalanche drove the rest of us out of Skygrass?" I asked. I was still amazed to be sitting by him, I couldn't move even an inch away and pressed my body tight against his side.

"My shame in allowing Grieg to capture you made me stay behind when the mountain exploded. The fire from the volcano burned much of the skin on my body and I rested for weeks in a cave. When my strength returned, I made my way across the Dhali Ra. Amid the storms of winter, I found Grieg wandering the side of the massif."

He looked down at his right leg and I noticed that his foot had an old injury. He had wrapped it in green reeds from the aquamarine lake.

"I sought his life, and we battled for a long time. Finally, we broke apart, neither of us strong enough to kill the other. I dragged myself into a cave and rested throughout the winter. Tell me of your journey with the First Blood Arrow after you left the Skygrass valley."

"Lord Rohr and I waited for you for many weeks at Halfhigh after the Avalanche. The rest of the Kosi returned to the Citadel and the miners returned to Talin. When the snows began, Lord Rohr insisted that we leave. I begged to stay longer, but my burns wept liquid and the fever would not leave me. We travelled across the mountain and made it to the Valley of the King by the beginning of the Moon of Snows."

"That was over a year ago, Sab-ra. What did you do in the Valley of the King while the seasons passed?"

I could have told him then about my pregnancy and the babies but I held my tongue. I would wait until he could see them with his own eyes.

"Lord Rohr and I stayed in the King's service until spring when I received a summons from Wirri-won, Healer of the Kosi people. Although he feared for me, Rohr took me to the Island of the Eaten. Wirri-won had established a leper colony and developed a compound that prevents the disease. She and I were able to save many leper children before the White River tore the Island apart. After that, Lord Rohr and I set out to find you again."

"Why is the First Blood Arrow not with you?" Say'f asked, frowning.

"Lord Rohr never broke faith with you, my Lord," I felt tears fill my eyes. "He protected me as long as he drew breath but a giant leopard took his life," I started to sob. "When he died, I cut myself and stained his arrows with my blood. I placed his quiver and bow on his chest. I promised that I would take his place. I vowed I would take his place. I would become First among your Blood Arrows."

"There is no need for Blood Arrows in the Lost Lake," Say'f said quietly. He looked out across the lake. He seemed accustomed to living here, resigned.

"The Kosi nation waits for you, King Say'f. I came into this valley through a pupil in the eye of the Goddess, a hole in the rock wall. If we can get through the opening together, I have my medicines at the Bearer camp. I can treat your foot."

"No," he told me quietly, stubbornly. There was a set to his mouth that boded ill.

I looked at Say'f and felt a trembling come upon me, like shock. The Kosi King looked up toward the range of mountains. Once again, he did not plan to come with me. Once again, the bars of his pride would not let him escape from the prison of his own making.

"Come with me, my husband," I said. "I beg you."

"Sab-ra, I cannot," he said, pointing to his foot. "I am crippled. No cripple could rule the Kosi."

"Must I get down on my knees again," I asked. My voice was low and I held his eyes with my own. I had said those words to him once before, when I begged for our union on our wedding night.

"I am King of the Kosi no longer," he said. The determination in his face was like rock.

"I think I know a King when I see one," I said keeping my voice calm. "Now I have something to say and you will hear me. I am no longer the terrified bride brought to the bed of a Kosi King. Lord Rohr and I survived a trip across the top of the Dhali Ra in winter. After helping Wirri-won with the leper children, I travelled to the Citadel to find you, but nearly everyone was dead. Hozro had been there."

Say'f took in a sudden deep breath, dread clenched his mouth. "Tell me of my few living warriors."

"When the tide of war turned in favor of the Kosi, Hozro retreated to the Citadel. He waited for your warriors to return and convinced them you were dead. He forced them to choose. Either they would honor his sovereignty or they would die. More than thirty chose death. He killed two women and their infants. He even killed a pregnant woman." I could still see the ranks of the dead in the Citadel and grimaced.

"Were no warriors left alive?"

"I found three Kosi warriors and one woman barely alive in a nearby ravine. It was Ghang, Lord Rohr, Argo and the woman Niffa. They told me what Hozro had done. Say'f," I looked at him with iron in my eyes. "You have no choice. You must resume your kingship. Your people need you."

I knelt before my husband and slowly unwrapped his foot. I was horrified to see that four of the toes were missing. The scars were raised and puckered. Red streaks rose on the sides of the foot. It was still infected.

"How did this happen?" I asked.

"After the Avalanche, when I stayed behind to seek Grieg's death, the Mountain God froze my toes. I had to cut them off." He sent me an image of removing his left boot and sawing off his toes with a knife in a snowstorm. I saw the blue toes, rock hard, blow away in the fierce winds. I saw his boot, skittering away and his desperate attempt to grab it, before it slid into an icy cleft. I saw his bare foot turn red and then blue as he hobbled away.

"You are a Warrior still," I said. "I applaud your courage."

He shook his head, saying, "I am King no longer, but when I see your face and feel your touch, I would still be your husband. Let us make our home here, in this beautiful valley."

I quieted the rage that was starting to rise inside me. "As your Queen, I will not permit you to remain here." I felt my body grow hot.

"You are not Queen of the Kosi," he said, shaking his head. "To be Queen of the Kosi, you must be a true warrior; you must have taken the life of an enemy of the tribe."

"When Justyn and I rescued the four Kosi from the ravine, I met Argo, the Kosi assassin. I ordered him to locate Hozro and bring him to trial before the Elders at Talin. I will tell them of his crimes."

"A trial by pacifists will not serve, my wife. Hozro must die," he said softly.

"If no man in Talin will take his life, I will behead him myself," I said.

Say'f looked at me stunned. "You?" he asked. "Your People are peaceful miners and Ghat herders. Your religion bans taking the life of any sentient being or even eating the flesh of an animal that can nurse its young. What has time wrought to make you like this, Sab-ra?"

"When I saw the Kosi dead at the Citadel something changed deep inside me. Some crimes are so horrendous that they require the perpetrator to pay with his life."

Say'f shook his head and looked at me in admiration, murmuring, "You are more warrior than I, Sab-ra. This night I release you from your marriage vows. Once Hozro lies dead, you can select one of the living Blood Arrows for a husband. Only then can you be Queen of the Kosi."

"I am already married to the King. I will have no other."

"The Kosi would despise me because of my injury. Injured women and children are cared for, but injured warriors are cast from the Tribe. Most join the Shunned. How I wish I had a son to take my place."

I was sorely tempted to tell him about Quinn then, but held my tongue.

"If you do not return to the Citadel," I said and heard the mooncat growl in my voice, "I will ask the Elders to spare Hozro's life. He will become King of the Kosi in truth. He will claim me as his Queen. He will force me to lie with him and give him sons. If he found my appearance displeasing, he would torture or kill me, even bury me in a pit of garbage as he did to Hodi."

I wanted Say'f to know what his pride would cost. I saw his eyes darken and felt the spark of his anger flare into flame.

"It is your duty to protect me," I hissed. "Your injury pales next to your responsibility to your Queen."

The Kosi's golden eyes looked off toward the blue and purple ranges of mountain. He needed time alone to determine his path. I left him to think on my words.


I searched out some willow shrubs, tore off their bark and made a powder from their marrow. The willow powder had a harsh taste, but it eased pain and erased inflammation. I climbed back up to Sumulus who lay where I left him. I forced it down his throat. After some time had passed, I could tell his pain eased. I sat petting him all afternoon. By the time the sun went down, he was able to stand. He licked my hand.

"Farewell Great Angelion," I told him. He left me slowly, climbing up toward the cave he shared with his mate. Just before he entered the cave, he turned and we looked long into each other's eyes. "May the Goddess of the Dhali Ra bless you and keep you. With all that I have and all that I am, I honor you," I said.

When I returned to the lakeside, Say'f had made a campfire. He found food in Grieg's small house. We ate in silence. After the meal, I stood and slowly removed all my clothing, piece by piece. I held the glowing eyes of my husband with mine. I lay down beside him. Suddenly shy before his melting gaze, I covered my breasts with my hands, but he pulled my hands away. As he had said on the night we married, he murmured, "I would not have you covered, not for all the gemstones in Skygrass."

Happiness waved across me. I thought him gone to the sky worlds. A warm blood song rose in my body. He gave a shuddering sigh and bent to kiss me.

"I want only you," I murmured. "You are my Lord and King, heart of my heart, blood of my blood. Four toes are nothing to give away—to keep your Kingdom and your Queen."

As we fell asleep on the white sand, I saw two glowing strands of stars form a great circle in the sky. Say'f and I were together again.

# Chapter 18
## Coming Down to Halfhigh

We emerged from the White Snake's lair the next afternoon. Say'f told me he had spotted the opening in the mountain months earlier, but his injured foot kept him from further exploration. I don't know what convinced him, but when I said I was leaving and stood to walk from the Lost Lake valley, he limped beside me. He wore only his left boot and cursed his injured foot all that day. I prayed his other boot was still in the camp where I left it. Walking into the narrow slice in the rock and then crawling on our knees forever until we saw the light, we finally made it to the other side.

When we reached the camp, all the Bearers had vanished. They had left only the war horse, the dweli and some pemmican. They had taken Jemma with them. Inside the dweli, to my delight, I found my husband's other boot. Lord Rohr's horse, Kys, pranced in delight when he saw the King.

After a night in the camp, we proceeded slowly down the mountain. Say'f rode Kys, I saw behind him. I quietly mourned the loss of Yellowmane and scanned the skies for her image dancing in the clouds. I would mourn her for the rest of my life. I knew Say'f still had terrible doubts about his ability to lead the Kosi. I had none. Although it seemed the Kosi were now an orphan nation, their willingness to defend the sacred Skygrass valley and my marriage to their King had made them my People.

"The Kosi have always been warriors for hire," Say'f told me as we rode. "In the time of my grandfather, the Old King, we were pledged to protect the people of the Twelve Valleys. One woman a year from your People chose to come to the Kosi. It was considered an honor and the People's women vied with each other for the privilege. When the Old King died and my father became Ruler, he left the Citadel with two guards to negotiate a new agreement with your People for more women, but he never returned. Hozro and my father's guards carried his body back to the Citadel. We gave him a sky burial."

"So you became King then?"

"I was so honored," he nodded. "Months later, one of the Bearer people came to me and confessed that he had witnessed Hozro kill my father. Because Hozro was my nurse brother when we were children, I believed his many lies." Sorrow crossed his face.

"The betrayer must die," I murmured.

"When I banished him from the Kosi territory, Hozro set up a separate camp near the Green River. He lured warriors away with promises of wives and children. When you arrived at the Citadel, I was making plans to attack his camp and take back my men."

"When Hozro lies dead and your warriors know you live, they will all return. I have seen you rule a great and numerous people. We will place Hozro's head on a post at the entrance to the Citadel and make the Shunned kneel there. If they would keep their heads, they will swear an oath of fealty to you. We will rule together and the Kosi will once again be the guardians of the People in the Twelve Valleys. Your daughters, Kim-li and Kensing will join us. They are with Conquin and her husband in King Ruisenor's palace."

"I want more children," Say'f said and his gaze made my body warm. I kept the secret of Quinn and Crimson alive in my heart, like two perfect bread rolls warm from the oven of my body.

We rode most of the way in companionable silence for the next several days. The Harvest Moon had begun; my birthday month. I had turned eighteen. On this day three years ago, I left Talin for Maidenstone in disgrace, banned from my People for leaving Hodi in the hands of the

Shunned. Today I was returning to the Twelve Valley's country as Queen of the Kosi. My son and daughter, future monarchs of the warrior tribe would be waiting for us at Halfhigh. Together with my husband, we would bring peace to the Blue Mountains. I felt a shiver of intense pleasure cross my shoulders. I had achieved my destiny.

I watched Say'f carefully for signs of pain and fatigue. When I saw his face turn white, I made him stop, saying I was too tired to continue. The autumn rains had ended and the sky was bright blue. The sun had scorched all color from the dry mountains, but along small streams, yellow and red trees flamed near blue water.

On the last evening before we reached Halfhigh, we camped by a tributary of the Green River. I disrobed and bathed in the water. Say'f joined me and together we washed the dirt from each other's bodies, playing, splashing and laughing. I found a large flat stone lying barely beneath the tumbling water. I laid down on it and let the river wash my hair. I poured water over Say'f and slowly unpicked his coiled braids. I washed his hair with soap grass and left it long to dry. It reached his waist, black and shiny as moonlight. Kosi Warriors never cut their hair unless they are defeated in battle.

"I have never been routed in battle, Sab-ra, but this battle you place before me is harder than any I have fought before," he said. "I cannot pretend that I am confident about the outcome."

"You will prevail," I said calmly and he smiled. Then my husband led me by the hand to the sandy riverbank and took me as I lay, half in the water. His hair covered us like a blanket.

"You are my husband and you will be King again," I vowed. The sun went down. We started a campfire and ate our evening meal.

The next morning, I did my hair in the fashion of the Kosi women. I consigned the King's torn dirty shirt to the flames of the campfire and buckled the leather band that held his arrowheads diagonally across his naked chest. I braided his long dark hair. I saw the old healed scars of injury on his body—a warrior's mark of honor. We had washed his leather trousers the night before. He stepped into them, balancing on one foot and holding on to my shoulder. I had sufficient willow bark powder to fill the toe of his boot. It would keep the pain down while we descended.

When the sun reached its height, I spotted two figures standing ahead of us by the trail. As we approached I saw it was Ghang and Argo. They held a leather bag. When we drew rein beside them, Argo held the bag up to Say'f.

"I greet you, King of the Kosi," Argo said. "In this bag, I have Hozro's head. I fought him to his death. As the fight turned and it was clear that I would prevail, he became a true Kosi. He refused the help of his followers and died honorably."

I shuddered inwardly, but forcing myself not to gag, I looked inside the bag. These warriors needed a Queen as brave as their King. A head was there. It was gray and looked almost waxy. I turned away but then quickly back again. This man had a white eye. Argo had failed to kill Hozro—instead he killed the Kosi Wolf who took Hodi's life.

"You have played me false, Argo," I said, in a sudden spasm of fury. "This is not Hozro. This is the Kosi Wolf who murdered my spirit brother, Hodi. While I am grateful he is dead, I ordered you to bring Hozro to Talin. The King demands his trial by the Elders."

"Let me see this head," Say'f said. He bent down and when he raised his face up, I saw him grin.

"Sab-ra, this man is Hozro. The man you call the Kosi Wolf, the man who killed Hodi and buried him alive, and I call Hozro—they are one and the same." Turning to the assassin he nodded, saying, "I am in your debt, Argo."

Argo bent his head and Say'f put his hand on the assassin's shoulder.

Turning back to me he said, "Well done, Queen of the Kosi."

I saw at last my husband's smile of victory, the easy smile of the Kosi King from the days in the Citadel. The death of Hozro had set him free. Just as he had killed my enemy, I had ordered the death of his.

Say'f took the leather bag from Rohr and tied it to his saddlebags. I fought the stench and my nausea, but knew it was his talisman. The King's confidence had returned and I had achieved justice for Hodi. I looked up into the sky and saw my little spirit brother's open-hearted smile. The King and I, with Ghang and Argo behind us, rode on to Halfhigh as the sun began its sky journey to the west.

We began to see more Kosi warriors. They stood silently on both sides of the trail, astride their horses, bows and arrows strapped to their backs. At first, we saw only two, then three. Soon there were more, twenty, thirty. Some looked afraid, some triumphant. There were women too, bare breasted on their horses, erect and prideful.

"Just as I told you, your warriors have returned, King of the Kosi," I felt jubilant.

As we passed the silent warriors, they fell in behind us, riding two abreast. When we reached the bottom of the trail that leads up to Halfhigh, Say'f stopped. He turned his horse around and faced his Warriors and their women. He raised his bow and gave a huge roar. I did not know the words of the Kosi cry, but the men made a giant dark circle around him. With their horse's heads bowed, they were a ring of satyr's—half man, half horse. It was the vision he showed me the day I asked him to defend Skygrass, the day I knew he would fight for us.

## Chapter 19
## The Twins Reunion

We thundered up the trail to the camp at Halfhigh. When the jingle of the horse harnesses died away, I saw a red-haired woman standing in the doorway to the dweli.

"Come out," I said, dismounting from the war horse. "I would see you now, my sister."

When the light hit her hair, I could see our hair was identical in color. It was eerie to see a replica of myself. For a long time we said nothing, silently surveying each other.

"I am pleased to meet you at last, my sister," I said formally, inclining my head. "What is your name?"

"I am Ruby, and have come half way around the world to find you, my sister. When I first arrived at Maidenstone it was winter and I was unable to travel to the high country. When it was spring, I left Namché to find you. While travelling through the great Kosi grasslands, I was kidnapped by a scout of the Shunned and taken to the Green River camp."

"Tell me what happened there. It was at the Green River camps that my spy partner, Hodi, was murdered."

"I met Hodi's mother."

"What became of her?" I asked.

"I am sad to tell you she died. The Kosi broke the bones in her foot because she tried to help me escape."

"I will tell my husband of this. I would have justice for her. Where do you come from, Ruby?"

"I live with our mother, Ashlin, on an island in the great sea. She sent me to bring you back with me. Will you come, Sab-ra?"

"I honor the arduous journey to have taken to find me, Ruby, but I am Queen of the Kosi and would have you remain here with me."

"Our mother, Ashlin, is ill and I promised I would return to her. Your land is beautiful, but it is not my land. Please, I beg you, my sister, on behalf of our mother, bring your babies and come with me," Ruby said.

"I hope the day will come when our mother is strong enough to come to visit me here and see her grandchildren, but I am married to the King of the Warriors. I must remain. Please stay, my sister, and learn about my adopted culture."

"I cannot stay," Ruby told her. "Someday, perhaps, I will return and bring our mother with me. But for now, I must leave here for Maidenstone. From there I will take many trains, what you call Iron Horses, and then a boat to return to the fair island of Viridian. It is a trip of many weeks, but I long to begin."

"My heart is sad that our lives have touched for such a brief time. I miss Maidenstone where I spent some of the happiest days of my life. When you arrive in Namché, please greet Mistress Falcon for me and tell her the day may yet come when I will return." Sab-ra said.

"I will," Ruby said and smiled.

"When you must leave, Ruby, I have a dear friend in Namché named Justyn. Would you also greet him for me while you are in the city?"

"What message should I give him?"

"Tell him that the King of the Kosi lives, as do my children. They have a father now, but I will never forget the love he gave to them. Or to me."

"I was asked to give you a final message from our mother. She said to tell you she has lived with regret every day since she left you at Maidenstone. She asks for your forgiveness."

"Tell our mother that she gave me the gift of life and the gift of love for the Angelions. There are no greater gifts. When I left Maidenstone, Mistress Falcon said our mother asked that I find Sumulus, the baby Angelion she raised with our father. Tell her I found him. I held his great head in my arms and told him of her love," Sab-ra said.

"Then he is real?" Ruby asked. "I must admit I doubted."

"He lives, but only in the highest ranges. There once were many Angelions in the Blue Mountains but he and his mate may be the last. Perhaps he lives only within the Lost Lake valley. Beyond the boundaries of that sacred space, I think he is only white smoke."

"Our mother told me I would understand everything if I could see him, but even without seeing him, I do. Have you any other messages for our mother?" Ruby asked.

"Please tell her that regret must no longer reign in her heart. There is nothing but love between us," Sab-ra said.

"She will know of your triumph, and finding Sumulus," Ruby said. "I came to Halfhigh with Deti and your children. They are very thin but alive. We were all near death from a leopard attack that killed Hent and nearly killed Ambe. Deti and I tried everything we knew to save them. When Lord Sta'g came to Halfhigh and saw our desperation, he went for Wirri-won. She came and cured your children."

"You have been brave and loyal, my sister," Sab-ra said. "I will miss the chance to know you better," my voice quavered. "I am and will be in your debt my whole life long. Come with me now. I want you to meet my husband."

"Did the Kosi abduct you and force you to join with him in marriage." Ruby's body seemed braced for a terrible confession.

"Oh Ruby," I shook her head and laughed. "You don't understand. I wanted this marriage in every part of me. He was the reluctant one. I had to go down on my knees and beg, but at last he agreed and we were married. If you would stay here, I would marry you to one of my husband's Blood Arrows."

Ruby looked at her in frightened amazement. "Dearest sister, I thank you, but there is a man in Namché, a soldier I think I might just love."

"It is good you will marry a warrior," I said. "When you two are married, bring him to meet me. My husband will make you both honorary Kosi. It is time you met your father, Quinn," I said reaching for her little boy who had walked out of the Aid Station.

Refusing his mother's arms, Quinn dashed between the feet of the warrior's huge stallions and came to a halt before Say'f, still mounted on Kys. Both Sab-ra and Ruby held their breath, afraid the stallion would stomp on this small brave boy.

"Pad-ma," Quinn said. He lowered his head and went down on one knee.

"How did he learn this," Sab-ra asked Ruby. "It's the proper welcome for the King."

"Lord Sta'g must have taught him," Ruby said. Baby Quinn raised his head, his dark green eyes shining and laughed aloud. Sab-ra looked at Say'f. He seemed completely baffled.

"Sab-ra, who is this boy who calls me father and kneels to as King?" he asked her, frowning.

"This is Quinn," I said. "He is your son."

Seeing the still confused expression on the Kosi King's face, I motioned for him to bend down and whispered, "Conceived on our wedding night in the light of the moon."

Then I picked Quinn up and handed him up to Say'f. Holding his son in his arms moved Say'f so deeply that tears sprang to his eyes.

"Kosi Warriors, I present my son." He held Quinn high over the warriors and the assembled Kosi roared. Little Quinn held his fists in the air and roared right back at them.

Ruby had returned to the dweli but came forward from the shadows, carrying Crimson.

"Who is this woman, Sab-ra? Did you die after all? Is she your revenant?" Say'f asked as alarm waved across his face.

"This is Ruby, my sister and twin. She and Deti saved our children from starvation."

"Then I am in your debt," Say'f said and Ruby smiled tentatively at him. "Is this your child, sister to Sab-ra?" he asked, looking at Crimson.

"No, this one is also yours, Kosi King," Ruby said. "She is your daughter, the Princess Crimson."

Say'f held out his other arm for his daughter and she went to him eagerly, talking in a continuous string of words. Say'f looked at her in wonder. "What is she saying?" he asked.

"I believe she is saying she is pleased to meet her father, although she speaks a tongue I do not yet know. My sister also brought your gazehound with her to Halfhigh. The dog was still waiting in your sleeping space when I arrived at the Citadel. Starved, dehydrated and nearly dead, she waited for your return. I have named her Dusk. She will be the mother of future generations of our gazehounds. I am sorry, my King, but your eagle was not at the Citadel. I can only hope someone released him."

When I said the word eagle, Quinn began struggling to get down. Say'f handed him to me and I put him down on the grass. As Ruby and I clutched each other's hands, Quinn dashed to the very edge of the mesa and cried out loudly, "Sky Dog! Down!"

An enormous golden eagle descended, racing down from the sky, talons outstretched. All of us feared he would rip Quinn's arm off, but he settled—light as a songbird.

"I believe your eagle has returned, my Lord," I said, unable to keep from laughing. "Apparently, Quinn, future King of the Kosi, can already call him from on high."

As the Warrior King smiled at me, I knew the destiny I sought for many years was mine. I had rescued my husband, the Kosi King. I met and loved my twin sister, Ruby. The silver cord of marriage and the golden cord of motherhood could now honorably join the red cord of the Healer and the white of the Far Reader around my waist. I was whole.

# Epilogue

Many decades have passed since that dark day when I was sent on my first mission with young Hodi to take Lethal Sleep berries to the Kosi of the Green River camp. When Hodi was murdered by the Shunned Kosi the Elders of Talin blamed me. I was banned from Talin and sent to the city of Namché and the terror of what I believed Maidenstone would be.

Before all is lost in the mists of time, I must confess to the terrible part I played in the war with the Harn Army, the destruction of the Skygrass valley and its blue diamond mine, the slow disappearance of my People and a near end to the Kosi tribe. Everyone knows of these terrible events. People call it "The Saga of the Fall."

But looking back through the years, I also know that a miracle rose from the ashes of that war. The Lost Lake valley came to the People of Talin—a place even more transcendently beautiful than Skygrass. The blue diamond mine vanished and would no longer cause wars. I found Sumulus, an Angelion of the high peaks, an animal both real and evanescent. I married the Kosi King and bore our children, the Princess Crimson and Prince Quinn. The People of the Twelve Valleys and the Kosi became one Blended People.

Now my hair is white as snow. I have grown old. I sit writing this history in the beautiful white tower of Maidenstone, looking down through the colored web of bridges at the dreaming spires of Namché. As Justyn had known I would, when Say'f died honorably in a war with the Hakan, I returned to Maidenstone and became Mistress of the Lamasery. When I rode through the Leopard Gate that day, Justyn was waiting. In the evenings now we take tea together and talk of the days when we were young and the world a far different place.